Welcome, Scholar

Welcome, Scholar

A novel by Jake Fuchs

GRIZZLY PEAK PRESS
Kensington, CA

For information contact:
Grizzly Peak Press
350 Berkeley Park Boulevard
Kensington, CA 94707
grizzlypeakpress.com

Welcome, Scholar
is published by Daniel N. David
and is distributed by Grizzly Peak Press.

Book design and layout
by Sara B. Brownell • sarabbrownell.com

ISBN Number: 978-0-9988310-1-5
Library of Congress Number: 2017933592

Printed in the United States of America

For David Kubrin

The author is grateful to friends who read this book in various stages of composition, foes of Dulness all.

Part One

"A Study of Reading Habits"
–Philip Larkin

When Derek Rosenblum was in first grade, he couldn't learn to read, just couldn't get the hang of it, and so was "left back." But his then energetic mother, Mimi, talked the school principal, or whatever authority it was, into making Derek's failure to promote contingent upon his flunking a reading test at the end of the summer. Then she got him a tutor. Although Derek must have passed the test, as he was advanced into the second grade with the rest of his class, he never remembered taking it. What he did recall was the delight felt one morning that summer when words suddenly spoke to him; for that was how it seemed then and later, for a long time. Though not always.

It was probably a funny book that summer morning. He always liked funny books, like the stories about Freddy the pig and one about a mouse who lived in Ben Franklin's hat. Of course he outgrew kids' books at the usual time to outgrow them, and after that not everything he read and enjoyed had to be funny. In fact, it could be sad or even tragic. But what he felt when he liked something was always the same. He forgot where he was. He was carried to another place, where the people were more interesting than in the real world, where he often wasn't. He could feel what they were feeling. Outside of a book, with real people, that wasn't so easy.

Derek's teachers distrusted him and complained when he laughed or exclaimed during silent reading time, and the children's librarian at the local branch of the Los Angeles Public Library tried to ban him from the room. His mother put a stop to that, but she worried about him and said that he read too much and that it was bad for his eyes. Perhaps the teachers and librarians would have been more tolerant if he had worn glasses like the "inch-thick specs" in the Larkin poem, but dark-haired Derek was a big, strong boy with 20/20 vision and an uneven temper. The other kids knew better than to tease him about his reading habits.

1

In high school in the early seventies, while all his smart male buds were doing math and science and were gaga over computers, he was the only boy in eleventh-grade honors English. The girls in the class seemed to resent him just for being there. He resented them for ignoring his opinions about the fiction and poetry they read. They acted as if his voice hurt their ears. There was one girl he wished he could impress, Tracy Chatham, a sexy, full-racked blonde, a cheerleader, who must have taken the class just to fill a hole in her schedule. Books seemed not to interest her, and neither did Derek.

At least the teacher, Mrs. Magner, liked him. He liked most of what they read, as long as the words spoke to him, which, of course, they weren't actually doing, though it seemed that way to him. They were speaking among themselves, to one another, but he got to listen. Not everyone gets that privilege.

Perhaps thinking of him, Mrs. Magner had the class read *The Rape of the Lock* by the eighteenth-century poet Alexander Pope, and he loved it. He then read Pope's *An Essay on Criticism* on his own and liked that almost as much. What Derek was responding to, without realizing he was doing so, was Pope's excellence at wit, a verbal condition in which the words not only converse among themselves but also poke one another in the ribs. The delight factor manifesting itself full force, he wanted more. Having somehow acquired the idea that college professors got to read and even talk about such stuff all the time, he asked Mrs. Magner how he could go about becoming one. She told him. She also mentioned another poem of Pope's, the *Dunciad*, which he might want to read but not until later in his career. He went home.

"I'm going to get a Ph.D. in English," he told Mimi.

"A what?" she asked.

"A Ph.D. You know."

"I do?"

He explained as well as he could. Eventually she understood that he needed this advanced degree in order to teach English in a college.

"Well, all right," she said, doubtfully.

When Derek's father, George, came home from the menswear store he owned, Mimi greeted him at the door with this underwhelming news. Derek couldn't get either parent to understand what he got out of words, especially the words of a hunchbacked satiric poet who had died in 1744. They had never heard of him, and the name made them suspicious.

"Pope his name is?"

He told them not to worry about it and passed a few hours struggling with the *Dunciad*. Magner was right. He should have waited. It was funny, but in a scary way. There seemed to be hundreds of characters, all in constant motion. There was a gigantic woman, too. What they were all doing together was not clear to him, and so he soon gave up. He didn't understand, but, strangely, he could almost see them, the horde and the lady. Well, later he would read it. He would read everything by Pope.

Derek didn't inform his jock friends, the guys he played with on the basketball team, of his professorial ambition; but he had brain friends too, being sort of one himself, and he did tell them. They were not impressed. Doing stuff with computers and making tons of money, that was their ambition. That was their delight.

Now we will see what became of his. For Derek did become a Professor of English. His fate was a matter of temptation followed by a giving way, a sequence common to most people and their destinies. But Derek's case may stand for something larger, the decline of English as professed in our colleges and universities. It may even have had something to do with causing that decline.

Professor Rosenblum

May 15, 2024
Kansas
Enola Gay State University
Engl 204
Professor Derek Rosenblum, Ph.D.
The Eighteenth Century: Pope and his Contemporaries

Kazoot! And again, kazoot. Two times. Giving vent in his classroom. Some smart guy with an adolescent sense of humor? But they weren't humorous, these seminar students of his. They never laughed. Oh, at the beginning of the quarter some had chuckled occasionally, but the noise soon ceased. The professor surveyed the table. Blank faces. Eyes half-closed. The usual. He became aware of a female student, her face concealed by the book held up before her, reading something aloud … something. The assignment, no doubt. And what was that? The professor hadn't looked at his syllabus lately. It was online and he had forgotten just how that all worked. Nor had he been paying attention to the student, her reading style being incredibly monotonous, as if she hated the lines she spoke and it was an awful burden to speak them. It was a poem, he could tell that much. Iambic. Very iambic. Now she was reciting something about bees, "The buzzing Bees about their dusky Queen." She flopped the book down on the table. Someone else's turn to read.

What happened to the boy who loved books? Thirty years in academe, that's what.

Reading aloud was all that the professor let students do in his seminars. They might get something out of it if they listened to themselves, and it was easy on him since it required no prepping. This was the teaching technique of his adviser in his own grad student days at Heartland University, Professor Lucia Luteplucker. Her example had encouraged him to employ it himself, even though she had never actually said anything to him about its virtues. Luckily,

4

he was resourceful enough to grasp them on his own. At first, as her student several decades back, he hadn't liked the reading aloud, as much as her students had to do it; but eventually it had grown on him. It was restful.

Occasionally Professor Rosenblum wondered where Lucia might be now, if alive. Probably she was. If she'd died, he'd just know it, as she'd been an important part of his life. He just knew that, too, but couldn't recall anything she'd done that helped him besides setting an example of how to run a class. She had never been seen after the video screen fell on her during the Loma Prieta, the big San Francisco earthquake of '89. At least, not by anyone he was aware of. Ah well. Either she was, or she wasn't. Alive.

He mused. Dusky queen. Dusky queen. Now, who the devil could that be ... ah, yes ... of course. She was Dulness, the huge presiding deity in Alexander Pope's notorious satire, the *Dunciad.* That's what the assignment must be, the crazy mock-epic that heaps scorn upon writers, now unknown, whom Pope despised. They only continue to exist in the footnotes the poem is stuffed with, and some of these notes, composed by Pope himself, are not easy to make sense of. He made them that way deliberately, the cranky little guy. But notes should make things easier, not harder, right?

These poor kids. Even the name Dulness was off-putting, with its single 'l,' but that's how Pope insisted on spelling it. It was also a scary poem; that's how the professor thought he remembered it. As a young man he had read it many times, starting in high school. At least he had tried then. After that experience he tried again, repeatedly, and at one point thought he understood the *Dunciad* well enough to write about it, but his adviser, that Luteplucker, wouldn't let him. Some day he must read it again, perhaps on a plane going someplace nice, like an academic conclave in San Francisco. He could probably finish the whole poem on the flight. Maybe he was a little weak on what might be construed as the *Dunciad's* meaning, but he remembered a lot of the details.

He had never assigned it before, not even for the eighteenth-century seminar he called *Pope and his Contemporaries.* He'd had a feeling there was something icky about this particular poem; if he'd known what that was he'd forgotten, but he still had the feeling. Maybe he shouldn't have assigned it this time. Why, come to think of it, had he? He didn't remember doing it. Oh, well.

But these poor kids. Did they even know what a mock-epic was? Well, if they had to tackle the *Dunciad,* he'd better fill them in. Nothing to it, really: a poem satirizing someone or something in the poet's present that alludes to ancient epics about heroes doing heroic things; thus, whatever's being satirized looks even worse than it would without the implied comparison. This description struck him as slightly abbreviated, as if he'd left something out, but he was sure it was what all the handbooks said. If there still were handbooks, actual books. Professor Rosenblum wasn't sure about that.

He really should also say something about Alexander Pope, his career, the time in which he lived, that sort of thing. All he had given the class so far was a lengthy paragraph he'd typed up for another class taught long ago that in fact wasn't supposed to be about Pope or any kind of literature; it was an off-beat kind of language class, but somehow he got into it. It had seemed important to the prof then that Pope (1688-1744) was a divided person. With half his mind he thought that since God was in charge of the world, everything always worked out for the best; with the other half he seemed convinced that his country (England) was entering a period of steep cultural decline.

The decline was what the *Dunciad* was about. Besides savaging the authors of crappy poems and plays, Pope went after teachers and scholars and scientists, dunces all. What was Pope's problem, anyway? Did he think all these characters *wanted* to be stupid, to be dull? He might have, but did they?

Professor Rosenblum cast an eye upon his students. Several were yawning without troubling to cover their gaping mouths. Is that what *they* wanted, to be stupid? That might answer some questions he had about them. But he, the professor, was doing okay. For a moment he congratulated himself on how well he remembered the *Dunciad*, like he'd just reread it yesterday. He could almost see what Pope describes, a mob of deformed halfwits rushing up to Dulness, a huge, enthroned female, begging her to certify them as 100 percent dumb. Something, a layer of something, lay across her face, but she could still see them and gladly own them as her subjects, her dunces. Maybe he was remembering too well, or too vividly. It seemed to him that the *Dunciad* was supposed to be funny, a regular kick in the ass, but now that it was reviving itself in his mind, it was more like a nightmare. Is that how Pope felt about the world he was living in, that it was a nightmare?

Maybe, but he also wrote a once famous poem all about how "Whatever is, is right." This, said the prof's paragraph, was the philosophy of Leibniz but he couldn't remember how he had known that, since he now had no idea who Leibniz was or what university he taught at. The interesting thing was that Pope also wrote satires that seemed to say that whatever is, is wrong. Of these satires, the most sweeping, profound, scary (none of these words was quite right) is the *Dunciad*, the poem the female student was reciting.

Oh, sure. Of course. The dusky queen is Dulness, the goddess who rules the crazy world of the *Dunciad*, and she's called that, the professor was almost sure, in the poem's fourth and final book. The *Dunciad* was first published in three books in 1728 (or was it 1727?), and what became the fourth book came out separately as the *New Dunciad* in 1742. Then it became Book 4 when Pope tacked it on the first three, revising everything, in 1743. Pretty darn complicated, but he was still on top of it, all those details.

Anyway, in Book 4 everyone in England or maybe the world is being drawn to Dulness, like buzzing bees to a queen. All these people come bringing odd things to give to her as presents. He remembered that, but at the moment he couldn't recall what these items were. Well, then, after about five hundred more lines, something bad happens, and here the prof's capacious memory for details again failed to serve him. It was a great catastrophe, like a plague or flood, but neither of those sounded right. How about an earthquake, like the earthquake he'd narrowly survived several decades ago, but even worse? Could be. He could go to the library and look it up after class, if he felt like doing that. Usually he just went home at that time and watched a little TV. Judge Judy was always interesting.

Now, wait. Was he right about that dusky queen thing? He had a bad feeling.

"Gimme that," he said, seizing a student's Pope anthology (one-volume Twickenham edition).

"Hey," said the student, drowsily, raising her head from the table.

Soon he located the queen reference in Book 4 and found that indeed it was just a simile involving bees. No one actually addresses Dulness as that in the poem, with its cast of thousands, though she is regularly hailed as "Goddess" and occasionally as "Empress" or "Mistress." Good! He'd corrected himself, as a proper scholar should do. Idly he skimmed the pages. He chuckled at the couplet that began the brief section that concluded with "dusky Queen."

And now had Fame's posterior Trumpet blown.
And all the Nations summon'd to the Throne.

Dulness's Throne, of course. Good stuff. Really should reread. Maybe then he could recall what the point of the whole thing was.

He had a pile of pieces of poems in his head. Fragments. More Pope fragments than other kinds. At one time in his life he'd read Pope for about six hours a day. Trouble now was, it was hard to put the pieces together, even when a particular poem he was trying to interpret to a class was short, like a sonnet. Not that he'd done any of that lately. Not that Pope had written any sonnets. And the *Dunciad* was by no means short. He had a feeling that somehow it was *about* fragments or fragmentation, which made him think of explosions, but he doubted an actual explosion was the big disaster in the *Dunciad*.

He pushed the Twickenham edition back across the table to the student who owned it. It was christened that by its publisher, Yale UP, because Pope had lived in a village of that name; students usually called it the "big Twick." He felt the heavy book hit something and heard a clonk.

"I think you broke my iPad, " the student complained, lifting it from the floor and holding it out to Professor Rosenblum as if she wanted him to take it home and nurse it back to health.

"Did not," the professor replied. "I understand they're practically unbreakable. Now, don't be silly."

Mental picture of an iPad with a nuclear bomb dropping on it. He should get one, an iPad, not a bomb. They were handy for finding out bits and pieces of things. Long ago, when doing his seminal work on Laurence Eusden (poet laureate 1718-1730), he had spent many hours in libraries unearthing long interred details concerning old Laurence. It would be so much easier now.

Now the student reader, the current one, was complaining. "Should I go on with this, Professor? No one seems to be listening. Don't they give a shit or something?"

"Oh, sure they do," he said, smiling at her. "Let's hear some more."

Pretty little thing. He took off his glasses and polished them with his tie, a very old, narrow one from his dad's menswear store in Santa Monica.

Now, wait a minute. Those toots he heard (funny that no one else had shown any sign of hearing them) must have come just after the then student reader had recited the line about the queen. So the blasts had escaped—or been forcibly thrust—from someone's posterior, or mouth, just about when Fame blew her "posterior Trumpet," summoning the nations to her throne. That was it. Now he had it. The monotonous girl had read the line, and then some wise-guy student had farted. kazoot. Twice. kazoot. kazoot. Hopefully, just with his lips.

But hold the phone. No. That would require a real wise guy and he had none. He always made sure of that. If a student showed symptoms of wise guyness—a smirk, a giggle, an impertinent question when he wanted to just sit quiet—Professor Rosenblum made sure to quash him or her with an icy glare or, in a severe case, a B grade instead of the standard A. The farts had probably been real, touched off by the potent formula "posterior trumpet." Neither the gaseous one nor his classmates may even have noticed what he had produced, so dull were their senses. They were so mechanical, his students. A good thing they had him for a teacher. Reading aloud was as much as they could do. They could hardly be expected to understand anything. And Pope was hard, or so he recalled. He thought about the funny couplet again.

And now had Fame's posterior Trumpet blown.

And all the Nations summon'd to the Throne.

Well, so what did Fame farting signify in the poem? His memory seemed stalled. Was this one of the hard things? Then he remembered. The posterior trumpet was supposed to announce the coming of Dulness, the goddess, and the imminent collapse of civilization, whatever form that took. She, Dulness, did something to cause the collapse, but he couldn't remember that either. Damn! And how many times had he read the *Dunciad?* Well, many, though not lately. Again he considered a trip to the library after class. He looked out the window to make sure the library building, constructed in 1892, was where he remembered it.

Actually, it didn't matter who kazooted. Whoever did it hadn't meant anything, and it was probably just an accident. Perhaps he was the one! That was funny. He smirked, then chuckled.

"What's so funny, Doc?" The reader had stopped reading again, but it wasn't her question. That had issued from the professor's favorite student, an undergrad PE major and reserve defensive back on the Enola Gay Battlin' Bombardiers. Rocky had enrolled in the class under the misapprehension that the Pope of *Pope and his Contemporaries* was Bucky Pope, an NFL wide receiver known as the Catawba Claw. After learning what Pope it really was, he had stayed in the course because it fulfilled a breadth requirement and was easy. He wasn't a real wise guy, just friendly in the bumptious style of athletes. Professor Rosenblum had had to caution him against massaging his crotch in class, but he was a good boy.

"What am I missing here?" Rocky asked. He was a curious soul, was Rocky, but he meant no harm with his occasional questions. "What's the big yuck?"

"Oh, nothing," said the Doc. "Not really."

"Hey," someone protested, someone new. "I'm reading now."

Yes, there had been a sort of hum in the seminar room. It was the new student. "Please continue," said the professor.

The kazooting. Maybe it had come in from outside. Would have to be mighty loud for that to happen. Someone with a real medical problem. Ah, well. What difference?

He glanced at the reading student, who wore glasses so enormous they appeared to be floating in front of her expressionless face. The lenses were quite dark. How could she see? Not much light was coming into the room from outside, the prof observed, shifting his gaze to the seminar room's lone window. Dark out there, very dark, although it was only about three in the afternoon. Could a tornado be coming? His colleagues had told him Kansas tornado stories so hair-raising that he thought they were just trying to scare him, and there hadn't been one since he'd accepted his tenure track position at Enola Gay more than thirty years ago. Full professor for most of that time. Outstanding record of service on departmental committees.

Now he discerned a heavy layer of mist settling on the grass outside, like nothing he'd seen before. Not here, anyway. It had often got misty in England, when he was teaching there. But might the phenomenon here be a prelude to one of those savage twisters?

"Let's quit early," he told the class. "I want to go home and make sure everything's closed up."

Where had he parked his car? He had two favorite spots. He would try both. No problem.

But why, after he had suggested quitting early, had no one moved? No shuffling of notebooks and big Twicks. No squeaking of chair legs pushed back. Were they all asleep?

"Hey, everybody." No response.

He tried the relatively energetic athlete.

"Rocky? Rocky, do you think you'll get in the game on Saturday?"

But the backup back said nothing. He appeared to be napping, head down on the seminar table.

Well, one student was awake, the big glasses one, or was she reading in her sleep? The words, the noise she was making. No, it wasn't her. Like the kazoots, that humming sound was coming in from outside. It washed over him like surf. A picture formed in his mind of a gigantic, enthroned female. Her. Dulness. My dusky queen. No, that was a bee. My Empress. My Goddess. He loved her so. Where the fuck was all this coming from? He had no idea. Something, perhaps something from his past, was stirring inside him. There was a blank spot back there, somewhere. He'd always had dreams about it, about going back and seeing ... what? Then he'd wake up. Lately the dreams had been coming more often. In them he was first confined in a small space, but then it opened up and he saw something or someone bearing a special message for him that he couldn't recall upon waking. But why was he thinking about this now?

Suddenly the professor was in something of a panic. Nothing made any sense, and he needed to go home and rest. He lumbered to the classroom door and crashed through it, but somehow then turned wrong and entered a narrow, dark room he didn't remember. Nor did he remember exiting from the room, but suddenly he found himself outside. It was dark there, too, with barely enough light, a sickly, yellow light, to show the path before him. He saw his friend, Shelley from the grounds crew, sitting on one of his mowers, hunched over as if something was wrong with him. He called out to him, but Shelley showed no sign of having heard. Curious what bad weather will do. Goddess, Goddess. Are you coming? Did he say that or just think it in his head?

He'd never noticed how dingy and decrepit the library looked. What a shame for such a fine old building, as if no one visited it anymore. He should tell Lozange. No, that was at the other school, the one in England. He stumbled and barely caught himself. His balance was off. His left arm hurt, must have banged it when in that little room.

The professor looked up at the sky. It was turning from gray to black.

Home Invasion

April 23, 1983
Heartland City
Derek's Apartment

His place had been "tossed." Isn't that what you say, "tossed"? It would be good to use a word the cops would take seriously. "I've been burglarized" was what an old lady might quaver, lamenting purloined antimacassars. Were he to say it, the sturdy midwestern lawmen he'd noticed around town might not laugh, but they would be less apt to take him seriously. He'd had more than enough of that, of scant regard, in San Francisco, at the Eighteenth-Century Studies convention from which he'd just now returned. There the college recruiters actually *had* laughed. They laughed when letting him know what a fool he was to think he had a chance for a job at their institutions. This, even though they had invited him to interview after he, following his adviser's counsel on where to apply, had made the initial queries.

Standing amid the rubble of his small apartment, the scattered contents of looted drawers and clean swept shelves, he picked up the phone.

"This is Derek Rosenblum at 695 Pleasant Meadows Lane. I just got back here from a trip and found that my apartment's been tossed."

The cop or dispatcher, or whatever she was, said, "It's been what?" She sounded faintly amused.

"Burglarized."

She asked him to say his name and address again. Then she said, "Okay, what's missing?"

"Oh." He hadn't really looked. Now he glanced around.

"My Selectric," Derek told her. "My stereo. Books."

"Books?" she queried. As if who cares about books? But some of those missing were valuable and not even his. They came from the university library or from other libraries via interlibrary loan, rare scholarly books he'd needed for ...

"My dissertation! I don't see it!"

She said something about "cash value." He wasn't listening. "I'd better look," he said. "In the mess."

This learned work, 'Laurence Eusden: Laureate Little Known,' had been recently accepted by his adviser, Professor Lucia Luteplucker; she was then supposed to have a copy made for donation to the Heartland University library. It hadn't been there, however, the last time he'd checked. The professor's actions were difficult to predict. Perhaps she had thrown it away. She had never been at all enthusiastic about 'Laurence Eusden,' even though she had insisted that Derek write about laureate Eusden, who had served two British kings from 1718 to 1730. She had also insisted on the clunky alliterative title.

Derek scrambled about on the floor of his apartment, where everything he owned seemed to have been pitched, except for those items stolen: Selectic gone, also his stereo, fuzzy-screened TV, barely functioning camera. The thieves (too much disorder to have been caused by only one person) had even taken the bag containing his bowling ball and shoes, which seemed needlessly cruel. How much would a fence give for an old rubber bowling ball? And the way all his things had been thrown around—plates and knives and forks dumped on the kitchen lino, pole lamp knocked over and broken—suggested some personal grudge, not the swift, businesslike approach of professional criminals.

Enemies? Well, sometimes he lost his temper and frightened people who were giving him a hard time. He'd had to restrain himself at the convention. He was a good-sized fellow by any standard and he seemed close to huge here in the middle Midwest, whose both male and female citizens averaged about five-nine, rarely shorter, rarely taller. Occasionally he'd given some unfortunate person a shake or two, but this wanton destruction of all that he possessed seemed far too much payback for anything he could remember doing to anyone.

He discovered the dissertation spread out across the bathroom floor, directly in front of the commode. Gingerly, he assembled the disordered pages, a task swiftly performed, there being only 120 of them, considerably fewer than in the average dissertation. As Eusden was, indeed, very little known, there was no criticism to take issue with, and Derek could think of little to say about him and his poetry. That was where the hard work had been, squeezing something out of this mediocre man and his mediocre verses.

There. The title page. Putting it on top of his meager pile, he noticed that the thief, while perched upon the bowl, as he must have been, had scrawled something just beneath the "by Derek Rosenblum." The message was faint, in pencil. Derek carried the page into his living room, righted the pole lamp and turned it on. It blinked, but gave enough light for him to read. "This is shit," he read.

"Why, you son of a bitch," he whispered. And then, "It's not *that* bad." And then, "She made me do it," meaning Luteplucker, who had kept rejecting his proposals to write about anyone else from the eighteenth century until only Laurence Eusden was left.

That had been an excruciating hour. She led off with Eusden. He said he wanted to do something on the *Dunciad*. If she had asked him what, he couldn't have told her. It fascinated him, that was all. But she didn't ask. She just said no. Well, perhaps she had something against that particular poem. There was a story he'd heard. So could he do other things by Pope? Or by Swift, or Johnson, or Behn? No. When he asked about working on such minor players as Henry Mackenzie and Robert Blair, for even they were more interesting than Eusden, his adviser didn't even bother to speak. It was Eusden or nobody, and he wanted that Ph.D.

Their session had concluded. Professor Luteplucker had another engagement. Rising from her desk, she turned to pluck her leather jacket from its hook. It seemed to Derek that she posed thus, backside to him, for a long moment. Her buttocks were round and firm-looking. He began to feel aroused and thought it best to leave. That afternoon he began work on his dissertation. Now, seated in his turn upon the toilet, he contemplated his first page.

"This is shit," huh? Well, what other perceptive comments might be written here? Derek glanced at the following pages and noticed what seemed to be corrections for grammar and style, but as he began to look at these more closely the law arrived. Derek left the bathroom to admit the policeman, who stood exactly five feet nine inches tall. The yellowishness of his complexion suggested that most of what he ate was made from corn. He was a city cop in tan, rather than one of the campus officers, who wore blue uniforms and silly London bobby-style helmets.

After poking around and finding no signs of forcible entry, he asked if Derek might have left his door unlocked while away. Derek said it was possible. The cop shook his head. Did Derek have renter's insurance? No, no. Again a shake. Tsking, the cop made a list of items stolen, the Selectric and other stuff.

"No great value," he commented. "That's good."

The cop became curious about 'Laurence Eusden: Laureate Little Known,' probably because Derek was holding it to his breast as they paced around the apartment.

"Looks like a dissertation," he commented.

Well, it's a university town. Any hunk of paper is likely to be a dissertation. Derek said, "Yeah."

"Oh, let's see." The cop extended a hand. "I'm always interested in what you guys do."

"No."

He didn't want to have to explain who Eusden was. Besides Luteplucker, he'd met only one person who knew, Professor Sheldon Glick, encountered at the convention recently concluded in San Francisco. Which didn't give him shit. That is, a job. And now here was "This is shit." The cop might laugh at that if he saw it.

He laughed anyway. He knew. "Bet he wrote on it."

Derek did not respond. With one hand he clutched his manuscript; with the other, he removed items from a drawer, making room for 'Laurence Eusden.'

"There's a gang of 'em," said the cop, who appeared to think it was all very funny. "Call themselves the ABD gang, whatever that means. Always leave a comment behind. Sometimes they're pretty witty. Sometimes it's a kind of manifesto about not being allowed to teach because they haven't got a Ph.D. Here, let's see what they wrote this time."

Derek plunked his "This is shit" dissertation into the drawer, which he slammed shut.

"They didn't write anything," he lied. "In fact, that's not even a dissertation. Actually."

"Oh, really?" said the cop. "That's not what you said a minute ago. Come on, guy. Gimme a look."

"They took my bowling ball. That's what concerns me most. I'm in a league."

That too was a lie, and he was a terrible bowler.

"Have it your way," grumped the cop. Soon, tucking his brief list of Derek's stolen valuables into his shirt pocket, he made ready to leave. Derek had a question.

"Fingerprints?" he asked. "You're not going to dust?" Perversely eager to see what else the thief had written, he didn't bother protesting when the cop huffed, "Dust. Dust? Hah!"

He exited, repeating "dust" and shaking his head.

Alone, Derek sat at his desk, surrounded by mess, and proceeded to read. Yes, there were corrections, though not for grammar; having taught nine sections yearly of remedial composition at Heartland University (thus releasing regular faculty for less onerous tasks), he knew the proper place of every comma. But the thief did seem intent on simplifying Derek's sentence structure and shortening his paragraphs. One para became three. One trickily subordinated sentence became three choppy shrimps.

My thief, my editor. Brilliant suggestions in the bathroom. He had begun with Derek's very first sentence, which as Derek wrote it was: "Although modern taste places the traditional panegyric well down in the hierarchy of genres, formerly it ranked as one of the noblest of the literary kinds, and it is unreasonable to consign Eusden to literature's lower depths simply because it was his occupational specialty." With a few strokes of what probably was Derek's own pencil, filched from the desk, this became: "Modern taste places the panegyric well down the genre ladder. Once, however, it was a noble literary kind. It is unreasonable to ['consign' written and crossed out] deposit Eusden in literature's lower depths just because he wrote them."

Derek considered. His own beginning wasn't exactly a grabber, but it was much better than the choppy revised version. "Just because he wrote them" wasn't too bad. It's not always a mistake to write simply, as he told his students when they got fancy and therefore completely unintelligible. But still, this guy was way *too* simple. Anyway, how dare he presume to touch another's prose! Now Derek was sorry he hadn't pressed the lawman into taking fingerprints.

On page twelve there were no comments. Thirteen was free of them as well. All the pages following were unmarred. At least the thief hadn't wiped his ass with them.

Derek returned to page eleven, where the last comment was.

"Who was Laurence Eusden? Shouldn't you say, college boy?"

Eusden

Yes. Who indeed? In those pre-Wikipedia days, it had taken Derek a good deal of time and trouble to learn not very much. Let us review.

He was born in Yorkshire in 1688, attended Trinity College, Cambridge, and became an Anglican minister. In 1718 he was appointed poet laureate of Great Britain and continued to hold that office until his death in 1730. Thus he served as well as he could (Lord knows he tried) two kings, the Georges I and II, though for only three years of the latter's reign, which rumbled on until 1760. In the *Dunciad* Pope refers to this father and son team as Dunce the First and Dunce the Second, so it was probably a good thing that they got the laureate they deserved, one as dull as they were.

Eusden is the least known of all those who wore the laurel; hence Derek's title. While literary historians almost never mention him, when they do, the word "mediocre" always turns up sooner rather than later. There was, then, nothing Derek could find to do with him except to argue that Eusden deserved critical attention for being so distinctively mediocre. Indeed, his tenure sits as an absolute low point for mediocrity, coming as it does after the not quite so dismal terms of Richard Shadwell, Nahum Tate, and Nicholas Rowe and before those of Colly Cibber and William Whitehead, who represent a slight improvement. All these are mediocre too, but Eusden set the standard for all time.

Mediocre, not exactly bad, which might be more interesting. He could rhyme, and he could count: ten syllables to a line, iambic pent, da-dum, da-dum, da-dum, da-dum, da-dum. Equal syllables. If you had one line, you always knew what the next would be. "Where-e'r you find the cooling Western Breeze,/In the next line, it whispers thro the Trees." That's Pope, in *An Essay on Criticism*, being critical, as was his wont, though not in this case of Eusden or of anyone in particular. He often did attack specific targets, certainly; he went after Cibber hard, appointing him king of the dunces in the 1743 *Dunciad*, but Eusden receives only two mocking lines, also in the *Dunciad*. Always the *Dunciad*. Everyone's in it, and everything.

Oh, and what sort of poetry did Eusden produce? Whatever he wrote before his laureateship is unknown, even to people who know everything or who pretend they do, like Professor Lucia Luteplucker. As poet laureate, he did what all of them must do, he flattered. That's the job, and it's okay to be obvious. Consider Eusden's blatant "Poem on the happy Succession, and Coronation of his present Majesty." Admittedly, considering the character of the first two Georges, only a particularly ingenious poet could have produced words of praise one could take at all seriously. John Dryden, a rare example of a truly literate laureate, might have been up to the task, but Eusden was no Dryden.

Eusden's "present Majesty" is George II, succeeding his father after the latter's death in 1727. A happy succession indeed for the new king, who had hated his father as much as the latter hated him. (The ever restive British public detested both of them.)   Neither George took the slightest interest in poetry. Indeed, the elder, imported from Germany when Britain ran out of Stuarts, never learned to read or even to speak English. What subjects for the Muse! But here that lady is, down in the dumps upon the first king's death, slopping around like a San Francisco street person in the twenty-first century.

> The Muse, that late on dangling Pinions hung,
> Her Voice neglected, and her Lyre un-strung.

Or here the lady *was*. For now, with the second George in charge, happy, She,

> Chear'd with sweet Prospects, spreads sublime her Wings,
> Tow'rs in bold Flights, and, flush'd with Rapture, sings.

Hideous? Well, no, for hideous would have been better in the sense that these lines would have made an impression. They would have made you shudder. These lines have no effect at all; they are mediocre. That was Eusden's achievement in everything he wrote (with one possible exception to be discussed later). What was his secret? It was at least partly a matter of following the rules too strictly. Thrusting in the Muse was a rule, for example, in this kind of verse.

Although they weren't all written down, there were several rules for writing panegyric. In this era, there were rules for writing anything, every genre. However, in the *Essay on Criticism*, Pope observes that there are occasions for breaking rules. This is good, nay, valuable advice, but Eusden seems never to have broken any, thus creating poetry of impeccable dullness. Isn't that worth talking about? Why not give mediocrity a break for once? That was the question Derek posed, hoping it would interest other eighteenth-century specialists, even the big shots, who are finding ever less to say about the poets and novelists thought to excel in one way or another. But there was no response from the professoriat. No one noticed either his question or him.

Understanding how ridiculously obscure his subject was, Derek had thought he might begin his dissertation by seizing upon the virtual emptiness of Eusden's personal and emotional life as an opportunity for all kinds of adventurous speculation. Indeed, fueled by vodka and desperation, Derek would eventually employ his imagination in just this way. But then, when he mentioned his planned introduction to Professor Luteplucker, she shook her head and murmured, "No." At least he got a word out of her. She didn't explain, but that was no surprise. As was well known at Heartland U, she rarely explained herself; in fact, she rarely used words and relied on gestures and postures. Thinking about it later, Derek provided his own explanation. She didn't care for speculation, for, it was her pride just to know a host of things about the century, especially little things, and she had a way of finding out about them.

He didn't understand this then and so he wondered why she made him revise 'Laurence Eusden: Laureate Little Known' four times, with an eye to including more and more little things. These tidbits, though often lacking any perceptible connection with Eusden, were often fun to uncover. He particularly enjoyed learning about the heroic Admiral Edward Vernon, whose victory over the Spanish at Porto Bello became the subject of a pretty good mock-epic by Henry Fielding, *The Vernoniad*. That Vernon's naval triumph occurred in 1739, nine years after Eusden's death, caused Derek some difficulty when fitting it in to his dissertation; but he did his best to make it fit and was thus considerably frustrated later when, for his final revision, Professor Luteplucker insisted on removing everything about Vernon. In fact, everything not directly connected with Eusden had to go.

In the following year, though Derek didn't know about it at the time, his professor published a two-page note about Edward Vernon and Fielding, based on his researches, for which he received no thanks or credit. That was her regular practice with her students, assigning, then appropriating, leaving in Derek's case a skimpy treatise focused entirely upon the pathetic Laurence Eusden.

Eusden! In San Francisco the recruiter at the convention who knew who Eusden was had burst into coarse laughter when repeating the name after Derek said it first.

"*Eusden?* You wrote about *Laurence Eusden?*"

It was only human of Derek to hold a grudge against scholarly wise guy Professor Sheldon Glick of Enola Gay State University.

Welcome, 18th-Century Scholars

In 1983 the American Association for Eighteenth-Century Studies, Literature Branch, held its annual convention in San Francisco during spring break time. It rained a lot, giving Derek a poor impression of that fabled city. No matter where he ventured, it had a dingy look.

Before his evening meeting with Glick, he had met with faculty recruiters from two colleges, one located in South Dakota and the other in north Alabama. Both men casually confessed to never having heard of Laurence Eusden. In addition, they seemed not to know who Derek was or why his name had appeared on their lists of interviewees. His presence made them scratch their heads. Glick, his last chance, though better informed on both counts, was obviously determined to get rid of him as quickly as he could. So why had Kansas's Enola Gay State scheduled the interview? Why had the other schools? Angered, the job seeker resolved to sit there in Glick's hotel room until morning, just to spite the fat little eighteenth-century specialist from Kansas.

"How can you consider living in Kansas, a fellow of your type?" Thus did Glick begin.

Your type? Derek didn't know what his interviewer meant by that, but it was easy to answer the question. "I've been at Heartland for four years, the Midwest. It's okay. It's fine."

Glick promptly responded. "Kansas is worse than Heartland, believe me. Dull, dull, dull, especially for us urbanites. From New York, am I right? Brooklyn, maybe? My home town."

Indeed it was. He had the brogue. He was sitting on his bed in the little room in the dingy Tenderloin hotel where the Association stored delegates from second and third-rate colleges. It was nearly midnight, and Professor Glick had his pajamas on, so it puzzled Derek that his thinning hair was all moussed up and combed over a still detectable bald spot, and that he had drenched himself with a cologne that made him smell like an aged salad.

"Am I right?"

"No, you're not right," Derek replied. "I've only been in New York twice."

"You should go more often."

Derek did not respond

"So. Okay. Where *are* you from?"

"L.A."

"Aha! Proves my point. Same thing."

"No it's not. Anyway, I don't like it there."

"You like tornadoes? We got them. And right-wingers? At a college named after the B-29 that wiped out Hiroshima? They have a big mock-up right in the middle of campus. You bet we got them. You wanna come to Enola Gay, really?"

Not particularly, but he'd go if they offered. After four years of grad school, coming up empty in his job search would be a terrible thing. And, absent a miracle, that was exactly what was going to happen. No one had taken the slightest interest in him, not even little prairie pisspot Enola Gay. Fuck them. He'd had enough. He changed his mind about camping out in the room of this Glick character. Better to get out, take a walk, get drunk.

"No, I don't really wanna," Derek said, "and you don't want me, anyway, which means there's no point in me taking up any more of your time. Nice chatting with you, Professor Glick."

But when he got up to leave, Glick lifted a restraining paw. "Hang on," he said. "Maybe there's some things I could tell you. Is it possible maybe you don't know these things?"

Derek settled again in his chair. Someone rapped three times on the hotel room's door. "Early," Glick observed, pronouncing it "oily," like his hair. "Hey, honey," he shouted. "Come back in ten minutes."

"They don't like us lingering in the halls," a woman answered, sounding aggrieved.

"You mind?"

Just as Derek realized that the question was addressed to him, Sheldon sprang from his bed, dashed into the bathroom, flicked the light on. Through the open bathroom door Derek saw the little man thrusting his face into the mirror. He emerged, stroking his side hairs, and admitted the lady in the hall.

"Two of you?" she inquired. "Why was I not consulted?"

"No, he's going," Sheldon said.

But Derek wanted to hear about the promised "things."

"The things," he said, "I may not know. Tell me, please. I may as well get something out of this." He meant the whole convention, the wet city.

"Yeah, okay. You mind?"

This to the woman, and again he did not stay for an answer. Confident little bastard. Derek found himself being amused by Glick, somewhat. The woman did not respond in this way.

"Meter's running," she grumbled.

She was short, busty, attired in a shiny one-piece garment. Whole thing probably peeled off at the touch of a zipper. She was almost cute, but Derek had too much worry in his head to take an interest. Too old, too. At least thirty-five, four years older than he was.

"I got another appointment in half an hour," she said. "UT Permian Basin guy in one of the suites. They pay. Oil money. Better get a wiggle on."

Sheldon ignored her. Huffing, she plumped herself down at the foot of the bed on which the pajamed professor had now stretched himself full-length. He pulled a pillow under his head and addressed Derek while staring at the ceiling.

"Look, Rosenblum. I feel sorry for you. I also feel sorry for me, for all of us. Something's gone wrong with the profession. But here's what's specifically wrong with you. For your doctoral dissertation, you chose to write on an unknown white guy. Why?"

Derek made no answer. He'd wanted to write about Alexander Pope, a known white guy, but that his adviser had forced Laurence Eusden on him was something he preferred not to reveal. Sheldon carried on.

"You couldn't find a woman to write about? Least you could have done. Better yet, a lesbian. A racial minority? Not easy to find in eighteenth-century Britain, that I'll grant you; but the truth is, Rosenblum, that it wouldn't matter anyway who you wrote about, cause *you're* not a woman or a lesbian or a minority."

"Jew," Derek said, meaning himself but knowing it didn't count.

"Very funny. Ha-ha. You know, it wouldn't be so bad if they looked at the person too, not just at the ethnicity. But they don't. And suppose you got a job somewhere. Unlikely as that would be, let us consider it. Let us, in fact, consider me. Me! Me!"

"Meter's running."

"Oh, yeah, you. What's your name?"

"Marigold."

"Pretty, and so appropriate. Okay, I publish. I read papers at meetings. Like in this one, I'm in a Samuel Johnson seminar. Johnson, he was a—"

"I know who Samuel Johnson was," snapped Derek.

"Well, it's truly amazing what people don't know these days. And what they do know."

Marigold chimed in. "Dictionary guy, right?"

"Geez." Glick sat up on the bed. Hard to tell if he was tickled or dismayed by Marigold's show of erudition. In either case, Marigold was irked.

"You think I'm stupid?" she said. "Just because I'm a sex worker, that means I don't know who Johnson was? I had the survey."

Unheeding, Glick rolled on. "So what am I teaching at EGSU? When it's not composition to illiterates, it's multicultural. Native American Oral this and that, Armenian diaspora free verse, Spanglish lit. I'm not saying all that stuff is bad, but they throw it at me, and it keeps changing. Eighteenth-century lit? My specialty practically since birth? One course a year, if I'm lucky. And such will be your lot. If you get a job. Which you won't. So go! I wanna get laid."

"I don't think I like your attitude," said Marigold. "Keep your fucking money."

To Derek: "Come on, let's blow this taco stand."

"Yes, go," said Glick, leaning back and shielding his eyes with one pudgy forearm. "Both of you go. I don't care. No one cares about me, so why should I care about them?"

"Just a minute," Derek said.

Though he felt somewhat responsible for Marigold, who seemed to want his company, he wasn't finished with Glick.

She took umbrage. "Now or never," she told Derek, strolling toward the door, and when he stayed put, "Don't need you, big boy."

As Marigold flounced from the room, while pulling down the zipper on her outfit, Sheldon Glick inserted himself beneath the covers on his bed. From somewhere he produced a ratty-looking newspaper and held it up above his face.

"Yes?" he said to Derek, through the paper. "You require something, I take it?"

Derek approached the bed and knelt so that his ear was six inches from Glick's mouth. Gently, he twitched the newspaper, open to a listing of outcall massage services, from the professor's grasp. A corner tore off.

He had a question, one he'd been meaning to ask of anyone who might have an answer, since his first interview, two days ago. First, though, he'd changed his mind about saying why he'd written about an unknown white guy.

"I didn't choose to write on Eusden. My adviser made me." This made him look weak, but better that than stupid. He hated looking stupid.

"Ah," said Glick. "That would be Professor Lucia Luteplucker."

"You know her?" asked Derek.

Glick lowered his voice to a whisper. "No. God, no."

Derek understood. She was not a friendly person and made everyone apprehensive. Hastening to his question, he found himself whispering also.

"Listen. Why did you choose to see me here? Any of you people. I mean, why did you pretend to want to see me, so that I came out from Heartland on my own dime to find out that no one wants me. Why put me through this? That's what I want to know. The other things you told me I sorta knew; this I don't."

"Her," Glick sounded frightened, possibly because of the uncomfortable closeness of his mouth to Derek's ear, or there might have been another cause.

"Her?" But Derek knew.

"Your adviser, that Luteplucker woman. She bullied us into it, all of us, just as she bullied you on your dissertation. She made us do it. She sees things, knows things. Say, would you mind backing off a little?"

Derek backed off. Glick continued. He ceased whispering.

"What does she know? What thinking? What scheming? No one can tell. But now she's far away. She can't get at us when we're out here on the coast. I hope. And listen, Rosenblum. She wasn't very enthusiastic about you, anyway."

"Oh."

"It's funny. We had to interview you, but we didn't have to hire you. Like I said, who knows about her? And the truth is we just don't have a slot for a person of your gender, ethnicity, and sexual orientation. In fact, nobody does. So turn off the light, my boy. Go! Get a non-academic job. The media pay well, I hear. If I were younger ... but I'm not. So go! Get out while you can. Let the darkness come."

Quite a character, this Glick. Such flamboyance, especially the bit about Professor Luteplucker knowing things. But his adviser was distinctly weird, and Derek wouldn't have minded hearing more from Glick, either about her or the profession he had hoped to enter since boyhood. Even though the little man seemed obsessed with his own sad lot, Derek sensed some concern for himself in what he had said, but Glick was all talked out.

Closing his eyes, he rolled onto his stomach. Derek flicked off the light and left the room. In the hallway Marigold was waiting before another door.

She turned, revealing now half-exposed bare breasts, and smiled enticingly as Derek, who didn't smile back, thus perhaps rejecting a potentially lucrative career as a pimp.

He went to his room in the hotel. Drinking no longer appealed.

What Glick had said suggested that while Luteplucker had forced the recruiters to talk to him, she had set him up for failure in the interviews. But why would she do that? It made no sense to Derek.

Luteplucker

The following evening found Derek standing amongst the detritus of his looted apartment. In the morning he drove to the campus, found a parking space for his wheezing Toyota Corona, and walked to the university library, where he reported the stolen books. He agreed to a $600 replacement fee, to be extracted in installments from his next year's monthly checks for teaching remedial comp. That was fine with Derek, since he knew there would be no checks. Now that he had the Ph.D. and was in theory ready to launch his academic career, even if he'd wanted the remedial job, the English Department would insist on giving it to someone new. And he didn't want it or to be at or even near Heartland U, where it now appeared he had wasted four years and become no longer young.

The spring semester had four more weeks to run, which meant he would have to meet each of his two sections a total of twelve times. He would sit there and try to answer questions if his freshmen had any, but he wouldn't bother them with quizzes or papers to hand in or, especially, lectures. He had nothing to tell them. He was finished here. The burglary seemed now to be a sign. Clear out, it meant. Go elsewhere.

It appeared that he was also finished with the profession of English. Sheldon Glick had given him the word on that. It wasn't fair, but there it was, a fact. Clear out. Go elsewhere. Do something else. Think of it as an adventure, why don't you? At thirty-one, he wasn't all that old, and he had no dependents. He was still strong. His pace quickened on the campus path. Then it slowed, as he recalled where he was heading, the classroom where Professor Lucia Luteplucker should be just now concluding a session of her eighteenth-century grad course. Telling her about his failed interviews was the only thing that presently daunted him. He forced himself up the steps.

One of the professor's students was reading something aloud, but so softly that Derek, as he stood in the hallway near the classroom's open door, couldn't tell if it was poetry or prose. There were no other sounds. His eyes closed. He'd had little sleep last night, after discovering the burglary and going through his burglar-annotated dissertation. He leaned against a convenient wall.

The class ended. Derek watched the students drift by. They seemed as dazed as he was and were probably short on sleep themselves, that being a regular part of a student's life—if it were not something else that made these young people shuffle along, eyes fixed upon their plodding feet.

Suddenly she materialized before him in the hall. Seconds before actually seeing her, he had sensed his adviser's presence, which had its usual effect of making him feel small. This was hard to explain. Oh, she was tall. In her high-heeled boots, Lucia Luteplucker stood just a few inches below six feet, but Derek, bootless, exceeded that level by the same margin. And while she was a large, broad-shouldered, though shapely woman, Derek was just as large and broad for a man. He wasn't used to feeling short and meager, but what particularly puzzled him after one of these odd encounters with her was that he found the sensation of smallness somehow comfortable, when it should have been spooky.

Had he spoken to the professor's other students, Derek would have learned that she made them feel the same way, pleasurably shrunken. But her students didn't talk about her. Nor did her colleagues. One didn't.

She was all in black that day, boots, tights, a clingy sweater. Her usual. Very ripe she was, enough, one would think, to arouse any normal male heterosexual, and Derek was as normal as a heterosexual could get. But often rather than concoct fantasies about coupling with her in conventional fashion, he imagined himself crawling onto Luteplucker's lap—physically impossible since he didn't actually shrink into a toddler in the professor's company—and being cradled in her arms while he nuzzled her large, bomb-shaped breasts. The urge beset him even now, when he had to deliver the bad news about his trip to San Francisco. Best to do it quickly.

Interviews three, job offers zero. There. He had said it to her, there in the hall. She said nothing. He had considered asking why she had packed him off to talk with uninterested recruiters, but now decided not to. He didn't know how she would react to the question, for he lacked a sense of what she was feeling. Anger, at him for returning jobless? Or at the three colleges for turning down one of her students, even if she hadn't pressed them to take him? If not angry, was she depressed, or bored, or anything at all? It was always this difficult to guess at her moods. Everyone thought so, colleagues and students alike. Were she normally verbal, that might have helped, but she could spend hours at a faculty tea in utter silence. Her eyes gave no clue, for she always wore sunglasses, indoors or out. Their lenses were red in color.

Today they affected Derek strangely. Though they hovered (it seemed to him) less than a foot from his own face, he felt that she didn't see him. No, not that. She did see him, but only as a dot in an unnaturally copious field of vision.

Suddenly his ears popped. The light in the hallway went dim. I must be tired, Derek thought. Or the stress. Now he felt that she was looking both down upon him and beyond him, way beyond, staring down from a perch impossibly high upon the whole Middle West, at endless corn fields, alabaster shopping malls, thick-thighed linemen sweating out spring practice on sunbaked gridirons. She saw all. Glick. It was Glick's fault that he was having this little fit, what the little man had said—she sees things, knows things. Derek shook his head.

The lights came back up. The professor was upon him, too damn close! Unnerved, Derek wanted out, out of the hallway, away from her, and why was she pressing ever closer to him? Or was he, now a tiny fellow, somehow being drawn to her by virtue of her superior mass? To crash upon her and lose all his breath! She was a killer! And yet he wanted never to leave her and knowing that he had to, because he was leaving Heartland, was for the moment life's greatest tragedy.

At last she nodded. From outside a sound penetrated to the place where they stood; a toot on a horn it could have been, emitted by a strolling student trumpeter prepping for band practice. She said something Derek didn't catch and, turning her back on him, walked down the corridor toward her office. He did not follow either afoot or with his eyes. He was glad to be released and knew he was unequal to the mystery of her.

Derek was not the only one to find seldom-speaking Lucia a mystery. Besides the eye concealing specs, she rarely changed her expression, which could not have been less readable had a small cloud lain across her face. What thinking? What scheming? These questions had no answers that anyone could provide, and only those new to Heartland ever asked them. But some continued to think about them.

Res cogitans. There had to be *something* at work in there, in her head, grinding out directions for the rest of her to follow. Her sentences were short and rarely uttered, but she did speak. Similarly, she often seemed simply to pop into existence before students and colleagues, as she had with Derek in the hall, but she had legs. Being human, she must think, and yet some of her colleagues, the old hands, were not so sure. It seemed to them as if something was controlling her, moving her about, guiding her actions, selecting her very words. But for what purpose?

Malone G. Malone, Heartland's original eighteenth-century man, still hanging on during Lucia Luteplucker's initial year there, may have thought he knew. Or he was just screwing around; he liked freaking out the newcomers, did old Malone, and had played lots of daffy tricks. What he did with Luteplucker was shuffle up behind her as she sat at a table in the Humanities Division Refectory and recite, as loudly as his emphysema would permit, two couplets from Alexander Pope's great and monstrous mock-epic *Dunciad*.

> Then blessing all, "Go Children of my care!
> To Practice now from Theory repair.
> All my commands are easy, short, and full;
> My Sons! Be proud, be selfish, and be dull."

Lucia ignored him, which made him angry. Malone stamped his right foot and huffed away, dragging his wheeled oxygen tank behind him. The only other person present, the department's poet and teacher of would-be poets, had always refused to read anything written in rhyme and meter, so she failed to recognize the quotation and merely remembered a garbled version of what she'd heard. When, however, she spoke of the encounter in the Refectory to the department chair, he figured out what the old man must actually have said. He was sure that young Assistant Prof Luteplucker wouldn't want the story getting around, and that if it did, despite her inferior rank, she could cause a lot of trouble. Thus he cautioned the departmental poet never to speak of what she had seen and heard, and he gave her four units of release time to make her more willing to abide by his request.

But either she disobeyed or the chair didn't follow his own counsel, for gradually the story did get around. To most it was meaningless and was soon forgotten, and Malone was unable to take matters further had he chosen to, being dead due to a mysteriously exploding tank. His head was never found. But of those who had read Pope, their numbers decreasing every year what with all the competition from the multiculture, some troubled themselves to try puzzling out the dead professor's meaning. Eventually the story trickled down to Derek Rosenblum, who easily identified the lines' source, but at the time did no puzzling about Malone's reason for reciting them. Just a senile quirk, he thought.

Well, maybe not. For if the old guy did have something to say, it might have been this: that then Asst. Prof Luteplucker was like Pope's goddess Dulness in the *Dunciad*. For in the poem she speaks the lines Malone recited. That was his source, and perhaps he meant to imply something akin to possession, rather than a mere likeness. But for now let's simply compare them, the goddess and the prof, who in her prime became a person of nationwide influence in English.

Begin with this. In Book 4 of the *Dunciad*, a legion of dunces appears before Dulness, their goddess, seated on her lofty throne. These are "the children of my care." Seeking her approval, they brag to her about their various pursuits, pursuits that Pope thought anti-human. Would-be scientists raid nature for specimens and bring their prizes with them: "A Nest, a Toad, a Fungus, or a Flow'r." Some who teach the Greek and Latin classics force their students to memorize without understanding and themselves indulge in philological study, dwelling on mere words, rather than simply reading and enjoying literature.

"Words we teach alone," says one of their number, words severed from sense.

Now consider the oral reports and papers and dissertations submitted to Professor Luteplucker by students whom she approves as graduates of a course or program or as Doctors of Philosophy, like Derek Rosenblum. In the poem, ever gracious Dulness declares each member of the mob of approval-seeking suppliants a perfect dunce. And does not Doctor equal dunce, and Lucia's Doctors, once she's done with them, more so than any other? Petty scholars these, in their generations, molded in her mind-quenching seminars. That she is laconic we know, but the result of her tutelage is as if she spoke the very words of Pope's dark goddess. "Go Children of my care," and away they trudge, her sons (and daughters, too), glassy-eyed and heavy-footed.

Derek, however, wasn't quite in that condition, which may explain why she was less than enthusiastic in recommending him.

Lucia may think that she restricts her students to reading aloud only because it renders preparation unnecessary and thus saves her work. She may (or she may not) think she has them write theses and dissertations on obscure writers so that she can pirate bits from them for her own scholarly notes (average length, 650 words), thus sustaining her reputation as one who knows a lot, even if it's all pretty fragmentary. But isn't she remarkably dull, both as teacher and scholar? And she makes others dull. For her brainy rep attracts students, who soon decide against warning other students about her tactics lest she find out who squealed. Soon they grow dull, then forget why such warnings should perhaps be given. In time they take their degrees and proceed to other institutions where they do as she did and thus produce more of their kind. And so the darkness grows.

Did Pope picture in Dulness something that actually exists? Did the poet give this dark entity the shape of a large, stupid female? Assuming that he did, can it (but let's call it "she") dwell in mortal bosoms, like the gracefully formed one of Lucia Luteplucker?

Knotty questions indeed. And Derek is so lazy! Unless forced to, he will not think of these things. Only I. And who am I? You can find me in that grand prophecy, the *Dunciad*, but not just there. In fact, I am everywhere, in every story, for I am Fame. Now I am poised to blow my posterior trumpet, whereupon all ends. But first I must tell this story, the story of Derek Rosenblum, Ph.D., which necessarily precedes it. Most times I am content to remain in the background, like any "omniscient narrator." But upon occasion I will present myself to you naked and unadorned. Watch for me!

Back Home

Derek's remedial students got to finish the semester early. He canceled the last week of class and gave everyone A's. Then he set about packing for the trip back home. Loading the Corona on the day of departure, he was depressed by how little stuff he owned. The thief had gotten a few things but had left most of his books, his own battered paperbacks, which now fit easily into one medium-sized box he'd pulled out of the dumpster behind the HyVee supermarket. This made him feel he had been something of a sham as a grad student, and therefore might not deserve a teaching job, even if he did know more about Laurence Eusden than did anyone else anywhere. He put both his dissertation and the copies he'd made of every known line of Eusden's verse into another, smaller, box, also a supermarket product. On his way out of town he returned to the dumpster and pitched it in.

"This is shit," Derek intoned, as the only known treatise on the poet laureate of King Georges I and II settled down within a stratum of rotting carrot tops and slimy, aged chunks of iceberg lettuce. While he meant what he had said as a comment on everything in his life, 'Laurence Eusden: Laureate Little Known' was the stupid worst of it. A muscular female employee, emerging from the store's rear exit, shouted at him for trespassing as he ran to his car. He drove west.

An hour later, at the Missouri line, he turned the car around. He drove back and rooted in the dumpster, looking in vain for what he had left there. Entering the market, he found the sturdy employee seated at the customer service desk, reading the dissertation, now badly stained.

"Gimme that," Derek said wearily. He didn't want it, he couldn't leave it.

"But why this guy, instead of, say, Aphra Behn?" Well, it's a college town.

He made no reply, which miffed her. She stuffed 'Laurence Eusden' back into its box with the Eusden poems and handed it to him without a smile, as if she'd just bagged his groceries. Derek stowed the box in the trunk of his car, where it would stay for almost two years. Passing through Kansas, he considered dropping in on Professor Glick, but Enola Gay State was too much of a detour. Glick was an asshole, anyway. Couldn't understand why he'd felt like seeing him.

So for three days more he forged on to L.A., his native place that he had told Sheldon Glick he didn't like. And he didn't. How could he? His youthful life there had consisted of one damn disappointment after another, causing him to liken himself to a cartoon character unable to dodge heavy pieces of furniture falling on him from the heavens or even to see them before they hit. It was worst in high school, worst of all in his senior year, from which derived his most unpleasant memories.

Big fellow Derek played basketball and had assumed that as a senior he would play a lot, perhaps even be a starter. Then, on the first day of practice a pair of burr-headed six-foot, six-inch twins appeared from nowhere—Montana, Derek learned later—and butt-bumped and elbowed him off the court onto the bench, where he remained throughout the season. What hurt him most wasn't their size and willingness to inflict pain, but that they were good players, which meant that he wasn't. He had been stupid to think he was.

Soon after that disappointment came another that caused him greater pain by far. One day after trig class, something got into him so that he marched right up to the sexiest cheerleader at Sam Yorty Senior High and asked her to be his date for the senior ball. She looked left, then right, gulped and said, "Well, all right, David."

He didn't let it bother him that she got his name wrong. She'd said yes.

"Derek," he gently corrected.

"Whatever."

This was Tracy Chatham, the girl in his honors English class who didn't care about books. Shiny blond hair, sleek tan, great rack. Her smile drove him crazy. It was slightly off-center, as if she thought something was funny but didn't want to talk about it. That smile made him wonder about her, while the rest of Tracy made him intensely horny. From his seat on the bench at basketball games he'd adored her as she pranced upon the court. Even after one of her routines had concluded, Derek's coach would have to slap him on the back of the head to make him focus on his assignment, which was to enter the game and lay a hard foul on the opposing team's best player.

She had a beautiful body, she *was* her body. It required and enjoyed vigorous motion, as do all healthy animals, and whether you watched her or not was of no concern to Tracy Chatham, especially if your name was Derek Rosenblum.

She had no need of books or to learn anything in school. Her flesh did her thinking for her.

On the night of the ball, when he arrived at her house, her obviously bewildered mom told him that the boy she thought was Tracy's date had made off with her half an hour earlier. Derek went home, ripped off his rented tux and hurled it into a corner of his room. Then he cast himself on his bed and cried.

Except for a possible encounter on a southern California beach, Derek didn't speak to Tracy Chatham, or she to him, for the rest of their lives. Many years after high school, at a moment when he knew where she was and could have spoken to her, he chose not to. Until then his memory of Tracy's athletic beauty retained its hold on him and prevented him from sliding entirely into the sink of academe. She was an anti-Luteplucker, but she wasn't enough. In the end, Tracy couldn't even save herself.

Derek found out after the ball (he was always finding things out after) that the earlier arriving date was the dudish senior class president he hated more than anyone else in the school and that on the dance floor he and Tracy had virtually sucked each other's faces off. Thus did several of his wise-guy friends make a point of telling him, just to see how steamed he would get.

But when he told them of his plan to lie in wait for the prez and punch some holes in his pretty-boy face, they said to forget it. The whole mess, his buddies said, was really his fault. He never should have asked her. Tracy was too hot for him, they explained, too hot for the likes of him and also of them. How could he not know that? There were plenty of okay girls around. Why hadn't he asked a lesser light to the ball, as they had? Maybe get some easy nookie, too. Think, buddy, think! Don't be so dumb. Well, with Tracy he couldn't help it.

But why be so dumb as to imagine he had a shot at getting into Harvard, Princeton, or Yale? That was the question he asked himself, when the rejections came.

His friends may have dated girls that were just okay, but they got into the top colleges, while he only made it to their wait lists. Harvard, Princeton, Yale—in the end, each one said sorry. It was his mom's idea that he apply, but her enthusiasm had so infected Derek that when the rejections came, all three on the same day, he was at first genuinely surprised. He'd thought at least one would come through. After a few hours, though, he recalled what a second-rater he was and accepted his fate. It wasn't so awful enrolling at his backup college, an okay school in Ohio. At least it got him out of L.A.

It was a bad habit, he recognized: expecting too much, so that he experienced bitter disappointment when he didn't get it. And a tough habit to break. He would be almost forty when life would finally teach Derek to savor the easefulness of expecting nothing and just letting things take care of themselves.

Los Angeles, his present destination, was surely not the place to begin learning that lesson, for, in Derek's estimation, nothing good had ever happened to him there. However, he couldn't imagine how anything, even in that blighted place, would have the power to make him feel worse than he already felt. After toiling in grad school and completing his degree there by composing a treatise on an unknown and utterly boring English poet, he had failed to get a job. Understandably, Derek felt like doing precisely nothing, and the only place where he could do that was his parents' apartment in Malibu.

For he needed to rest and he could stay with them and not have to worry about living expenses. For he'd had it with trying to be a somebody, even just a junior professor at a cow country college, and L.A. was the best place he knew of—if not for others in the city, for him—to be a nobody. That's what he had always been there. Later, rested, he might go about discovering what opportunities could lie ahead for a man hardly old, if not exactly young. He could summon some enthusiasm then, possibly.

In fact, he had already worked up a little of that precious quality for the Malibu condo that his parents now owned, having sold their inland house. Malibu was still L.A. In fact, it was probably more L.A. than any other section of the city except Hollywood. But at least it lay along the ocean. He could walk to the beach from the Rosenblum condo whenever he wanted to go body surfing, one of the few things he'd ever enjoyed in his youthful days.

After spending his last night on the road in a Nevada motel, Derek called his parents to warn them that he was coming. When he arrived, in mid- evening, his mother hugged him and his father shook his hand. Then, their voices chiming, each asked him about his "plans." He hadn't told them, but somehow they seemed to sense that no college had offered him anything.

"Could we discuss this later?" he requested. "I'm tired."

They fed him. He took a shower, after which he gazed at his naked self in the bathroom mirror. His pecs were drooping; he needed exercise. He then slept for ten hours and after waking spent two more throwing himself around in the Pacific surf. At brunch that day, he told George and Mimi, "You know, I don't *have* to be a college professor. There are other things."

Their faces said, "Like what?" He turned from them and jogged back to the adjacent beach, where he soon learned he didn't belong.

The community into which George and Mimi had settled for their golden years was reserved for the old. On sunny days blackened, wrinkled bodies, some sloppy fat, others shrunken husks, dotted the sparkling sands like an explosion of moles on an otherwise healthy complexion. The oldsters glared hostilely at Derek whenever they spied him emerging from the waves after a bout of body surfing. To get even, he dripped on them as he passed, perhaps an error.

Someone, anyway, ratted him out to management, for his parents soon received an official notice, hand delivered in the evening by a stern-faced minion. The legalese was hard to penetrate at first, but after several readings they determined it was a demand that too young Derek move out within thirty days, as per clause 4a.23 in the contract the Rosenblums had signed upon becoming members of Surfside Senior Sojourners.

It seemed to Derek that his parents were unnecessarily cheery about his having to leave, but what rankled more was their insistence that they would not be the ones paying the rent on his new place, wherever it was. Of course they wouldn't be! He'd been resting, which he'd needed to do; but now he was almost rested enough and knew he would need to earn, and not just for rent. He had to eat and to spend on other things. He knew this very well. What did they think, he was some sort of freeloader? They even went so far as to urge him to rise early the very next morning and start his search for work right then. George retrieved the *Los Angeles Times* from the recycling and started checking out the help wanteds. He found one he thought suitable, for sales trainees at a big insurance company.

George described this red-hot opportunity to Derek, who said nothing but directed his eyes downward toward his hands, clasped between his knees. While both parents, short, round people, paced around their living room yacking at him, Derek slumped on the couch, where he laid his six-foot plus every night.

George objected to his evident lack of interest in the sales trainee job. "What? You can't just try it? Give them a call tomorrow, see what they say."

Mimi had her own idea. "With his education," she began.

George interrupted. "Benefits. Retirement. You have to consider—"

They began interrupting each other. The effect was almost musical.

"A Ph.D. in English, a Doctor, can't get a job writing for the movies or the television? In this town? Don't tell me—"

"the long-term bene—"

"he can't do—"

"fits."

"that."

"You see, with a national company—what?" George had interrupted himself, having noticed that Derek was no longer in the room.

"Where'd he go?" he asked Mimi.

She shrugged. "He'll get something," she said. "He makes a good impression. And he's not stupid, you know."

"I do?"

In the elevator, Derek descended along with the stern and silent minion, who was no doubt paying calls that night on other violators of the condo agreement. Fucking was a violation, no doubt. Breathing might be. It would be good to get out of this old-age home with its grouchy tenants.

As he strolled along the beach, deserted at night, the surf-sound caressing his ears, Derek found himself considering his mother's suggestion that he write for the movies or TV. It was a long shot, of course. He knew that, even if she didn't; but if he kept his sights low enough, say at the level of daytime soap operas, maybe some little company would hire him as a writer. Were there a lot of such companies? In this town, there should be. Let them give him a writing test of some kind. No subject or assignment could exceed the powers of a man able to produce more than a hundred pages on Laurence Eusden. And Mimi had a point about the Ph.D. At the least it might impress a potential employer enough to secure an interview.

In the morning, while he ate the scrambled eggs his excited mother had thrashed almost to a soup, he scanned the West Side Yellow Pages under "production companies." There were four within a few miles of the condo. TV or film, or both? He couldn't tell. Well, he'd wing it.

"Guess I'll try these," he said to Mimi, who smiled extravagantly while waving the phone at him. Derek waved back at her, but dismissively. "Won't work," he grunted.

He had always hated talking on the phone, and, besides, how much of an impression could he make that way, begging for an appointment? But if, unannounced, he came surging into an office, young guy, big, energetic, that could make a hell of an impression on the office's tenants. Maybe then bring up the Ph.D., to impress them further. True, nobody in L.A. had ever thought he was much, but that was then, and he was different now. At least he felt different.

But he wasn't. By the end of the day, he wondered why he had ever thought he might be, even for a minute. It was his usual mistake, thinking that he was better than in truth he was, and L.A. was still his blighted city. Nothing ever changes, not for him, certainly not here. Two of the three receptionists he'd hoped to charm had interrupted him in mid-spiel with a "Writers? We don't need any *writers*." They made the word and the vocation sound ridiculous, no less so than if he were promoting himself as an Indian club juggler. The third had simply pointed at the door, through which he promptly slunk.

The day's rejections weren't as painful as being played for a sap by Tracy Chatham at the senior ball, but he thought of her because the three women who had scorned him all looked much as he imagined Tracy would at age thirty or so. Thus they all looked alike, and now that he thought about it, many of the youngish women he'd noticed as he'd traveled from office to office were Tracy types, neither tall nor short, but tan, blond, firm breasted. Types. Not as good as the original.

Of course, that was how one would expect thirtyish females to look who lived on or near the southern Californian coast, just as the seniors at Surfside Sojourners were mostly interchangeable within their sub-species of flabby and skinny. It was probably that way with old folks everywhere. Nothing odd about that. More difficult to explain was how many of the native Midwesterners he'd known at Heartland were all of average height. Students from other areas had joked about there being some genetic reason, a corn gene. But it did seem strange, as did the fact that this day, in the one interview he'd wangled, he talked with someone who reminded him strongly of Sheldon Glick.

This stubby individual called himself Ace Goldman and called his company Gold Man [sic] Productions. A framed print, three feet high, of the Oscar statuette hung from a hook on the office door. Ace may have been his own sole employee, or perhaps he was filling in for his resident Tracy simulacrum, taking time out for a mani and a pedi. In either case, he was sitting behind the reception desk when Derek entered his office and explained himself, his Ph.D., the opportunity he sought to take a test and show how well he could write. He was surprised when Ace let him utter several sentences, as none of the Tracys had let him complete more than one. Soon he ran out of things to say.

The little man sighed. "Rosenblum," he said. "Ah, Rosenblum. You know what? You remind me of me."

Derek was inclined to protest, having always assumed he wasn't particularly Jewish in appearance. Nor did Goldman's mournful air seem to hint at a job-opening as a video writer. Nonetheless, he held his tongue and awaited what came next, which turned out to be rather a lot.

"You know, Rosenblum, I was an English major and I too once thought literacy and a knowledge of the great classics such as *Moby Dick* and the *Divine Comedy* were just what one needed to cook up a good dramatic show or sitcom, but I had to forget all that and become a complete crudenik before I could get a toehold in the industry. Changed my name from Eliot to Ace, which sort of sums it up. We write about life here, okay? Real life, not what you can find in a book. Ph.D.? Don't let people find out. Is it possible that you didn't know this?"

There was no particular point in telling Ace Goldman that, deep down, he *had* known it. Somehow Derek had let his mother's enthusiasm infect him, so that he temporarily forgot what he knew, that in L.A. he never got anything he wanted. In fact, the Ph.D. really wasn't what was wrong here. It was just him, as always. He stood up, ready to leave, but he was mildly curious about Goldman's physical resemblance to the little man from Enola Gay State. And he remembered, too, that Glick had also expressed surprise about what he didn't know and almost in the same words. For a moment he fancied the two men were really one person cycling between Kansas and Los Angeles.

"You related to a Sheldon Glick?" he asked.

The question seemed to disturb Ace Goldman. Perhaps he was a Glick cousin or other relation and didn't want media people to find out that he shared DNA with a professor of English. Or had he known Sheldon back when he was still Eliot the English major and now didn't like being reminded of his deviant past? He pulled open a desk drawer and began extracting various items, three-by-five cards, post-its, pencils. "Wherethefuckis," he muttered. Then he looked up.

"So go. I try to tell you things and you ask me a nonsense question. So go be a professor already. You've been trained for it, yes? And what else are you good for? Now, go! Go! I got work to do. Real work." He fumbled in the drawer.

"Weasels," he muttered. "Wolverines."

"Nature show?" inquired Derek, still trying. But the producer continued to fumble, head down, and when he spoke again, it wasn't about the genus Mustelidae.

"You know, I used to like that stuff," he muttered. "I got high when I read, or sometimes low. But that was okay."

"You know," Derek began, but he had to break off. It had gotten away from him, whatever he'd wanted to say.

The video producer resumed. "Yeah, always had my nose in a book. *Moby Dick*. Read it eight times, then took American Lit and never wanted to read it again. No pleasure in it. Why doncha teach high school, get'em before they've gone dead?"

Ace might have explained, if asked, before which had gone dead, the books or the students; but Derek, revolted by the suggestion that he take his Ph.D. and crawl back to high school, swiftly turned and left the office.

The meager headquarters of Gold Man Video occupied a small part of the top floor of a three-story building full of similarly undersized offices occupied by an assortment of toilers within the industry. From behind one closed door came animal noises, growls and grunts. Nature shows must be big, concluded Derek, and wished there was some animal experience in his background. In the corridor and on the stairs he noticed several Tracys, striding legily, and two Aces (or Sheldons) scuttling. Were there people like himself somewhere? Or even just people who would give him a break, who would like him? There didn't seem to be anyone like that in L.A.

And elsewhere? No, not there either. He'd known people at Heartland, fellow students, but they weren't really friends, and there was no one he'd care to see again. Certainly not his treacherous and spooky adviser, Luteplucker. Returning to the condo, he donned his trunks and, having done nothing in answer to his mother's questions about the day except shake his head, jumped into the surf. It did not soothe him.

To placate his father, after a few days of loitering he entered the downtown headquarters of the big insurance company and took what seemed to be a standard multiple-choice intelligence test. On occasional breaks from checking the bubbles, he glanced around the room at the other test takers, obvious losers, ill-clad, coke-bottle-bottom lensed. Mediocrities. Did he really belong among them? He feared that he did.

Certainly the company thought so. Two mornings later his mother woke him at eleven and dragged him to the phone in the kitchen. It was someone from Oriental Insurance, telling him he had smashed the test and could start the trainee program right away. Had he not been still half asleep, he might have said something more articulate than a grunted, "I don't wanna." But it would have been the same message. He didn't wanna. With the video biz plainly out of reach, teaching literature in a college, his ambition since boyhood, was the only profession that appealed. He was sure he could analyze texts as well as anybody, and although the remedial composition he'd taught at Heartland wasn't much fun, teaching literature would surely be different.

Ace Goldman had told him he was good for nothing else, and that was probably true. But Sheldon Glick had told him he was unemployable as a prof, and that was probably true as well. It was as if the two look-alikes were cooperating to discourage him. Without having really started, he stopped looking for work of any kind.

One evening his dad presented him with a key to an apartment a realtor friend had located in Venice, a small city several miles down the coast from posh Malibu and decidedly different in character.

"Location's passable," sniffed George. "At least it's not the part of Venice where the gangs are. The Shoreline Crisps and whatnot. I'll spring for the damage deposit, but I'll expect you to pay me back. And of course there's the monthly rental. Can't help you with that."

"Told me already, Dad," Derek mumbled. He worked his key ring out of his hip pocket. It held two keys for the Corona and one more for his old, burgled place in Heartland. When he began pulling it apart in order to attach the Venice key, he pinched his finger and dropped the ring on the floor.

His father looked upon him with pity and perhaps a little disdain as well. Derek, bending for the key ring, knew why George was still standing there, what he would say. He said it.

"Well, you haven't found a job yet, so you can sell for me afternoons and evenings. I'll move the guys around, maybe cut their hours back a little. Hate to do it, they got families, but who's got a choice?"

Who indeed? Surely not unemployable, except by daddykins, Derek.

He chose to spend his last day of illegal residency at Senior Surfside Sojourners body surfing at the complex's beach. The oldsters snarled at him as they baked their repulsive bodies in the noontime sun. Maybe they called the minion, for as Derek rode a wave to shore he spotted the stern-faced man in his khaki uniform. Was that a pistol he wore at his side? Not wanting to get his parents into trouble by his illegal presence, he swam out beyond the point where the waves broke and then thrashed his way north. Soon he spotted a beach that was appealingly free of people, probably closed to the public and unused to visitors from the sea. Perhaps another minion would appear and order him back into the surf, but so what? Maybe he'd get into a little tiff with the guy. He felt ornery. Life was fucking with him. Time he fucked back.

But no one came to chase him off. No one came at all. After he surfed for a time, he sat on the sand and contemplated the ocean and the sky. It was so quiet. He fell asleep and woke up with his back all scratchy, but he rather enjoyed the feeling. One more ride, he told himself and then swim back to his starting place. He'd deal with the minion there, if he saw him.

Just as he entered the water a monster wave arose, perhaps the seventh in a set. It scared him, but he threw himself into the white water and was lifted up into the bright blue sky until being dumped on the sand on his belly. Rolling over, he discovered that he was no longer alone. For Tracy Chatham was there, bikini clad, with more of her revealed than had ever been displayed on the court at Sam Yorty High. She was beautiful. She shone in the sun. Tracy or a Tracy; for the moment that didn't matter. She was ... she was ... he didn't know what. Where had she come from, anyway? And so quickly.

Derek got up on his feet and sauntered across the white sand. He stood near where she lay, feeling awkward and hulking. He couldn't tell if she was aware of him. Her eyes were closed. Was she asleep? He looked her up and down. There was not one bit of her that wasn't golden and pretty. She stirred then. She opened her eyes and looked him up and down, showing no sign of alarm.

"Uh, David? Is that you?"

Well. Maybe she was a Tracy look-alike who knew a guy named David, who looked like him, Derek. Or maybe she was the real one, who had addressed him as David when reluctantly accepting his bid to escort her to the senior ball. That was the last time he had spoken to her.

"No," he said.

"What?"

He knew he should say something besides no. Unfortunately, he could think only of literary allusions. From the undergrad survey, no less. Joyce's bird girl, Wordsworth's "dear girl," etc. She would think he was nuts, especially if she were the real, literature-disdaining, Tracy.

The woman sat up on her towel. "Do you belong to the club?" she asked.

It wasn't meanly asked. But after that stupid "no," what more was there to say? He was afraid to be around her. He wanted to touch her, and that wouldn't do. Derek turned and ran into the ocean.

The surf was rough, and he had to fight his way out. Finally he got beyond the breakers, where he treaded water and caught his breath. Looking back toward the beach, he saw her, standing now and shading her eyes with her right hand. She was looking for something or someone, probably him. He had left so abruptly, she might have been wondering if he'd been there at all.

What if he had spoken to her? What might she have said to him?

He returned to Senior Sojourners. Emerging from the water, he was glad to see no minion. Derek was no longer in a mood for trouble.

Then began his working life at Rosenblum's Best Togs for Guys, located on the Third Street Promenade in Santa Monica, slightly north of his Venice apartment.

The Promenade was a prime spot for sales, always bustling with tourists, but in his first week at the store Derek sold only two silk ties by Countess Mara and three handkerchiefs that came together in a transparent plastic box. He also persuaded a nice old lady to pass on a seventy-five dollar silk ascot for her football coach son that another salesman had talked her into buying. After that, while his dad kept paying him a beginning salesman's wage, Derek spent the days and nights at the store reshelving and rehanging, vacuuming and bathroom scrubbing; he closed the store in the evening, taking care to arm the alarm system. Before his coming most of this work had been done by a high school boy, whom George was obliged to let go.

"Nice kid," he remarked. "Hate to do it."

Sky was indeed a nice kid, so it was a shame he had to go. The three salesmen, Spero, Merle, and Oren, were not so nice. While they lost no hours, because Derek did no selling, they disliked him on principle, as the boss's son. For a few days, whenever George wasn't around, they addressed Derek as "Dickhead"; finally he backed the snottiest one, Spero, up against a wall and promised to push in his face if this Dickhead business didn't stop. It did. But it was no fun hanging around the store, often idle, in the company of men who resented him and rarely spoke to him.

He never found much to do outside of business hours. Most of the people he noticed in his Venice neighborhood were board surfers and skateboarders who took no interest in anyone who didn't share their lifestyle and whippet-thin, sun-blackened physicality. He tried bodysurfing a few times at Venice Beach, but felt, as at the store, that he was unwelcome. It wasn't as if he was out of place by being too old. Though his neighbors all seemed young, some, Derek soon realized, were at least in their early thirties, slightly older than he was. What would they do when they hit their forties, not far distant? While this question lacked importance as far as it concerned them, it led him to wonder about himself at forty. What doing? Working for his dad?

That prospect, long-term employment at Rosenblum's Best Togs for Guys, was truly upsetting, and he took his vexation out on a local teenager, who seemed to sneer at him whenever the two met. Once, when Derek considerately halted his car to let the young surfer tote his board across the street, the boy overtly scorned his offer. Instead of nodding his thanks and crossing, or even just crossing, he stayed where he was and made a disdainful flicking gesture with his head. Somewhat incensed, Derek floored the Corona, which stalled. He thought he heard the kid laughing.

The next afternoon as Derek left his building to go to work in Santa Monica, he saw him unloading his board from an old van parked next to Derek's Corona, equally old.

"Don't hit my car," he said, though there was no danger of that. The boy, and he was just a boy, was taking it slow and careful. Maybe that was what he tried to point out to Derek, but he mumbled.

"What?" Derek asked, and without waiting for an answer, he immediately shouted "What?" again. This second time he was addressing not only the surfer, but also his own life, which had lately taken to addressing him in mumbles as well. Understandably, the boy understood the question as meant wholly for him.

"I don't want nothing," he said, while glancing around for other members of his tribe. He was considerably smaller than Derek. No help was in evidence. He implored, "Hey, man, can ya just chill out?"

Derek strode toward the boy, intending he knew not what. At this moment, however, a middle-aged woman came running down the street, screaming at him to "leave Dustin alone." Derek backed off.

"Don't call me that, Mom," said Dustin, beginning to snivel.

Derek gawked at the mother, the first adult he'd seen here in Surferville who actually looked like an adult. Probably her son insisted that she stay inside until the sun was down. She patted his back while addressing him as Speedo, evidently his nom de surf. Derek crept to his car and set off for Rosenblum's Best and a date with mop and pail. He regretted having gotten so pissed.

But in the following weeks there were similar episodes. People kept disrespecting him; he could read it on their faces, sense it in their flat, dead voices. And though he realized it was usually "nothing personal," his blood rose just the same. He never touched anyone, but he came close, and his face in those moments resembled a big, red fist. Speedo and his pals walked or skated rapidly away when they saw him. None of the salesmen at the store wanted to be alone with him. He couldn't blame them, for he knew how angry he was, and he even knew why. Because he felt stupid, his old L.A. feeling. Because he was scared of being at forty what he was now, which was nothing.

Anger was better than fear, better than feeling like a dummy. That was the way his mind always worked, it was one of the few things he understood about himself. Well, so be it. He couldn't help being the kind of person he was.

Big disappointment that Derek knew himself to be, he avoided his father at work and rarely visited his parents' condo. He knew that while George and Mimi worried about him, they were happier not seeing him. When they did, now they questioned him about his social life. Once his dad, noticing how morose and taciturn Derek was at the store, overcame the embarrassment he obviously felt and asked him straight out if he was "getting any." The answer to that was a shake of the head. As for his social life, broadly considered, Derek didn't trouble to explain that it consisted of chatting with the man who brought the mail, composed of bills and advertising circulars.

He was in no mood to meet people and try to have fun with them at "gatherings" and "functions" arranged by dating agencies. He did hit a few bars. There was a bustling pick-up bar scene in the Dogtown section of Venice, and he ventured out into it occasionally; but he was just as bad at selling himself there as he had been with plaid sport jackets and initialed silk dress shirts, called "shirtings" by Spero and the guys.

Same reason, too: he wasn't trying, he didn't care. On weekend nights the bars were rife with Tracys, some detectably aging and slightly desperate. Easy pickings for a man who wanted to get him some, but Derek couldn't maintain an interest. He hurt the feelings of a few when he turned away from them. He felt some sympathy; perhaps they too, these older ones, were wondering about themselves at forty. But what could he do about it? It wasn't their fault that they didn't turn him on. It wasn't the faint lines on their faces. Only two women could possibly interest him, and he had no hope of ever connecting with either.

One, of course, was the real, the genuine, Tracy Chatham. Occasionally he wondered what had become of her. Had that really been her on that lonely stretch of beach? He thought about returning there, but doubted he could find it again. Even if he did and she appeared and was the real Tracy, what could he say? Lines from old books just wouldn't cut it.

He tried not to think of her. It just made him feel bad. It didn't help that he had another woman on his mind: of all the world's females, Heartland University's Professor Lucia Luteplucker. In one sense, this wasn't strange; she had a lavish body. But she had treated him horribly. Derek wondered if that turned him on a bit. It was possible, though he had never thought of himself as a masochist.

What had brought her back into his mental life was a brief spasm of lustfulness for Speedo's mom, who was tall and dark and stoutly built, unlike her scrawny Dustin. For a brief time he considered seeking her out and, were she agreeable, slaking himself in her; soon, however, he decided to take no action, feeling it would never satisfy him. For one thing, he felt no desire to curl up in her lap, as he had with the professor. Additionally, though the mom had run to save the boy, Luteplucker would never hurry for or to anyone. Students at Heartland were drawn to *her*, often against their will, as a smaller mass is attracted to a larger. That was her power; that must be what made him desire her, even though she had never shown the least sign of liking him. Despite serving, or disserving, Derek as his dissertation director, she had been so impersonal with him that he doubted she remembered who he was.

And so his longing for her gradually ebbed. Like Tracy, she was too hot—in her frigid way—for the likes of him. Should he ever see her again, perhaps his feelings would revive; but there was no way that would happen. And he was sure he would never meet anyone like her. There was only one Lucia Luteplucker.

At least not in this waking world. It was different at night.

Frustration and Subsequent Resolve

Several times recently Derek had felt dizzy when getting up from bed in the morning and would have to sit down in a hurry. First he suspected low blood pressure, but he never felt dizzy at other times, as when he rose from his chair after a long session before the television. He began to wonder if he had been having a dream that disturbed him in this way. On his dizzy mornings he brought with him from sleep only a vague sense of a multitude of people caught up in immense bustle. Since the whole experience was repeated several times, he wondered if the dream, if he was really having one, might bear a special message for him. He had no idea what.

Thus Derek was now, in addition to being morose and hostile, also distracted by his musings about a possible dream. At the store, while he continued to do his humble chores acceptably well, his father noticed how little interest he took in them and began to badger him about it, delighting the salesmen. It got so that Derek hated coming to work. At this time he endured a particularly irksome episode with his father.

Every night, when the others left Rosenblum's Best, leaving Derek to tidy the place for the next day's business, George would remind him about setting the burglar alarm. "Arming the system," he called it, as if it were a line-up of anti-missile missiles. On one Thursday, he seemed particularly emphatic. He stood in the doorway, one foot in, the other out. So go, already, Derek wanted to say, but he had to listen since his father was his boss. It would have been okay if he were a kid, but he wasn't.

"Arm the system," ordered George, for the third time. "Don't forget!"

"I won't."

"It's important. Do you realize how important it is?"

"I do. I do realize that. Hey, when you come in the morning, is it ever off?"

"'Disarmed,' you mean? You don't need to take offence, Derek."

"I'm not taking—"

"I'm just telling you. Because if you did forget, Derek, and somebody got in, it would be a calamity. The insurance would shoot up, and you know it's killing me already." On "up," he raised his right hand above his head; on "killing," he brought it sharply down like the chopping stroke of a guillotine.

"Right, Dad. I'll do it."

"All right then."

"Like I always do."

"Umph! Wise guy!" But George left.

Derek then entered each of the four dressing rooms in turn, picking up the jackets and slacks customers had left behind. He replaced them on their hangers, then fetched the vacuum from the storeroom. Just as he bent to switch it on, he heard a tapping on the window. Turning, he saw a shabby, presumably homeless man hopping up and down while pointing at his crotch, a mute request to use the rest room at Rosenblum's Best Togs For Guys.

Derek shook his head, then set about his vacuuming. On his second pass, he observed the shabby man pulling down his pants in the street outside where Rosenblum's Best was crammed between a Greek restaurant staffed by Mexicans and a shop that sold T-shirts with printed sayings, such as "Life is a beach" and "Did you ever see a chicken shit?" That one came illustrated.

He opened the door and yelled at the man, who stumbled off, filthy denims binding his knees. A minute later Derek heard angry shouts in Spanish. He continued cleaning and straightening up, moving more quickly than his usual sluggish pace. He wanted to get out and go home, not that there was anything to do there except watch junk on TV. But maybe later he would dream. Maybe this time he would remember more.

At around ten that evening, after he had showered and gotten ready for bed, George called him from the store. He'd returned there for some reason and seemed greatly upset.

"Are you alive?" asked George. It seemed a serious question, but Derek chose to laugh it off.

"Last time I checked," he said,

"Well, check again. Do you know what you did or didn't do?"

Ah, distracted by the homeless man and his own desire to go home, he had forgotten to arm the system. That must be it. Had someone broken in? Hesitantly, Derek asked his father.

"Suppose you come up here and see," George snapped.

He got dressed and drove to Santa Monica. There he found a scornful dad, for he had indeed forgotten. And while the store was unviolated, that seemed not to matter to George.

"This can't go on," George said.

Derek started to get mad, as he often did for lesser provocations than this, but he knew that would be wrong. He had fucked up, no denying that. But his dad was acting as if he fucked up every night. That was unfair. With difficulty he retained self-control. Driving back to Venice on the Pacific Coast Highway, he repeated to himself what his father had said. This can't go on. It was true. He could bear no more of it, his life both in the store and out of it. But what else could he do with that life? He badly needed an answer.

That night he dreamed. It was in color, but the light was sickly; it was hard to see anything clearly. It had sound, too, though this consisted of shouted words mostly incomprehensible. Even so, this time he was sure he remembered it.

In the dream he first beheld a barren plain, featureless except for a small hill on which stood a metal chair of the kind that Heartland U bought for faculty offices from Midwest Prison Industries. Suddenly Derek's professor, Luteplucker, appeared before the chair, into which she slowly settled. As soon as her plump buttocks made contact with its seat, the humble chair morphed into an ornate throne. Then, as Derek felt something pop, both throne and occupant expanded to enormous size.

Was this gigantic female simply Lucia Luteplucker, grown suddenly huge? Derek didn't think so. She impressed him as considerably more than a mere supersized mortal. Indeed, this monstrous person was a being of immense power, and it was terribly important to make her happy. For Derek found himself among a scrambling horde of tiny suppliants gazing up at her from a nearly infinite distance, all vying for her favor, bellowing incomprehensibly and clumsily slapping and pushing at one another. Each held a gift he hoped fit for a queen, nay, the goddess that dream Derek was sure she was.

For he knew precisely where he had seen her in earlier times, when he happened to be awake: in Pope's *Dunciad*, Book 4. She was Dulness, receiving her legion of favor seekers, the dunces who give the poem its name. Despite the wisp of fog or cloud that lay across her face, she recognized and welcomed all, hailing them as "children of my care." Derek, the exception in the crowd, watched as two thieves wrestled clumsily over the stolen Greek coins each wished to sell to moronic collectors, until Dulness calmed them down. A college grad just returned from the Grand Tour was presented to

Dulness by his guide, who proudly boasted of introducing his charge to "ev'ry Vice."

One individual, frantically waving overhead what looked like a large letter F, was a caricature of the eighteenth-century classical scholar Richard Bentley. The apparent F was really a Greek digamma, pronounced "wau," and so-called because it looked as if one gamma had been superimposed upon another. Bentley had shown that the digammas had dropped out of the *Iliad* and *Odyssey* when the Homeric epics were written down, but Pope's response to this acclaimed discovery had been "So what?" For to consider what was not there, a practice maintained by scholars unto the present day, distracts from what is and flattens the whole experience. If you're looking for digamma, you don't see Achilles. And therefore Dulness saluted Bentley.

Finally, a host of eighteenth-century scientists charged the throne brandishing specimens wrenched from their natural settings: "A Nest, a Toad, a Fungus, or a Flow'r," just as Pope had written. Derek saw them all, was buffeted by them as they galloped past.

He had to go slowly, weighed down by his goddess-offering, a heavy scroll gripped awkwardly waist high, one hand at either end as if it were a concertina. What was written on the scroll he didn't know, at first. Then his feet, which he could not see, became tangled and he fell upon the rocky ground. For a moment the dunces, his fellow dunces, stood around him in a circle and jeered. "This is shit," they cried in unison, pointing at the scroll.

It was his dissertation on Laurence Eusden. Dulness agreed with the general verdict. Her blessing ("blessing all," in the poem) did not extend to him. She did not want his gift. He didn't need to be told, and he made no appeal. It was so little, what he had written. That short, simple thing.

The dunces scrambled off, heading toward the throne. Derek, in mournful condition, lay where he was. Squinting in the half-light, he could just make out a human shape, a manikin, slumped upon the goddess's broad lap. The figure was chubby, lacked hair, sported an imbecile's broad, what-me-worry grin. How wrong this was! In the dream, Derek felt usurped. *He* should be her favorite. But how could he be, with a rejected gift, one that was shit? Well, what would he have to do to be accepted?

In the morning—when, curiously, he experienced no dizziness—the matter of the favorite's identity seemed important to Derek, though he didn't understand why. In the *Dunciad* he who reposes in the divine lap is the buffoonish Colly Cibber, who succeeded Eusden as laureate, but Derek doubted it was

'

Cibber in the dream. But, then, who? Later, much later, the answer would present itself.

Sitting in his little kitchen, he reasoned that it was no wonder that any part of Pope's nightmarishly visual poem should have lodged in his memory and become the ore of dreams, for he had read it many times. Of course there were differences between poem and dream, besides his being a participant in the latter. Pope's Dulness is a goddess from the *Dunciad's* very beginning in Book One, where she lounges upon a regal seat. In contrast, the throne in Derek's dream had begun its existence as a humble office chair, and its occupant was the potent but surely not omnipotent Professor Lucia Luteplucker. What was she doing in his dream? More usefully, what did the dream tell him about her?

She turned into the goddess, was transformed. That's how it seemed, though it was possible that Dulness had *emerged* from the prof. From her carcass. That was an ugly thought. He then found himself thinking about Malone G. Malone and the lines he recited that day in the refectory, but Derek learned nothing from that. Soon he ceased to ponder the mechanics of how a mortal becomes divine.

This was what he finally got out of his *Dunciad* dream. What the goddess's rejection of his dissertation signified was that the professor's apparent acceptance of it was false. It had come, after all, without a single word of praise; rather than write her name on the title page, to indicate approval, Luteplucker had used a rubber stamp. She had approved 'Laurence Eusden: Laureate Little Known,' after forcing him to write it, only to inspire the college recruiters and ABD gang and who knew what others to mock him. She was his nemesis. He believed that.

Why? What had she against him? It was a purposive campaign. He had never heard of her going to such lengths with anyone else. Why him? To that he had no answer. The only thing Derek was sure of concerning Lucia Luteplucker, other than her unrelenting enmity, was that she was the dullest academic he'd run into in nine years of post-secondary education. Her tiny journal notes were devoid of thoughtful speculation and in her seminars, rather than encouraging students to discuss anything, she only allowed them to take turns reading aloud. No wonder he—his subconscious—had confused her with Pope's Dulness.

Derek had absent-mindedly risen from his chair and stood now at the sink, running water over a plate he had taken from the cupboard and not used. He dropped it into the sink, and it broke. He turned off the water. Thoughts shuttled through his consciousness at a rapid rate. What had he wanted for almost half his life? To be a college professor. How could he get it? By getting into print, for publication was everything. What did he want now, right now? To show Luteplucker and everybody else that he could write and publish something, a real article and not a little squib of the kind she wrote. That should be his goal, at least in the short term. Thus resolved, Derek stepped into the shower and bombed himself with hot water.

One thing still bothered him, that in his dream he had wanted desperately to please the goddess. Did that mean he wanted to please Luteplucker, after what she had done to him? There had been moments in their relationship when he had wished that. She was his adviser, so there was nothing odd in feeling that way, but there had been some weird experiences and weird feelings, going beyond conventional male need. Now, certainly, he wished only to humble her. That was what he told himself. So he took that element in the dream as a warning. Don't fall back into seeking her approval! Well, he wouldn't. He couldn't imagine why he had put up with her bullying back at Heartland.

The thoughts kept coming as he stood in his bathroom, dripping on the tiles. Should he attempt revision of 'Laureate Little Known' into a book? Besides eating up too much time, that would serve only to cast him back into the old futile struggle with Eusden's stunning mediocrity. Finding a new topic, though, meant digging in libraries before even beginning to write, with no guarantee of an ultimately publishable result. For a moment he faltered. Why try? He recalled the gibing mob in his dream. In real life these might be editors, human hyenas, laughing at him as Sheldon Glick had in San Francisco. For a moment he imagined himself shoved and elbowed by a multitude of balding Glicks, each with a hostile smirk upon his puss.

This cast him briefly back into the dream. The giant woman, the clamorous dunces encircling him—he could almost see them. He shook his head, cleared it. The dream was a nightmare, but it hadn't scared him, not after he woke up. After all, he'd been trained to analyze literature coldly, without getting his emotions into it. And that was good, as in this case. He had found what the dream meant, to him, so now he need not recall it or any part of it. Thus ran Derek's thoughts. Then he returned to the question.

Did he really want to do this, to try to write? Yes, he surely did. It shouldn't be impossible to find a topic he could handle. He would show the bastards, the Glicks, and Luteplucker, too. Especially her, and once he'd made his old prof admit who was by far, the better critic, she would cease to matter to him. He could forget her.

Indeed, for a time he did almost forget. But she would come back to him full force, to his thoughts, to his life, and when this happened he would be unable to dismiss the notion that she, Heartland's Luteplucker, and Pope's Dulness were related in some unfathomable way. Yes, one was real and the other just a poet's creation. He understood that. But still at such moments the goddess would seem real and the professor something on the order of her clockwork simulacrum.

This came later. Now, as he dressed for the day's deadly employment at Rosenblum's Best, he thought of Ace Goldman and what the video man who so much resembled Glick had said. "So go be a professor already. What else are you good for?" That had stung, because he had known deep down that Ace was right. But what was so bad about being a professor? He'd bet that the former Eliot the English major really wished he was one himself instead of an anxiety-ridden producer of videos about weasels and wolverines. No, professing's an ideal job. It's not even work. You get to talk about books and poems, and once you get tenure you're set for life.

Driving north to work, Derek found his thoughts turning toward his dissertation, even though he'd ruled out revising it into a book. Nor could he think of anything *in* it that could be worked up into an article of twenty pages or so. But there was something. He felt it, and it concerned Eusden, of all people. What, though, had he not covered in the dissertation?

Wait a minute.

He pulled over abruptly, causing several nearby cars to emit indignant honks. Now Derek remembered. There was one of the laureate's made-to-order products that had seemed to reach, as he had read it, a bit beyond the mediocre. Back at Heartland he'd sensed this, but since his approach in 'Laureate Little Known' was to extol Laurence Eusden as a master of the mediocre, he had no room to consider the single piece of work that had a different smell.

Arriving at Third Street Promenade, Derek pulled the Corona into a lot near his father's store. He walked around behind the car and keyed the trunk. In there, in the garbage-stained paper box with his dissertation, was the bundle of Eusden's panegyrics, machine copies made from the original eighteenth-century edition of his work, the only one ever published. He leafed through the bundle, found what he was looking for, and started reading. Spero, returning from lunch, drove into the lot and honked at him to get his ass into the store, but Derek didn't look up. As he read, he felt both excitement and relief. Yes, it was as he remembered. Something stirred there, pulsing against laureate

Eusden's customary offering of butt-kissing formulas. This would make an article, maybe a nice long one.

Three hours later Derek paused in the act of hanging up a $600 sport coat. He held the wooden hanger in one hand, the coat in the other. He had high hopes for something he hadn't even begun to write. Wasn't that asking for trouble? Before now, whenever he imagined future success in anything, that was a sure sign that disappointment was steaming his way. His best bet was to write the article, if he could, without thinking about the good things that might follow—publication, recognition, a job—or might not.

The title of the work by Eusden to which Derek would devote many hours of labor was "The Origin of the Knights of the Bath."

A Subtext Found

Perhaps Oren or Merle or Spero wondered why he had returned from late-afternoon break cradling in his arms a used IBM Selectric, sold him cheap because of the competition from the newfangled word processors, but the salesmen said nothing. Nor did the father speak, other than to grunt, "Okay, I'll call Sky," when the son asked for a week off. Though Derek usually drank nothing stronger than beer, on his way home that evening he stopped at a Venice liquor store and bought a bottle of vodka.

In his apartment that evening, while he never typed a word on his new machine, he spent several hours reading and rereading the 101 lines of "The Origin of the Knights of the Bath." At some point after midnight but before the dawn, having immersed himself in Eusden's vision of Britain at the time of Julius Caesar's second invasion in 54 BC, he began to see in his mind the scenes and characters that the little known one describes. Maybe the vodka was responsible, maybe not. In either case, Derek saw Julius stirring in his sleep, Venus soaping her divine armpits in her bath (although gentlemanly Eusden doesn't actually picture her there), her priestess Thamesia screaming her lungs out when besieged by a pair of English wolves. Derek even mentally pictured the wolves dashing back and forth while dragging their snouts along the ground like vacuum cleaners, for this was how his brain interpreted "scour'd for prey." These were crude, brightly colored two-dimensional figures that he conjured up. Had Derek spent any time playing the relatively unsophisticated video games of the '80s, he might have remarked on the likeness between those fantasies and the laureate's. In fact, the Professor Rosenblum of the later era enjoyed the simpler games, having by then forgotten about Eusden, as had everyone else.

Of all the poem's characters, there was one who held Derek's attention more than any other. This was Marcus Cassius Scaeva, a Roman soldier of fearsome competence in battle and incredible resistance to pain. His body, in Derek's crude mental picturing, was bespotted with blobs of red, denoting blood, yet he fought on. Though Derek didn't then know whether Scaeva was a fictional character or a real person (which he turned out to be), he sensed that the soldier's role greatly mattered in what Eusden was attempting to say, whatever that was.

Rising early the next morning, Derek tossed the half-empty vodka bottle into the recycling, plugged in the Selectric, and set about preparing an annotated typescript of "The Origin of the Knights of the Bath." It took him the week his father had allowed, including several lengthy sessions at the UCLA library. His original purpose was just to make the poem more comprehensible for himself, but soon it occurred to him that if a journal accepted his article its editors might want it to include a copy of the poem, with helpful notes. Those that he eventually composed fell between two stools, informational for his prospective audience and interpretive, directed at himself.

Eventually he decided against including the poem in his article. He summed it up, instead. It can now be found, reprinted for the first time in almost three hundred years, in the Spitfire College Press variorum edition of all Eusden's known work, edited by Professor Sheldon Glick, Ph.D. But since this volume is exceedingly difficult to obtain outside of Southampton, UK, confounding even Amazon, it is deemed advisable to include it here. Derek's notes will be found as well, for the reader's use in understanding some of Eusden's allusions and also because they indicate how, as Derek worked on the poem and its hidden meanings, he came to feel about Eusden in relation to himself.

The Origin of the Knights of the Bath[1]
Humbly Inscrib'd to his Royal Highness Prince William Augustus[2]

Hail glorious Off-spring of a glorious Race!
Britannia's other Hope[3], and blooming Grace!
Thou smil'st already on the burnish'd Shield,
And thy weak Hand the little Sword can wield:
Already, clad in Arms, Thou mov'st along,
The Love, and Wonder of each ravish'd Throng!
Awhile vouchsafe, young Hero, to retire
'Mid Streams, and Grottos, and th' Aonian Choir.
Apollo, God of Fore-sight, who with Ease
Thy distant, ripen'd Years, as present, sees,

Bids all the Muses Thee receive with Pride,
To all the Muses by all Arts ally'd.

Let future Bards describe in sounding Strains
Thy laurel'd Triumphs from deep-crimson'd Plains;
Enough for Me the Dawning to display,
That glows, the Promise of so bright a Day;
Enough to view, transported with the Sight,
The Royal Warrior-Boy, Bath's foremost Knight.

The Learn'd in antique Rites have labour'd long
To trace an Era, whence this Honour sprung.
They still Re-searches make with fruitless Pain,

---

[1] Here the little known laureate lauds the revival, or it may be the founding, of the Most Honorable Order of the Bath by King George I on May 18, 1725. There's some disagreement about whether the medieval Knights of the Bath, whose rituals included a purifying bath, constituted an official order; if they did not, then the Order was founded by George rather than revived. But this possibility Eusden chooses to ignore, as the poem celebrates the order's "origin," backdated, with absolutely no historical justification, to the time of Julius Caesar's invasion.

It is extremely unlikely that German George I took any interest in founding/reviving a British knightly order. Credit for this idea and all others conceived in his dull-witted reign must be granted his supremely manipulative de facto prime minister, the flamboyant Robert Walpole. Certainly Walpole was acquainted with the poet laureate, and his celebrated arrogance doubtlessly exacerbated the resentment Eusden must have felt for serving such a king as the thickheaded, poetry despising—in fact English language despising—George.

It is worth recalling that the interests of the prime minister's son, the literary-minded Horace Walpole, lay in the gothic novel, of which genre he may be termed the founder, and in the Middle Ages generally. It is beyond my comprehension that this hip, poodle-fancying aesthete would not have scorned Eusden's weary old neoclassicism. Knowing that (for how could the poet laureate not be aware of the tastes and predilections of the PM's son?) could only have lacerated and enraged poor Eusden even more. Okay, so at the time of the writing of "The Origin of the Knights of the Bath" in 1725, Horace was only eight years old, but he was precocious and also had a deeply waspish nature. Look at what he did to poor Tommy Chatterton!

Incidentally, why no Eusden bio in Samuel Johnson's *Lives of the Poets?* He has one for Isaac Watts, and who gives a crap about Watts? Did something about Eusden warn the intuitive Johnson to stay clear?

[2] Prince William Augustus. Second son born (1721) to the future George II and so second grandson to George I. Eusden addresses him further on as "Royal Warrior-Boy" in recognition of warlike talents displayed even at age four, as he was at the composition date of this poem. Several honors were conferred upon him then, including a junior membership in the Order of the Bath.

Warlike, indeed! As the sadistic Duke of Cumberland, William Augustus would fulfill his early promise in the aftermath of the Battle of Culloden (1746) by ordering his troops to bayonet all supporters of the Young Pretender lying wounded on the field. For this he was known ever after as Butcher Cumberland. It's easy to imagine what Laurence Eusden must have thought of this aggressive little prick, who in all probability teamed up with mean-spirited Hory Walpole to drive the laureate to drink. He struck back by the only means available to him, his verse. He knew that no one would recognize his true intent until after his death. But did he know it would take *this* long? Sense his frustration.

[3] "Britannia's other Hope": Besides William's elder brother, Frederick, Prince of Wales.

As Nile's high Fount of old was sought in vain.
Let their own Arts the Muses then avail,
Daughters of Memory can tell the Tale,
Where Selden, Dugdale, Ashmole, Anstis fail.[4]
Not Volusenus[5] a Descent could boast;
He only viewed a-far Britannia's Coast:
But Caesar came, with mad Ambition fir'd,
Yet Caesar, not too gloriously, retir'd.
With our brave Ancestors but ill He far'd,
And Storms destroy'd those Ships, the Battle spar'd.

Still He, whose Soul could Fortune's Frown disdain,
The Spring returning, bold return'd again;
True to Herself, She now a Smile bestow'd,
His Troops were landed, and his Navy rode.

'Twas Night, yet sleepless the great Roman lay,
When sudden round Him shot a Blaze of Day,
And to his wondering Eyes, un-doubted, shone
The Queen of Beauty, by her Beauty known.
Six silver Swans her golden Charriot drew,
Her Mantle ruby, and her Vesture blue.
Quick from her Eyes bright Emanations broke,
Then with the Voice of Harmony She spoke.

"Oh Heroe, worthy of my heavenly Line!
In Thee how fair the Aenean Virtues shine!
But whence for Albion's Conquest such a Flame?
Whence this fond Thirst of an unhappy Fame?
Alas! Thou know'st not, what Thou would'st destroy,

---

[4] John Selden, William Dugdale, Elias Ashmole, and John Anstis were, among other things, antiquarians. Eusden, presenting himself as an inspired bard, claims to top their researches with his Roman invasion story. Anstis supported the re-founding (as he understood it) of the Order of the Bath. He also presided over the coronation of George II in 1727. That Eusden asserts that Anstis "fail[ed]" shows his hostility to the royal establishment.
[5] Volusenus: An officer of Julius Caesar's, he voyaged along the British coast looking for likely invasion spots, but didn't land anywhere.

But, Trojan-sprung, would'st burn a second Troy!
With marks of Ruin a fair Land deface,
And half extinguish thy own native Race![6]

"Learn, Caesar!-Brute, thy Blood, these Regions sought;[7]
His Laws, his Subjects, and his Gods he brought:
Here, Neptune seconding his great Design,
An Ilium rose, once more, by Hands divine.
How thy first Navy perish'd hence is plain;
Still dread another Tempest on the Main.
Invasions on their Rights the Gods displease,
Whose Sons, in rouling Ages, He decrees
His delegated Rulers of the Seas.

She paus'd:-the mighty Victor, startl'd, cry'd,
"Bright Author of my Stemm! be Thou my Guide;
Shall now my eager Legions back be led,
And Rome, with Blushes hear, that Caesar fled?

"Undaunted Chief!" the Goddess made Reply,
"Conquest pursue!-Thee Fate forbids to fly:
But Conquest won,-Oh! The dire Use forbear,
And teach the unrelenting Sword to spare!
Thy Veterans, blind to Wounds, and deaf to Cries,
Forget, that Nature lent them Ears, or Eyes.

"Yet I one Veteran, greatly good, must name,
And strive the generous Act to pay with Fame.
Near thy Pavilion, on a rising Green,
To Venus sacred is a Temple seen:

[6.] Julius's family, the Julian gens, claimed Venus as an ancestor. Thus the goddess, appearing to Caesar in a dream, remarks that he is "worthy of my heavenly Line," and he hails her as "Bright Author of my Stemm." As a Roman, Caesar is "Trojan-sprung": Vergil tells how the fleeing Trojans, after the sacking of Troy, sailed to Italy and became ancestral to the Roman people. But Venus refers to the Britons as "thy own native Race," because they too are Trojan-sprung, as she immediately explains.

[7.] Venus tells Caesar the story of Brute, or Brutus, who led another boatload of vanquished Trojans to safety in Britain, a false but popular fable. Since Romans and Britons share Trojan ancestry, it's inappropriate for one to "half extinguish the other."

Thence, soft-descending, spreads a mazy Grove,
The Seat of feather'd Warblers, and of Love.
There by my Bath, amid' the tufted Wood,
My favourite Priestess, poor Thamesia, stood.
The Shades began to chace declining Day,
When lo! Two Wolves the Thicket scour'd for Prey.
Wing'd with her Fears, all-pale the Virgin flies,
And rends with lamentable Shrieks the Skies.
Scaeva[8], tho' cover'd o'er with many a Wound,
Shieldless, and faint, yet struggl'd from the Ground;
Then, as the doleful Shrieker drew more nigh,
He, now too conscious of a Woman's Cry,
Far, far beyond his strength rush'd furious on,
Both Wolves engag'd, tho' scarce a Match for one,
And sav'd Thamesia's Life, but risqu'd his own.
Him, Julius, to Equestrian Honour raise,
And be the Bath the Knight's distinguish'd Praise.

"Nor shall, with Scaeva, Knights of Bath expire,
But unborn Heroes, proud, that Name acquire;
That Name in hallow'd Rites, and pompous Dress,
That Name in Tilts, and Tournaments profess.
Ensigns of Dignity, the solemn Day,
The slow Procession, and the crowded Way,
Thro' a long Train of Centuries, yet unroll'd,
With Pride, and Pleasure I at once behold.
But Caesar, if thy founded Order fails,
And not o'er Time's devouring Rage prevails,
Then shall a Brunswick Albion's Throne adorn,
Whom Caesar could not for a Rival scorn,

[8.] [Marcus Cassius] Scaeva. Now Venus recounts the chivalrous deed of Caesar's toughest soldier. When two wolves attack Thamesia, the priestess who attends Venus's bath, Scaeva appears, and "tho' cover'd o'er with many a Wound" from preceding conflicts, routs the wolves. Venus then counsels Caesar, "Him, Julius, to Equestrian Honour raise,/And be the Bath the Knight's distinguish'd Praise." Caesar obeys his divine ancestor, so Scaeva becomes the first knight of the Order of the Bath, with Caesar as the Order's original founder: "Nor shall, with Scaeva, Knights of Bath expire,/But unborn Heroes, proud, that Name acquire." So Scaeva, whoever he is, is important in the poem. Sense something here. Key?

To found, and to revive, both, Praises claim,
And oft the Founder shares the nobler Fame:
But then, the great Reviver merits more,
When That shall never sink, which sunk before.

The Goddess ceas'd, and waiting no Reply,
Swift on her towering Swans regain'd the Sky.

Finis

Any additional notes have not survived. Perhaps there were no more, since note eight indicates that Derek felt he was headed in the right direction. Indeed, Scaeva proved to be the key.

Well then, who was he?

Marcus Cassius Scaeva was a real person who performed deeds notable enough to qualify him as the hero of a poem crafted by a laureate whose gifts far exceeded Eusden's. But he was the stalwart type and would never have complained about being so poorly paid for prowess. He was certainly good at his job, which was killing, and his career has not been forgotten even today.

In the twenty-first century, anyone curious about this old Roman would soon discover the website "Bad Ass of the Week," which in 2010 accorded Scaeva full honors as "a motherfucker who dedicated his entire life to beating the fucking shit out of the most vicious barbarians the world had to offer." It took Derek a full Sunday of stack digging at the UCLA library to find out essentially the same thing. Scaeva showed how bad was his ass on two occasions, one being the Battle of Dyrrachium in 48 BC. There, fighting for Caesar against the army of Pompey, he performed as a virtual killing machine despite assorted damages wrought upon his body and an arrow protruding from his eye.

But that was Scaeva's *second* great battle, and what mattered to Derek was the first one. For the Bad Ass of the Week had notched at least as many victims as at Dyrrachium in the earlier conflict from which he also emerged victorious, though somewhat hacked. His enemies fared far worse, however, and this blood bath occurred in Britain during Caesar's second invasion, the subject of "The Origin of the Knights of the Bath." Scaeva slaughtered *Britons*, but British laureate Eusden *makes a hero of Scaeva* and appoints him the founder of an order of British knights. Lightbulb time for Derek.

For this seeming paradox underlies what came to be known as the Rosenblum Thesis: Derek's proposal that "The Origin of the Knights of the Bath," on its surface a sycophantic paean to a destructive four-year old, is actually an ardent protest by a scorned, resentful poet against the stupidity and brutality of the Hanoverian dynasty of George I and his descendants, especially that same William Augustus, the soon to be Butcher Cumberland.

It took Derek several weeks of writing and rewriting, usually in the morning before reporting for work, but eventually he could declare himself almost finished. He had spent himself. A closing paragraph or two were all that was needed.

In his essay Derek had gone so far as to speculate that Laurence Eusden may have supported the Jacobite cause at the time of the '15, also known as the First Rising, when the forces of the Old Pretender descended upon the north of England. It is a fact that appreciable numbers of northern English rallied to the Jacobite cause, which sought the overthrow of George I, and Eusden was a native of the northernmost of the three Ridings of Yorkshire. It is not known where Eusden was or what he was doing in 1715, leading Derek to suggest that he had kept his Jacobite involvement hushed up. That almost nothing is known about every year of the little known one's life before the conferring of the laurel in 1718 did not seem worth mentioning.

But what Derek wished to emphasize was the exquisite irony of the four-year old William Augustus being the first member of the revived Knights of the Bath as Briton-butcher Scaeva was, in the fiction of the poem, the first knight of the original order. For one thing, since Eusden's Caesar makes Scaeva the first Knight of the Bath, as George knighted young William, George is thereby likened to Julius, whose absolutist reputation among a people who claimed to venerate liberty was far from good. "Rule Britannia, rule the waves/Britons never will be slaves," etc.

What, however, really quickened Derek's pulse was that just as, in Eusden's version of history, first Knight of the "original" Bath Scaeva was a butcher, so did first Knight of the revived Bath William Augustus become a butcher, and was actually labeled as such! And how interesting, given Eusden's putative status as a Jacobite supporter in the first of the Risings, that William earned his unofficial title of "Butcher" by committing atrocities after finishing off the second Rising at Culloden.

Now, at the time of that horrendous bloodshed, Eusden had been dead for sixteen years, which might seem rather to blunt the irony of it all and possibly even reduce the parallel of the two knightly butchers to mere coincidence. Luckily, Derek knew just enough about the styles of criticism in vogue to say that he, having engaged in knotty dialectic with the poet, had succeeded in flattering the long-deceased Eusden into conceding that his poem had been prepared for just such an occasion as William's bayonet order. Thus the poet, aided by Derek as co-poet, could claim, if only he were alive, the William-Scaeva hook-up as a legitimate implication of his original intention. At last the poem's meaning was complete!

And so the Eusden heretofore dismissed as the dullest of laureates, became a master of prophetic irony, given his just deserts at last. Given him by Rosenblum, which meant a lot to Rosenblum in a quite personal sense.

For, as Derek realized midway through the writing of "Laurence Eusden's Subversive Vision," *he* was like Eusden, likewise undervalued and scorned. He was endeavoring to rescue the reputation of an undervalued poet. Or, rather, to create a reputation for him since almost no one knew who Eusden was. But who would do as much for Derek? There were no possibilities he could think of. He became mildly disgusted with himself. How could he have imagined that any scholarly journal would accept an article about an unknown *by* an unknown? What was he supposed to put for title and affiliation? Derek Rosenblum, Ph.D., janitor, Rosenblum's Best Togs for Guys?

It appeared that he had made his usual mistake, hoping, more than hoping, believing that something great was about to happen. Then, as surely as the sun's rising, disappointment would follow. At least this time he'd waked up before ... before what? Before he sent his article to a publication that would promptly send it back. But would that be so terrible? It wouldn't kill him. Moreover, if he could submit it assuming it would be rejected, then, when that happened, he would just accept it without getting all upset. And you never can tell, maybe ... no. No.

But wasn't it a bit premature to consider how his article might be received? It wasn't finished. Almost, but not quite. So he would write the final paragraph and then decide what to do with "Eusden's Subversive Vision." Such as throw the thing away. Or mail it to an editor someplace so that he or she could throw it away. And after that? Work on improving his menswear selling technique, enlist with the big insurance company, whatever. But it was necessary to finish. He owed himself that, even if no one else would care.

So then. What made Laurence Eusden so acutely resentful that he would risk his laureateship by slipping a dose of poison into verses that someone in the court just might possibly read and even understand? But Derek thought he'd explained all that: the indignity of having to grind out poems for German philistines plus frequent contact with the arrogant Walpoles, father and son, and vicious little warrior boy William. No point in saying it again at the end. It would be nice to bring out something innate in Eusden, a particular sensitivity, and Derek toyed with suggesting that the laureate was gay. For it would be easy to unearth this vein in the poem as in any poem, a simple matter of playing with words. But Derek decided not to take that facile route. *He* wasn't gay, and he felt that the poet's rancor he had uncovered in "The Origin of the Knights of the Bath" was identical with his own. He realized then what he wanted to do with his concluding paragraph was to talk about himself and how the Academy had screwed him.

But he didn't want to look like a complainer.

Derek then bethought himself of the countless others similarly screwed, like the hordes of young Ph.D.'s serving as underpaid part-timers, as he had at Heartland. And the junior instructors who actually had full-time jobs, real jobs, what did they get to teach? He knew from Glick: lit from the Armenian diaspora, Native American Orature, and comp, always comp, to freshmen who grew more illiterate with each passing year. Well, maybe it was as bad as Glick said. It was still teaching. Far worse was the plight of the many who had no job at all and had to struggle to survive in the great world beyond academe. Like Derek.

This is the concluding paragraph he finally settled on:

"Laurence Eusden's has been a talent long unrecognized. One hopes that the present essay will entice others to explore the woefully uncultivated field of Eusden Studies. Indeed, it is not impossible that some prospective explorers will map the territory with particular zeal. I refer to the anonymous multitude of humble scholars sharing desks and manual typewriters in overcrowded, ill-lit offices, teachers of composition, usually on a part-time basis, along with every trendy, politically correct multi-cultural subject that comes along. For they, as did Eusden in his time, have talents that the powers that be—in the present case, the fat cats of academe with their tiny teaching loads—have chosen to ignore. And think of the Ph.D.'s frozen out of the ranks entirely, the burger flippers, secondary school subs, and men's clothing store employees! Just as they are effectively forbidden to do what they planned and were trained to do, so was Eusden, perhaps elated when made laureate, compelled to write birthday ditties for royal oafs. With "The

Origin of the Knights of the Bath" the poet struck back. If only we could do as much."

At the bottom of the page that held this excoriating finale, Derek typed:

> Derek Rosenblum, Ph.D.
> Salesman in Training
> Rosenblum's Best Togs for Guys

Where would he send this thing, with this conclusion? Fat cats of academe ran the journals. If one such should chance to read "Eusden's Subversive Vision" all the way to the end, a prospect scarcely possible, that diatribe against the system would surely make him reconsider any favorable response to what had come before. And upset him, perhaps grievously. Now, that was promising.

"I am outraged!" croaks the old professor. "Who is this Rosenblum? How dare he attack ... ack ... ack ... ack." He flops upon his desk, quite dead. When the news gets out, junior faculty and part-timers secretly rejoice.

Derek sent his article to *Poetics Now*, one of the most prestigious publications in English, not merely of studies of eighteenth-century texts, but of those of all the periods. By being aware that it would surely be rejected, he hoped to lessen his disappointment when the rejection came. At least he would have shown that he wasn't ashamed of championing Eusden, whom he now thought of as his alter ego. With luck, too, he might succeed in pissing off any posh editor/professor who chanced to read his doomed submission. Not that he seriously expected to hear of the death by apoplexy of distinguished Professor Such a One, but it was fun to think about while rehanging Italian sport coats at Rosenblum's Best.

"He died doing what he loved," said a spokesman for the respected quarterly edited by the grand old man, "with his red pencil in his hand."

Privately he confides to colleagues, "The look on his face still chills my blood."

This faint amusement was all that Derek felt he could reasonably expect for his labor of months.

Another month passed. The mail came at eleven. Derek was due at the store in two hours.

Why an envelope from *Poetics Now*? Hadn't he enclosed an SASE? It was a remarkably attractive and impressive envelope formed of thick-textured, cream-colored paper, as was the brief note inside, which he read with one eye while scanning the rest of his mail with the other. Bills and ads. He was also spooning yogurt into himself. Mysteriously, he felt good. That was funny.

He realized that he had no clear sense of the contents of the letter from *Poetics Now*, despite having just glanced at it while admiring the high-quality paper. Now he picked it up again. It began, "Thank you for submitting this stunning work of neo-historicist criticism that we plan to run in our forthcoming issue."

Derek reread the letter, this time holding a ruler under each line. He went into the bathroom and looked at himself in the mirror. There, perched on the commode, he read it one more time, aloud. Exiting his apartment, he saw Speedo the surfer standing by his old VW bus and waved the letter at him, shouting, "Hey, dude! Check this out!" The boy dropped his board and ran. No one else was in view, so Derek went back inside. He phoned Malibu and told his mother, who said she was glad it had happened, whatever it was, and did he feel all right because he seemed a little distracted.

"I'm fine," he said.

Then Mimi said she had to fix George his lunch.

Derek, deflated, sat down on his couch, holding the letter with both hands. The person who had typed it had not typed his name or her name, and he or she had so scrawled the signature that it was impossible to read. The first name was completely undecipherable. The second started with an M, followed by what might have been an o, but after that was just a squiggle. There was something suspicious about that. Derek knew that the editor in chief of *Poetics Now* was the aging Renaissance hotshot, Lodwick Lvov, both names lacking even a single m. This was probably some junior guy who had to do all the shit work for the mag and also coach Lvov's granddaughter's soccer team. Maybe he was just a grad student. No one more established would have easily tolerated Derek's polemical conclusion, which M had characterized as "zesty."

And why had M praised the essay as "something entirely new to the field of Eusden studies," when Derek was positive that he himself had just founded that field? He began to feel as he had on entering his apartment in Heartland and finding it tossed. Everything was upside down—In his head this time.

Now he began to wonder if the acceptance was real. The letter had the flavor of a prank with its reference to a nonexistent "field." Derek imagined the letter's author chuckling as he typed "neo-historicist criticism." That could be nonexistent too. And even if the letter meant what it seemed to say, *Poetics Now* might go out of business before his piece appeared. Such was his luck, He knew better than to get his hopes up; he knew what had always followed.

Better to just remember that than to eagerly await publication and be crushed with disappointment when his Eusden essay never made it into print.

And if that happened, he would be all right. He was adjusting to existence where he was. The guys at the store had been friendlier lately, and his dad might consider giving him another shot at sales, if he asked him about it. A Venice Tracy he saw occasionally in the bars seemed to be coming on to him. He was getting used to his life here, for it was easy and simple. The days passed swiftly enough.

So when "Eusden's Subversive Vision" didn't get published he wouldn't mind. Nothing would change, and that would be all right.

But something did.

Part Two

What Changed

Oh, it wasn't all that much. "Eusden's Subversive Vision" did appear in *Poetics Now*, and Professor Lodwick Lvov died, though not in a spasm of rage occasioned by reading it. It was a skiing accident that carried off the old professor, and not before he sent Derek a note, handwritten on that exquisite paper, praising his article for its "spunk." In the space of eighteen months, four articles about Eusden were published in as many journals, and each cited Derek Rosenblum's pioneering study. Each critic also noted the similarity between the unappreciated, exploited Eusden and today's academic helots, but none of them got too excited about it. "That's just the way it goes" summed up their feelings, which made Derek wonder if he'd gone too far himself in what he had written. In any case, he no longer felt as aggrieved. It didn't seem to be his problem, really.

For his success, such as it was, had had what might seem an unlikely effect on Derek. The day after his article appeared, he strode into Rosenblum's Best an hour early and demanded that George let him sell. Before he went home that evening he had disposed of eleven thousand dollars worth of coats, slacks, ties, and calf-length silk socks. He continued to have very good days and the other salesmen, buoyed by his newfound energy, started calling him Dickhead again, but this time as a term of affection. The store cooked, and George, delighted, started taking days off and sunning at the beach, laying his blanket down on the side of the chubby oldsters and gaining weight.

On the evening of that first big selling day, Derek visited a few bars in Venice's Dogtown and eventually found the firm-haunched blonde he'd recently noticed smiling in his direction and looking glum when he passed her by. She wasn't Lucia Luteplucker, but Lucia didn't matter much at this point in his life. Nor, though there was a general resemblance, did it matter that she wasn't the real Tracy. He didn't realize that he was taking his old buds' advice and settling for second best. In his apartment on that first night he drove into his new friend with such zeal that the couple who lived above him came down to complain about the noise. Wrapped in a blanket, he invited them in to party, but they declined. Two nights later he had another bout, with another pick-up.

So he sold and he screwed. For a time, that was all he wanted. It didn't seem strange to him that after establishing himself as the pioneering Eusden scholar (despite what M had written), he hadn't foraged further in the field. Nothing more needed to be said. He was no longer interested. Now he wondered why he had ever likened himself to the little known laureate. There was at least one big difference. Eusden was forced to write poems, generally bad, about people he didn't like; that was his job. But he, Derek, was free to do whatever he wanted.

Oh, he found it puzzling, when he occasionally reflected on it, that he hadn't sent English departments around the country any queries, concerning jobs, in which he could have boasted about the Rosenblum Thesis. Somehow he had forgone his long held ambition to become a college professor. Not that this was unreasonable in itself. For which was more satisfying, when you really looked at the alternatives: teaching (mostly composition, the only steady work in English) and writing articles of interest only to a handful of fellow scholars or making lots of money (30% commission on sales) and getting lots of sex? The answer seemed pretty obvious.

So much was reason. The rest was instinct, when his published article had made a career in English at least thinkable, leading him in a different direction altogether. For something in Derek, something other than his brain, knew what such a career could do to him. It could turn him into a dunce. He was a Luteplucker product, like it or not, and wasn't ready to combat her influence, to which entering the profession would expose him. Would he ever be? That was a question he didn't know how to ask. Something else he was too dim to realize was that his present existence as sales maestro and man about town wasn't exactly anti-dunce insurance.

But it took time for Derek to tire of that sort of life and to consider English once again. Therefore he was only slightly interested when Spitfire College Press sent him a copy of the *Variorum Laurence Eusden*, forwarded from Heartland, where he had left his parents' address with the town post office. Leafing through it, he guessed that it contained all the little known one was known to have written, plus editorial notes and intro. Derek hadn't known about this publishing venture; nor had he heard of Spitfire College Press, located according to the *Variorum's* title page in Southampton, UK. This same page also bore the tiny imprint of a prop-driven plane from whose stubby wings streamed little dotted lines representing machine gun bullets. Later Derek was to learn that during the Second World War the factory that produced the famed British fighter plane was located near Southampton on the Channel coast. For a short time his daily walk from bus to class at Spitfire College would take him past the granite replica of one. So too, during his lengthy tenure at Kansas's Enola Gay, would he often cast an eye upon the half-scale B-29 as he ambled across Bombardier Quad. But these experiences came later.

Now he casually leafed through the *Variorum's* introduction, which was brief and contained nothing about the poet he hadn't already known, including the proposition that Eusden was a secret subversive. Of course that was his idea, the Rosenblum Thesis, but his name appeared nowhere in the text. This constituted a flagrant breach of academic propriety, but since Derek now specialized in selling clothes and balling youngish women, he resisted getting worked up about it. He was also somewhat distracted from whatever resentment he might otherwise have felt—had every right to feel—by the editor's expressed indignation, in the introduction, for having once been compelled to teach the poetry of the Armenian diaspora. His memory jogged, Derek took another gander at the title page, on which only the little plane had previously attracted his attention. Of course the editor's name was there, too, though in extremely small print.

Indeed, it was he, Professor Sheldon Glick, who had told him that writing about Eusden was the stupidest thing Derek could have done. And now this Glick creature had scored a publication surely made possible only by the interest in Eusden created by himself, Rosenblum, true pioneer of Eusden Studies. Rosenblum the unmentioned. But it still didn't matter. Not in view of the life, both lucrative and carefree, he was presently enjoying.

Nonetheless, during a lull on the sales floor the following afternoon, Derek thought it would be fun to give Sheldon Glick a call. He wanted to remind the little man of what he had said about how unsatisfying a subject Eusden was and also to inquire, as snidely as possible, about the omission of the weighty name of Rosenblum. In the storeroom he stood, surrounded by clutter, leaning against the wall next to the phone. It took a few minutes to get Enola Gay State's number out of Kansas information and then to get through to the Department of English. At one point, salesman Spero rushed in, thrusting an index finger into the opposite fist, the gesture that meant "rich customers, let's fuck them"; but reaching Glick and telling him off seemed, if only for the moment, more important to Derek. Spero shrugged and departed at a trot.

But Derek could not speak to Glick, who was no longer at Enola Gay. The English Department secretary said that Sheldon had "moved to greener pastures" and when asked where those pastures were, replied that she hadn't a clue. No one did. Sheldon hadn't said. It was a New York voice telling Derek these things in an accent like Glick's. Maybe everyone in Kansas now came from New York.

"We don't miss him," confided the voice. "He's a smarty-pants."

That Glick wasn't missed almost made up for his not being there to chide. It didn't matter, anyway. He felt no sense of rivalry. They led different lives, he and Sheldon Glick.

In the following weeks, however, he surprised himself by occasionally wondering what life might be like for Derek Rosenblum, professor. The arrival of the variorum Eusden might have had, in a delayed fashion, something to do with this development. Whatever its cause, it was not to be acted upon in any way. Now that his article was no longer new, to try again, to send out queries again, would be a waste of time, and he'd already used up enough of that vital commodity in getting a useless Ph.D. Who would want to be a professor, anyway, a slave to classroom routine and preoccupied by the struggle for tenure? Well, lots of people, he was well aware of that. Of course, if you got to the top, full professor, you reaped rich rewards, infrequent teaching days, an easy life. That wouldn't be so bad as a long-term goal, but it was too late for that.

He thought about teaching a course or two at nearby Santa Monica City College. Some day, when he had a little extra time, he could go over there and ask. It would just be composition, of course, probably remedial, and he knew he'd soon get sick of that. Still, it would be nice to be back in the classroom, telling students what to do. This prospect attracted him more as his current, thoroughly routinized life style engaged him less. For now he was slowing down in both the store and the bars. George had taken to directing well-heeled customers to Spero, rather than Derek, and on some weekends Derek stayed home rather than prowling for fresh tail, of which there never seemed to be any. It was as if the same women kept coming back evening after evening. Like them, the months rolled by.

One afternoon, calling it a whim, he thought to thank M of *Poetics Now* for accepting an article by an unknown critic about an unknown poet. Derek had thought of M as a flunky, but maybe the unknown editor had some status and would prove to be a useful contact if he ever decided to reenter the job market.

Not that there was much chance that he would. But the person Derek spoke with at the journal (and this time no fellow employee rushed in to urge him to the selling floor) said they had no M, that there had never been an M. And what a shame about dear Professor Lvov. At least he died doing what he loved best. Skiing, she said, in case Derek hadn't known.

Lvov had written him a nice letter, and he hadn't bothered to respond. That might have led to something. Now the man was dead. Crashed into a tree probably, just when he was really enjoying himself. It gave Derek a chill. He actually shivered as he hung up the phone. Was *he* doing what he loved best? Didn't feel like it. He hoped he wouldn't die soon.

A year passed. He called Samo CC a few times. No openings.

He admitted that he was bored. He admitted it only to himself, as no one else gave a crap. Maybe it went beyond boredom, the state he was in. He thought slowly, lived slowly. Every day slower.

He wondered what Tracy Chatham was doing. He phoned a few old high school buddies who had long since returned to Los Angeles from their colleges in the East and asked them if they knew. Just curious. They didn't know, and although no one of them actually said he couldn't bring cheer squad captain Chatham to mind, that was the feeling Derek got from talking to them. He found this strange. Her legs at least he would have thought unforgettable, she having flashed them upon the b-ball court night after night before everyone at Yorty High. Every guy he knew was hot for Tracy. What seemed to him yet stranger, however, was that his erstwhile buddies experienced similar memory gaps in trying to place *him*. They weren't being snotty. They were simply quite vague on the subject of Derek Rosenblum ("math whiz, right? No?"), and, besides that, they who had once been remarkably quick in all their responses now seemed remarkably slow.

They were doing things with computers, "programing," "coding." Derek speculated. Could that sort of work, with machines, cause a kind of dislocation to the personality, making one seem stupid, or be stupid?

The same question, he finally understood, could be asked about peddling costly duds at Rosenblum's Best Togs For Guys. He certainly felt stupid when there. All of his energy had leaked away, and he contributed almost nothing to the daily sales totals. At the store, Spero, Merle, and Oren kept on calling him Dickhead, though now as a term of abuse. He didn't do anything about it. George stopped taking days off and grew lean. One day he asked Derek to start coming in later and staying after closing to clean the store.

"What's happened to Sky?" Derek asked.

The nice high school kid, now a student at Samo, had been rehired for flunky work when Derek hit his stride as a salesman.

"Let him go, too bad, you're it."

A menial once more and earning no commissions, Derek made only enough to cover basic expenses and could no longer afford to hit the bars. But he didn't miss them, as it had been some time since he'd enjoyed that kind of activity. Sitting home and watching TV, with scant concern about what crawled across the screen—that was enough to keep him going. Once when he went out for a walk, his only recreation besides the tube, Speedo dared to flip him off and Derek did nothing. Nothing was all he did in his free time, and he almost enjoyed it, felt obscurely satisfied switching on the set, settling in for an hour's viewing, half asleep. In his more lucid moments, which only happened upon him while driving to or from the store and had to be halfway conscious, he knew that was bad. He was rotting.

On those drives, he found himself thinking that college teaching was, after all, the trade he should have pursued. It was stupid in some ways: the classroom grind, the countless papers to grade, tenure to be won, and all for not much money; but maybe—no, probably—it was his kind of stupid. It was certainly a better fit than selling menswear or playing the seducer in noisy bars. Goldman, the video guy who had said that teaching was all he was good for, had given sage advice.

Sometimes Derek thought it was unfair that he was that way. How much choice had he been given in the matter? He had been, he surmised, conditioned as a child, virtually predestined. Books had taken him then, seized him with a delight that might well be called treacherous; for it had fueled his desire to become an English professor before he knew how hard it was to find employment in that profession, or what might become of the delight if employment were somehow found. Now he had suspicions.

He would never be able to test them. Employment was not to be found, so why try? His credentials were zilch. By now his Eusden article was even more obscure than Eusden. He would never teach again. There was nothing out there for him, and if by freakish chance an opportunity ever staggered into view, it would be in a southern swamp or northern bog, and his courses would all be in remedial comp or in subjects he knew nothing about drawn from the multiculture, like Sheldon Glick's poetry of the Armenian diaspora.

Glick! Arrogant, cynical, thieving Sheldon Glick! Only thoughts of Glick could fully rouse Derek and were at least part of the reason why he couldn't stop thinking about his old goal of entering the professoriat; for Glick had ripped him off with his *Variorum Eusden*. Though this hadn't bothered Derek particularly at the time, now it did, and what annoyed him most was the total omission of his name. So how pleasing would it be to outshine Glick, to teach at a ritzier joint than Enola Gay, to outpublish Glick, to be the one to tell *him* some things *he* ought to know. But not about Laurence Eusden. Glick having contaminated the field, he was done with Eusden Studies.

The idea of Glick as competition actually tempted Derek to reread the most difficult of all eighteenth-century works, the horrendous *Dunciad*, to see if he understood it as well as when he was a grad student. Before he began, however, he considered that Pope's mock-epic had been the source of the dream that he would rather not dream again, and so he got Oliver Goldsmith's *Vicar of Wakefield* out of the library instead. He found several things in it to talk to a class about and examine students on. He could teach it. So could Glick, probably. He was a Brooklyn smarty-pants all right, but he was no dunce.

Unfortunately, in pondering how best to cut the *Vicar* into bits for a class, Derek failed to enjoy what he read. It might have made him laugh with delight, as when a boy, if he hadn't been so intent on making it a test.

At least he knew he was still smart. But this knowledge did him no good and even made him bitter, because he knew he would never find employment. So he chose not to apply. Then employment found him.

Deliverance

One October morning the postman brought Derek an envelope from *Poetics Now*. Made of cheap, thin paper, it could only contain another of their appeals for money. These arrived regularly, nearly every month. "Dear Contributor," the letters began. He had never sent them anything. He tossed the envelope at the trash basket in his kitchen. It missed and, being late for work, Derek left it lying on the lino as he decamped.

Arriving at Rosenblum's Best, he found his father in a state of considerable upset because someone had invaded the store in the night. Derek, last man to leave, as usual, had again neglected to turn on the alarm system. Nor, it seemed certain, had he remembered to lock the front door. In fact, he was sure he hadn't locked it and told George so when asked about it.

"I can't believe," said George, in a tone of mild wonderment. He said it three times, followed by "wow." He shook his head.

He seemed more perplexed than angry, probably because the only thing taken was a three-pac of silk boxer shorts decorated with red and yellow colored replicas of tarot cards. No damage had been done to the store's windows or the door left providentially unlocked.

"We were lucky," Derek explained to his dad. "It was a good thing I forgot about the door. Otherwise they might have broken in."

George was stung. "Lucky? Derek, he used the bathroom, the *bathroom*! The light was on when Spero got here this morning."

"That might have been me who left it on. But—"

"If the insurance people hear about this," George interrupted, "it would be a calamity! The premiums!" He thrust his right hand above his head.

"Dad, I'll pay for the shorts." It was all Derek could think of to say.

George dropped his hand to waist level and made a fist. He gave the air an uppercut.

Now thoroughly pissed, "That's not the point!" he shouted. "Anyway, it's twenty-nine dollars. Do you have that much in your pocket? I sincerely doubt it, Derek."

Although he knew better than to tell George, Derek was sure he knew who had gotten into the store, snatched the shorts, and left the bathroom light on (if not himself). In the past weeks he had allowed the homeless man who stalked the Third Street Promenade to come in and use the toilet. Last night, however, this occasional guest hadn't appeared before it was time to arm the system and lock the door, both of which chores he'd left undone, being already mentally hunkered down half-conscious in anticipation of the evening's television viewing.

Later the man had come along, tried the door, entered, relieved himself, and noticed the underwear, which, with their loud colors, were hard to miss. Hadn't been selling either, so why the big fuss? Derek took out his wallet. He had a ten-dollar bill and a one. He offered them,

Mr. Rosenblum didn't want his money. "Go home," he told him, wearily. "Just go. I'll call in Sky for the day. You can come back tomorrow. I'll just have to keep reminding you about the system."

Then he sighed.

Spero was standing by the door as Derek passed through it. "Dickhead," he hissed. This angered Derek, first time he'd felt any strong emotion in months except when thinking of Glick. He was in no mood to take his usual shit from the sales force, not on top of his dad being disgusted with him over a package of gaudy underpants.

"Push your face in," he whispered to Spero, who ducked away. But Derek did not pursue him. He was sick of the store. He wanted out and, at that moment, wished that his dad had simply fired him and ordered him never to come back.

In his apartment he picked up and opened the envelope from *Poetics Now* without thinking, the way he did many things. He walked into his living room, where the television was, holding between forefinger and thumb the sheet of paper the envelope had contained. Absently, he rubbed, and felt a rich texture. That got his attention. Perhaps this wasn't just another appeal for funds. Perhaps a complaint had come to them from a senior prof somewhere, pissed off by the Eusden article's polemical final paragraph (that until now had provoked no such responses that Derek knew of), to which the journal sought an authorial reply. He knew this was unlikely, given how long it had been. Years, but it felt like decades.

But what he held in his two hands and then proceeded to read was a letter sent to Derek care of *Poetics Now* from someone who called himself Lewis Lozange, M.A. Scrawled in pencil at the very top of the page were the words "sounds promising," followed by a question mark and then the letter M followed by what was probably an o and then a squiggle. His friend. His phantom friend. Derek's interest quickened. The paper was indeed nice, high quality. Directly under M's penciled message was the imprint of a tiny fighter plane, the same as that on the title page of the variorum Eusden he'd been sent, and beneath the plane, printed in red capitals,

SPITFIRE COLLEGE OF HIGHER EDUCATION.

"Dear Doctor Rosenblum," Derek read and then stopped reading, baffled for a moment at being addressed as Doctor. He wasn't used to that. But he then recalled that as a Ph.D. he was a doctor of sorts and could be addressed as such, though the guys at Rosenblum's Best preferred Dickhead. He began again.

"Dear Dr. Rosenblum,
Greetings from Spitfire College, Southampton, UK! I am Lewis Lozange, M.A., Head of Literature.
As you may possibly know, it is our practice here to employ editors of books published by our press as instructors in the college for terms of one to three years. These rare scholars, acknowledged experts on the authors profit-obsessed major presses see fit to ignore, add a unique dimension to the education of our appreciative students. To speak only of your area of eighteenth-century literature: can any Oxbridge college boast a staff member who has edited the earthy lyrics of Ambrose Philips, Pope's great rival in the genre of pastoral? I think not, but our Bernard Simkin, M.A., may be found on the Spitfire campus every day, except when not feeling well, and his complete Philips is available in the college bookstore.
And who can forget the rigor and wit of Soame Jenyns's masterful essays, only available from Spitfire Press, whose esteemed editor, Mr. Gil Gomal, contributed a uniquely Asian flavor to the Spitfire Experience until stuffy British morality necessitated a return to his native land? And we are indeed fortunate in having secured Mr. Bert Bangles, M.A., he of the *Collected Poems of William Topaz McGonagall*, as a permanent member of our faculty.

No longer with us is the exceedingly clever Sheldon Glick, Ph.D., editor of the *Variorum Laurence Eusden*. His was a two-year appointment beginning last year. Unfortunately, he failed to fit in, and no one here was terribly displeased when, after only one month's time in the present year, he suddenly announced that he was leaving us. 'Greener pastures' was the whole of his explanation.

We would like you to replace him, if you are free to cease doing whatever it is that you do. Dr. Glick has told me that you are employed in some species of retail, but as several things he has told us have proven to be less than accurate, I hesitate to believe him on this. That you are not an editor of one of the press's volumes is a point that has occasioned much discussion in the dining commons. You will be pleased to know that your status as the founder of Eusden Studies was thought to overcome that deviation from form (although dear Doctor Glick insisted that he knew about Eusden before you did)."

Lozange concluded his letter by mentioning that Spitfire College would provide Derek with housing free of charge as well as a monthly stipend that amounted to 2500 American dollars. He was to phone with his acceptance or rejection of the offer ASAP. Derek found the number under the little plane along with a Southampton street address.

As it was one in the afternoon in Venice, California, Derek thought no one would be in at the college in England if he should call then, but he picked up the phone nonetheless.

"Hello, Dad? I quit."

"You do? The store? No kidding? Well, we'll find you something else someplace. That big insurance outfit might—"

"No, Dad. I've got another job. Got it today."

"Oh? Doing what?"

George uttered these words in a snotty kind of way, as if the job must be something contemptible, more so than cleaning the bathroom at Rosenblum's Best. Rather than try to explain the rather complex Spitfire offer, Derek said only, "I'll tell you both about it later. I think you'll be impressed." (They weren't.)

"Does it have benefits?"

"Sure." They had free medical care in Britain, far as he knew.

Derek then stayed up until two a.m., which he thought would be a good time to call someone in Southampton, UK. While waiting, he began to worry. This was what he wanted and needed, a college teaching job, so he had to take it. And it was in England; that was exciting. But what if they made him teach classes in Shakespeare or Milton? It had been a long time since he'd read or even thought about anyone outside of his period.

Or what if he were asked to teach authors inside his period about whom he knew next to nothing, such as Ambrose Philips and Soame Jenyns?

He had a related concern. Why would any press choose to publish the books the Head of English seemed so proud of? They made him wonder about the standards of the college. Jenyns and Philips weren't really obscure, as Eusden was or had been before Derek led him briefly from the shadows. Most people in eighteenth-century studies knew who they were. They were universally recognized as bad, that was the problem.

Jenyns, convinced that a benevolent deity had schemed creation so that all was good, speculated that beings on other planets enjoyed watching humans suffer; thus, our afflictions—from disease, from strife—were made to contribute to the general good and all was well with the universe. Pope had also preached the doctrine that whatever is, is right in the *Essay on Man*, but without any hideous examples, and he'd had the good grace to contradict himself in other writings. As for Jenyns, in a famous review Samuel Johnson had torn his ghastly hypothesis to shreds, leaving its author in a similar state.

Ambrose Philips wrote clunky pastoral poems in which (such was the general opinion) English shepherds were made to speak like Tarzan. "Ugh! Me bring ram to hump sheep." Pope, who enjoyed smacking people on the head, gave the talentless Philips a few satiric whacks, just as he had Eusden, but Ambrose was hardly important enough to be anyone's great rival in anything. It was hard to understand why, after several centuries, a scholarly press chose to republish these two. Perhaps Spitfire had hoped for a minor Philips or Jenyns revival, as there had been with Eusden, but the circumstances were different, Eusden having no reputation, the others bad ones.

And who was this William Topaz McGonagall? Derek had never heard of him. Was he an eighteenth-century writer, too?

Finally, Derek was uneasy regarding Sheldon Glick. So he claimed to be the first to know about Eusden. That didn't matter to Derek, who was perfectly willing to let him occupy the fertile field of Eusden Studies all by himself. But how did Glick know that he worked at the store? The contributor's bio in *Poetics Now* that described him as an "independent scholar" hadn't mentioned his job. What else did that little fart know about him?

It was also disturbing that Glick, according to Lozange, had "failed to fit in" at Spitfire College. While Derek was positive that he didn't resemble Glick in either appearance or character, they were both Americans, so maybe that indicated he also wouldn't fit in. It would be interesting and perhaps useful to talk to Sheldon, much as Derek disliked him, about this strangely named institution, but that wasn't possible.

Now Derek was almost sorry he'd told his father he was quitting and had hinted at a great new job. He could have waited and given himself at least a little time to consider whether this abrupt departure to another country was really a good idea. But Lozange's offer had arrived just when the store had become, for the second time, unbearable, and when he was on the point of admitting to himself that teaching was the only thing he was qualified by temperament to do. That meant something. It meant he should accept the offer. He made the call to England.

"Delightful!" boomed Lewis Lozange. He sounded as if he were seven feet tall, and his accent was the kind that Derek would learn to call "plummy," or high-class, "hoity-toity" his mother would say. Its effect on the sometimes cantankerous American was to make him timid.

"Could you please say what I'm going to teach? The classes?"

"Oh, I don't remember offhand. You'll be informed when you get here."

"It would be nice to prepare."

"Prepare?" chuckled Lewis Lozange. "Prepare? Performance teaching? No, Dr. Rosenblum, just get here. The term has already begun. Tell me when you want to leave—it had best be within the week—and what airline you prefer, and we'll buy your ticket for you."

He hadn't thought about that. It was a good thing the college was paying, since he had been earning practically nothing working for his dad. "How ... how nice," he stammered.

"We have a graunt," Lozange announced airily.

"Ah, yes," replied Derek, baffled by a ordinary word made unrecognizable due to the plum Lozange kept in his mouth, but feeling obliged to say something. It wasn't until he was well settled into his duties at Spitfire College of Higher Education that he understood that the institution's real business was the obtaining of graunts, that is to say, "grants." Being named after a fabled RAF fighter plane didn't hurt.

He told Lozange that any day and airline would do.

"Economy class acceptable?"

"Sure."

He found out later that Glick had demanded and flown business. Always pushing, that guy.

He had to pay an agency to get him a passport with two days notice.

On the day before his flight to London, Derek drove to the UCLA Library to research William Topaz McGonagall, who turned out to have lived and written in the nineteenth century, not the eighteenth. There were specialists in bad literature, Derek was astonished to learn, who all agreed in judging McGonagall's "The Tay Bridge Disaster" the worst poem ever written in English. UCLA didn't have the Spitfire Press collection of the poet's work, and he found "The Tay Bridge Disaster" in an anthology called *All-Time Literary Losers*. He read with a growing sense of alarm.

> Beautiful Railway Bridge of the Silv'ry Tay!
> Alas! I am very sorry to say
> That ninety lives have been taken away
> On the last Sabbath day of 1879,
> Which will be remembered for a very long time.
>
> 'Twas about seven o'clock at night,
> And the wind it blew with all its might,
> And the rain came pouring down,
> And the dark clods [sic] seem'd to frown,
> And the Demon of the air seem'd to say—
> "I'll blow down the Bridge of Tay."
>
> When the train left Edinburgh
> The passengers' hearts were light and felt no sorrow,
> But Boreas blew a terrific gale,
> Which made their hearts for to quail,
> And many of the passengers with fear did say—
> "I hope God will send us safe across the Bridge of Tay."
>
> But when the train came near to Wormit Bay,
> Boreas he did loud and angry bray,

And shook the central girders of the Bridge of Tay
On the last Sabbath day of 1879,
Which will be remember'd for a very long time.

So the train sped on with all its might,
And Bonnie Dundee soon hove in sight,
And the passengers' hearts felt light,
Thinking they would enjoy themselves on the New Year,
With their friends at home they lov'd most dear,
And wish them all a happy New Year.

So the train mov'd slowly along the Bridge of Tay,
Until it was about midway,
Then the central girders with a crash gave way,
And down went the train and passengers into the Tay!
The Storm Fiend did loudly bray,
Because ninety lives had been taken away,
On the last Sabbath day of 1879,
Which will be remembered for a very long time.

As soon as the catastrophe came to be known
The alarm from mouth to mouth was blown,
And the cry rang out all o'er the town,
Good Heavens! The Tay Bridge is blown down,
And a passenger train from Edinburgh. . .

There was a bit more, but Derek was too rattled to finish.

Compared to this, "The Origin of the Knights of the Bath" was the music of the spheres. Derek recognized "The Tay Bridge Disaster" as splendidly laughable, but he was unable to laugh. It could hardly be a good sign that Spitfire published the very worst poet. He slept poorly that night and in the morning boarded the London bound plane with reluctant steps. Another bad year loomed before him, even though he was leaving hard luck Los Angeles and getting to teach, which he thought he wanted to do.

But it wasn't bad at all once he'd settled there and became accustomed to the Spitfire Experience. He was grateful to everyone for helping him fit in, especially the kids in one of his classes who made a point of telling him what was what.

An Older Culture

They sat, the ten or twelve of them, in what was supposed to be a seminar, the only form of instruction in use at a college where lecturing was frowned upon as "performance teaching." But seminars are ineffective, Derek had always believed, unless the participants occasionally speak, and this bunch would rather sit in silence while they looked out the window or at the clock buzzing on the wall. Their faces were pale, their eyes sparkless shades of watery blue. They had big noses and protruding ears. Fascinated, Derek watched them yawn, lay their heads upon the table, mumble to one another about unliterary matters as if he weren't present. They only came, those who did come, because it was a morning class and the college pub didn't open until noon.

This particular meeting of British Lit, 1700-1820, was only his third with these people, and he was still trying to teach as he had in his classes at Heartland U. There he would come in with some things to say about the assigned text, usually a brief essay, that would entice the kids into a discussion. Some of the time this worked, at Heartland. Not here. On this day, however, the students consented to address him.

A young man wearing a greasy leather jacket. "Too much, Derek, the books. Much too much." He pronounced it "moch."

It was either the department's policy or the college's—Derek hadn't asked—for students to address instructors by their first names. That went for the visiting American, too, Lozange troubled to inform him, despite Derek's Ph.D. and title of Doctor. His colleagues, lacking these things, claimed to be mightily impressed by them. They expressed their awe in a rather sarcastic way perhaps, but that may have been just his imagination working. What he surely was not imagining, however, was his failure to get through to his students. The relationship would possibly improve if he addressed them by *their* first names, which was policy also, but connecting names, first or last, to these faces was difficult for Derek. All the young people in his classes looked alike to him, same eyes, noses, ears. They did not, however, sound alike, possessing various regional accents that served to baffle him all the more, since he often failed to understand them when they spoke.

Thus he was unsure of what greasy leather was complaining about.

He ventured, "You mean they cost too much?" They all laughed at that.

"No, Derek, no," said greasy leather. "Too much reading. That's what is too much, you see."

An affirmative grumble arose from the class.

Oh, that was it. Derek essayed a mild protest. "Book One of *Gulliver's Travels* doesn't strike me as too much for a week. It's often read as a children's story, you know."

"Then why are we reading it here in college? Eh?"

From the class. "Ees rye, ees rye, int he rye?"

Translated by Derek as "He's right, he's right. Isn't he right?"

The student continued. "Now, if we'd had it for A-Levels, that would be more acceptable like, but fact is we didn't. Nor did we have this other one, this *Sentimental Journey* by Sterne. I've looked at it, Derek. It's daft, you know. Isn't it daft?" He appealed to the class, which collectively muttered something that sounded like "aye-aye." A few began to smoke, ignoring a No Smoking sign.

Sentimental Journey was a bad idea, he could see that now. Too, well, daft. He'd thought about ordering Sterne's blockbuster, *Tristram Shandy*, for this class but decided that it might be too hard for undergrads. It was fabulously difficult and might be too hard for him, too. He'd never read it since it hadn't been on the list for his qualifying exams at Heartland; this made him a bit like the Spitfire students who became resentful whenever he asked them about something that hadn't been assigned for the A-Levels they kept talking about. Then, after he passed his exams, Luteplucker had kept him occupied with Eusden and Admiral Vernon. He'd managed, however, to find time for *Sentimental Journey*, 98 pages in the Penguin edition, and loved it, even though it was about (1) the incorrigible shiftiness of language and (2) death. It was clear now that his students wouldn't respond in the same way. To point out that 98 pages wasn't long would change nothing. Maybe for them that was long. This wasn't Oxford. It was a college of higher education, with higher meaning lower—i.e., teacher prep. He should be sympathetic.

"People," he began, and there he stopped.

He began again. "Friends." And stopped again.

The pale faces turned his way. He realized there was only one thing he could say. "See you next week."

And for the rest of his time with this class Derek got by with the anthology they all carried around containing tidbits of prose and poetry written between 1700 and 1820. In this slim volume, published by Spitfire Press in 1949, *Robinson Crusoe* was represented by six pages, Pope's *Rape of the Lock* by eighteen couplets out of around 400. The *Dunciad* wasn't represented at all, which didn't make him unhappy. If they thought *Sentimental Journey* was daft, he could imagine their protests about having to read even a tiny chunk of the *Dunciad,* which he preferred not to dip into himself. The slim volume would do. It was good enough.

Everything was good enough, really. The other teachers were civil and some became actually friendly after he asked them to please stop addressing him as Dr. Rosenblum. Bernie Simkin, mentioned by Lozange in his initial letter and nicknamed "Gentle" after a "Gentle Simkin" in a Dryden poem, turned out to be a fellow American. This one, however, lacked the Ph.D., despite having written a doctoral dissertation on Ambrose Philips at Heartland under the direction of that institution's eighteenth-century expert, Professor Lucia Luteplucker. She had compelled him to do Philips, just as she had forced Laurence Eusden on Derek. While she had then approved the dissertation without enthusiasm, as in Derek's case, poor Gentle could never pass a single one of the required foreign language reading exams and so the university would not grant him the degree.

He was living in New Jersey, teaching middle school English and coaching girls volleyball when Lozange somehow found him and offered him a chance to do the *Variorum Ambrose Philips* for Spitfire College Press. Then, as was the grant-supported custom, he joined the college faculty. Derek got along very well with Gentle Simkin whenever the Philips man, a serious drinker, managed to transport himself to campus. He usually seemed slightly dazed, as did a good many others in that place. It was easy for Derek to talk with him about sports. Regarding literature Gentle wished to speak only of his poet's crude pastorals. Occasionally he declaimed a line or two.

One subject he absolutely refused to discuss was their mutual acquaintance, the good Professor Luteplucker. Something had happened with her and him, he wouldn't say what. Once, when a curious Derek pressed him on it, he got up from their bench in the campus pub and stomped away.

"Won't talk to you anymore," he huffed as he stomped. Eventually, of course, he returned. Everybody liked the college pub.

It consisted of a single large room, the largest in the college, where all other structures were broken up into small offices and seminar rooms. There were fewer than 400 students at Spitfire, and at least half of their number could fit in the pub and often did. To accommodate their collective thirst, large trucks loaded with beer visited the campus most days of the week. Faculty also drank at the pub both before and after their classes. Though Lozange had two offices, for he was not only Head of English but Principal of the College as well, he also preferred the pub. He was there that day.

"Sensitive chappy, Gentle," he boomed, pointing at Simkin's departing back. "Now he won't speak to you for a few hours, but never mind that."

Derek understood from this that he had done a bad thing but wasn't to feel bad about it. He shook his head and produced what he intended as a sheepish grin.

Lozange stood just a few inches above five feet and so was remarkably tiny to have such a big voice; it was a sign of the abundant energy he possessed in his small frame, as is common among small people. Besides the numerous administrative chores that came with his two jobs, he was always ready to help out behind the bar when the pub was packed. Often it was, but this was a slow period. Even so, he jounced energetically in his seat.

Derek grinned at Lewis Lozange. Lozange grinned back. Bert Bangles, the McGonagall man, who was sitting next to Lozange, simply grinned. He did so constantly, even when no one was near enough to him to be grinned at. Perhaps he felt this made up for his vocal shortcomings, for it was not often that he spoke. Days could pass. He was very old and thin and, as the poet's editor, knew more about William Topaz McGonagall than did anyone else in the universe. A few of the dimmer students believed he *was* McGonagall, who, however, had been born in 1825 and was presumably dead.

Bert's almost unbroken silence reminded Derek of Lucia Luteplucker's stinginess with words, but they were not the same in this; or so he felt at first. Professor Luteplucker chose not to speak, while Bert seemed unable. At times he wanted to, but the words declined to come; you could see it in the workings of his face. But the face of Luteplucker rarely changed its expression, which was no expression, signifying her lack of interest in communicating her feelings or anything else.

But was it possible, Derek once wondered, that she, almost as much as Bert Bangles, was simply incapable? He remembered how the older professors at Heartland had rumored that she was a kind of golem, a being that would probably lack aptitude for conversation. That Luteplucker only spoke— at some length, anyway—if prompted by some alien force situated in her interior, was a genuinely crazy idea, yet Derek couldn't entirely dismiss it.

He would have liked to laugh about it with Simkin had the Philips expert been less sensitive concerning the strange woman who had directed both of their dissertations. But Gentle wouldn't talk about her, and, really, why did it matter? Luteplucker was far away, across the sea followed by 1200 rugged miles of American soil. Far away in time, too. Four years now, wasn't it, since he'd seen her? Five?

In fact, it was good not to talk about her, think about her. His memories of Luteplucker weren't pleasant. She was the star of his *Dunciad* dream, too, until she turned into someone else. It always made him uncomfortable when something—a sudden dimming of the light, a bustling crowd—made him remember the dream and the goddess.

Simkin said little about anything besides the pastorals of Philips. Bert rarely spoke. Indeed, no one had a lot to say in the pub. You went there to sit and drink, maybe snooze a little. But who needs a lot of jabber, anyway? Just because people have always talked, that was no reason to keep on doing it. Derek thought this more and more. We talk talk talk, producing mostly profitless noise about things useless to worry about, whereas silence was restful and regenerated body and mind. Bert was a favorite with students for that reason, and they filled his classes to the max every term. There they also said next to nothing, preferring just to sit with him and breathe in the quiet. After a session with old Bert they felt refreshed, as if newly arisen from a midday nap. As Derek grew accustomed to life at the college, he considered going silent himself; either that or he might employ the Luteplucker reading aloud technique, also undemanding. Maybe he could combine the two approaches, eventually.

Of course there was no reason to do anything in a hurry. Hurrying uses energy at a great rate, and he had to be careful with that. He'd felt tired lately. Not tired exactly, more like sleepy. Back in California, working at the store, he'd been more tired than sleepy, and that wasn't good. Sleepy was all right, basically, as long as he didn't pass out in company. In fact, everything about the college was all right, in Derek's opinion.

It was a remarkable place in its way. The powers of Dulness (assume for a moment that she's real) were concentrated there, so perhaps some force stronger than mere contingency had led Derek to the Spitfire College of Higher Education. The institution made him dull, but he didn't care—until circumstances led him to resist.

Before then, when Derek wasn't taking his ease in the campus pub, he took it in his classes. He had two first year Intro to Lit seminars in which he showed instructional videos originally aired by the BBC of poets and novelists reading from their work or others' work. Lozange had hipped him to that. All the teachers showed these videos, of which the Division of English owned nearly five hundred. They boasted of this trove in their brochures.

Once a week in the late afternoon, Derek was assigned a class in the history of literary criticism, to which no one came. His students were supposed to be keeping notebooks on the essays they were reading in a 64-page pamphlet called *From Aristotle to Derida* [sic], Spitfire Press, what else? He would look through the notebooks at the end of the term. And the class that had complained about too much reading? Well, they were coming around, working as hard as they could, and when he felt that they weren't learning much, he only had to tell himself that eighteen couplets from the *Rape of the Lock* were better than none, eighteen times better.

All was well, or at least good enough. But why had Sheldon Glick quit in the middle of the term? That question still bothered Derek. Oh, probably smarty-pants Glick had just alienated everyone. Still, if he had committed some particular offense, Derek would have liked to know what it was. Lozange, when Derek asked him, simply repeated what he had written in the letter, that Glick had failed to fit in. As for the students, they hardly remembered him, though he had been their teacher before Derek came. They also seemed a little uncertain about Derek. They would squint at him as if trying to remember who he was and occasionally asked how to spell his last name, which might have been a polite way of finding out what his name actually was before they forgot it again.

But he didn't let this bother him much. Why make a fuss? Whatever had gone wrong for Sheldon Glick, he was fitting in just fine. That was because he had learned that at Spitfire College everything worked out by itself if you just let it. He remembered how he had thought the leather-jacketed student was complaining about the costs of the books and how the class had laughed when the boy corrected him. Now Derek had learned that government grants paid for any books the students needed for their classes and, more importantly, for the Spitfire Press editions each was required to buy. These were expensive books, 20 pounds apiece for very slim volumes of prose or poetry that no one in the world wanted to read. But the students didn't mind, as it wasn't their money, and all they were required to do was take the books off campus before throwing them in the bin.

Lozange did everything that might be considered wearisome. He attended meetings of student organizations, recited the names at graduation time, and did his best to recruit minority students, venturing into their purlieus bearing brochures and reciting useful phrases he had learned in Hindi and Gujurati. No minorities ever came to Spitfire, but he deserved full credit for trying. The most important thing Lozange did was to fill out time-tic sheets for everyone on staff, so that they'd all get paid. Like the others, Derek's only chore was to appear in class, and there he did less "performing" with each week that passed. It was quite pleasant being part of the Spitfire Experience, even if at times he felt sort of, well, hollow. That was probably just the state of being peaceful and comfortable in this older civilization.

But that civilization was changing, in the estimation and to the displeasure of everyone in the college. Derek had only a vague notion of what was happening, but he understood that they blamed it all on the woman his colleagues called Thutcher. And then they learned that Thutcher was coming.

That changed the way people behaved at the college. It woke them up. Now they talked more in the pub. They talked too much, in Derek's opinion. They yammered. It woke Derek up too, to the realization that his colleagues weren't as nice as he had thought. They could be aggressive and pushy, and he didn't like being around them. They were like the swarming dunces in Pope's poem.

The Iron Lady

Everyone at Spitfire claimed to stoutly oppose Prime Minister Margaret Thatcher, the Iron Lady. When Lozange had collected Derek at Heathrow, he had said something about Thatcher watching them, as if she were Big Sister. Pointing at a wall-mounted camera, he had said, "She tapes everything. She knows everything." At the time Derek assumed he was joking. Later he realized that Lozange might have meant what he said about Thatcher. Or, that is, about "Thutcher," as if with a 'u' instead of an 'a,' for that was how everyone at the college pronounced her name, making it into a handle that sounded like a Dickensian villain's. Indeed, she was a villain to them, and soon she would be paying the college a state visit.

Lozange suspected the worst and called a meeting of the faculty to alert everyone. The pub was packed.

"Mark my words, she'll cut away our graunts." Thus did Lozange begin. That was a great worry, as Derek readily understood. A free market champion, Thutcher insisted that government should both do and spend less, except on arms, and grants to students were thought to be her favorite target for cuts. And grants kept the college running. Very likely no students would want to come to Spitfire if their grants were eliminated or even sharply reduced. That it was a free ride, with a special provision for ski trips to the Alps and other continental enjoyments, was the college's principal attraction. Moreover, even if the cuts, the initial cuts, were relatively slight, that might still mean the end of the funds allocated students to buy Spitfire Press books. Then, since no one else ever bought any, the press, which Lozange ran all by himself, would become defunct, and the press was the principal's pride and joy.

Derek understood the general concern about grants. Harder for him to grasp was how the prime minister could be responsible for the epidemic of rudeness said by many at the college to be infecting the entire UK. His colleagues harped on the subject: no one was civil anymore, the way they used to be, and Thutcher was the reason. Being foreign, Derek just didn't get it.

He hadn't done any traveling in the country, preferring to relax on the weekends with some excellent British television. But the citizens of Southampton, where he lived as well as taught, seemed not at all rude. On the bus he rode to the college they became even more polite when it got crowded. That was a good thing, as they then tended to crash into one another while getting on and getting off, but with apologies always at the ready. Even assuming, however, that elsewhere ordinary Britons were as rude as his colleagues apparently thought, how would a mortal woman, even a prime minister, exert such a powerful and far-reaching influence? That was a question he never asked anyone. It would have been rude to, as they were all so convinced about it.

Something else puzzled him that he dared not ask about. They hated Thutcher at the college; that was plain to see. But sometimes what they said implied affection or even something stronger. When the college males, who were most of the staff, talked about her, they reminded Derek of little boys telling dirty jokes, their heads together, their expressions half-smirking, half-ashamed. Their breathing quickened, their faces reddened; all it took was the mention of her name, always in its altered form.

Thutcher.

Then it would sound to Derek like the name of a porn star who whipped people and trotted them around on leashes. Elizabeth I, Victoria—did they elicit similar responses? He wondered, but said nothing. He wondered at himself, too. Was she turning him on a bit, this middle-aged lady? He always woke up slightly when she appeared on the telly.

The few women he heard chatting on campus—beneath the replica Spitfire fighter was a favored spot—seemed vitally interested in the prime minister's clothes and makeup. Their conversations always seemed to end, however, with "Of course, she's terrible."

Well, soon Derek would learn what effect Thutcher would have up close, on him, on everyone. The official occasion for her visit was the 50th anniversary of the production of the first Spitfire fighter plane, but that wasn't even a purposeful attempt at a lie. Or so huffed Lozange in the pub, from which on this occasion students were banned. He reminded the group that the current year was 1987.

"Is it?" inquired Bernie "Gentle" Simkin. "Well, so what?"

Now that was rude, but Simkin was an American whose last stop had been New Jersey, so he couldn't very well be blamed on Thutcher.

"Fifty years ago," Lozange replied level-voiced, as if speaking to a child, "was 1937."

"I know that," Simkin said tartly. What was wrong with him today? Even for an American, that was rude. Nor was Lozange exactly polite in replying.

"Glad you do," he snapped. "Well, the first Spitfire saw the light of day in 1936, fifty-*one* years ago. So the fiftieth anniversary was last year, and she didn't come then or even send a note. Now is it clear to you, Gentle? I trust so."

"Don't like you," Simkin muttered, staggering to his feet. He'd been drinking steadily for two hours. For several more minutes he wandered about the vastness of the pub, thrusting through the crowd, before finally locating the door.

"Sensitive chap, Gentle," Derek risked saying.

"Oh, is that what you think?" challenged Lozange, as if he had no right to say anything. Derek then proceeded to surprise himself by mentally reviewing a number of doubts about the English Head and College Principal he hadn't realized he harbored.

Lozange was a bundle of energy, but his various enterprises all seemed to fall short of success. No persons of color had ever enrolled at Spitfire even after Lozange had appeared before them in their meeting places dressed in native costume. Frequently he made mistakes on the time-tic sheets so that staff were paid too much or too little, occasioning much tedious correction. One month Derek had received, in pounds, the equivalent of $1800, the next $3200. Although this was merely inconvenient for him, colleagues who had to pay their own rent complained and asked to do their own time-tic sheets, but Lozange wouldn't let them. And there was his Spitfire Press, the value of whose line-up of anti-masterpieces was certainly questionable.

Derek looked around the pub, until recently such a peaceful place. Lozange had succeeded in rousing the troops. Though still a bit foggy on the nature of the crisis, today they were almost fully awake, as was Derek. He wondered if he should be present in this meeting, as his was just a temporary faculty appointment. He supposed it was all right. At least no one had said anything, and the gathering was unusually diverse, with representatives from all four departments: Microzoology (the study of small animals, such as shrews), Art for School Children, Communications Science, and English.

Lozange continued furious about the trumped-up reason for the official visit. "Fiftieth anniversary your bleeding arse!" he snorted.

One of the art ladies objected to his tone, or to his words. Derek observed that her own arse was firm and round. He hadn't been interested in such female parts in quite a long time, both back home and here in England, but now women were turning him on again. Maybe it was the proximity of Thutcher, that sexy minister.

"Oh, Lewis," fussed the art lady. "You're just getting us all tiddly-widdly."

Rather than respond, Lozange tucked his chin down into his chest and mumbled to himself. Derek, sitting near the principal, heard him softly articulate, "Motherfucker."

The art lady then said, "By the bye, is Denis coming as well?"

Denis was Thutcher's adoring husband. Derek found that out later by asking Lozange, who seemed to despise the man.

"He is," he told the lady. "Damned wally! Why do you care about him? It's pounds and pence you should care about. She wants to find reason here to slash our funding. That's why she's coming, don't you see? What if she makes a classroom visitation and no students are there that day. What then, eh?"

"We could say they're ill," said a man who was the official college chaplain, although no one knew what sect he belonged to or what he thought about God and all that. Several in the group nodded and made approving noises.

"She can't expect them to come then," he continued. "Not if they're not feeling well. She can be very demanding, I know, but I'm sure she would have pity on the sick."

But Lozange rudely ignored the chaplain's suggestion, possibly thinking, as Derek thought, that if Thutcher found empty classrooms and was told that the students were all sick, she might instantly shut Spitfire down as a plague spot.

"Where's Bert?" he asked, standing on tiptoe and craning his neck.

"I here," gasped Bert Bangles, who was sitting, unnoticed, on the floor.

"All right, then," Lozange said, as if Bert was the answer to all their troubles. "We'll direct her to your classes, Bert. They're always well attended. But could you get the students to speak? She might notice if they don't."

Bert tried to speak then himself, but could not. He nodded fiercely, though, and wrinkled his nose. There was a positive air to all this movement. Yes, he would try.

"She can't complain about that, the old cow." This from Lozange, who had told Derek at the airport that the prime minister taped and therefore knew everything.

Here though, in the pub, with no wall-mounted cameras in view, he seemed not to care what bad, rude things were said about Thutcher. That was strange, but stranger still, thought Derek, was the way nice things were said about her by the same person and sometimes in the same sentence, as just then by the college chaplain.

Now the pretty Art for School Children lady spoke as if to herself. "Her hair looks nice the way she does it this year. Thutcher. "

"I know," exclaimed a Com Sci man, addressing her and sounding excited. "Why not have a contest among your children to draw Thutcher? Have her award the prize for best likeness! That would please her, would it not?"

The art lady did not welcome his suggestion, and she was rather rude about it. They were all not as nice as they had been.

"Oh, what a clever idea. But of course, we don't actually *draw* anymore, not with crayons and that sort of thing. We do computer graphics."

The communicator, unabashed but a little grouchy: "Well, then, have the contest on the computers with those graphic things, if you know how to do them."

"We soon will, you can bank on that. But the real problem with your little plan is that we have no actual children in our program. We just study about them. If we went out and got some, they might be the wrong kind."

"Oh," said the com man. "But she must love children. You can see it in her face. She's a mother, right? Not that I'd want her for *my* mother."

"Well," said the art lady "What I see in her face is an appalling arrogance. What can you but think of a population that would vote for such a person? But I must say she looks wonderful in blue. Saw her last week on the TV, wearing a round blue hat. We could paint the walls of this pub blue and receive her here, or she could receive us. Whatever the protocol is when the prime minister comes to call."

Soon the meeting ended with a decision not to paint the pub's walls any new color but to have Thutcher meet the assembled faculty there. Indeed, it was the only room spacious enough to contain even a sizable fraction of their number. Lozange knew of a large chair purchased as a prop for a play the students were supposed to do one year but didn't. Almost a throne, he said. Perfect for Thutcher.

"Thinks she's a queen, right?"

Lozange's question seemed to baffle his audience, whose members exchanged troubled glances. They got no help from Lozange, who moved on to the husband.

"Denis can stand. Don't know what she sees in him. Plays golf every day, and he's not even good."

So Thutcher would sit in the big chair, and before her would pass a brief procession of delegates from the academic departments and from Spitfire Press, each bearing a gift. Communications Science would have to be left out of this ceremony because their radio and TV gear was obsolete and shabby, as well as too heavy for one person to carry. The prime would then visit one or two of Bert's classes, tour the microzoology museum, with its stretched skins of little creatures, and examine the new Acorn computers in the Children's Art lab. Someone had better learn how to operate them by the day she would come, which was December 2, or at least know how to turn them on. Lozange intended to steer her away from his press, whose physical plant consisted of one small, unimpressive room.

In the days that followed it became clear to Derek that whether or not Thutcher thought herself a queen, many in the college did. That they were far from wholly approving of her didn't matter. There are bad queens and good ones. Thutcher's power over the minds of men and women was of the kind possessed by queens, or goddesses. It had nothing to do with morality or ethics.

Thatcher also possessed the power of a mum, for she was that too, rivaling in motherliness even the ancient Queen Mum. While the libidos of the male faculty throbbed for Thutcher, both genders at the college sometimes yearned to have her pat them on the head and murmur soft encouragements. Derek could tell that from the things they said. And yet everyone, save the silent Bangles, regularly accused her of despising working people, though of working-class origin herself. Therefore, in the logic of the faculty, she wished to deny education to common folks, she whose Oxford scholarship had boosted her from grocery clerk to her present post. Finally, she was making everyone in the country rude. They believed these things. They may not actually have hated Thutcher, but they surely disliked her very much. At the same time, they loved her.

All wished that Thutcher had not chosen to visit their college, whose grants she would then find reason to cut. But it was also plain to Derek, rendered quite uncomfortable by the tension and confusion that seemed to be overcoming everyone, that her appearance made them all giddy with excitement. "Appearance." That was the word they used, as if she would arrive by other than the usual, mortal, means of transport.

But when she was driven up in a car, one of a procession of cars, no one seemed disappointed.

The Appearance

They waited in the pub. She would be coming there soon. Derek, however, remained outside, waiting to make his own appearance; for he had been chosen to assume the role of gift-bearer in the ritual designed by Lozange. He was wearing what the principal said was a faculty commencement gown, but had the look and feel of an old terry cloth bathrobe. In his left hand (it had to be the left for some odd, old British reason), he held the *Variorum Laurence Eusden*, edited by Sheldon Glick, Ph.D. This would be his gift to Thutcher on behalf of the Spitfire College Press. He and the other three suppliants, also clutching the gifts they would bestow, stood by the pub's wide rear door, where delivery trucks usually unloaded kegs and cases. That was how Lozange got the throne in. They were all calling it the throne.

The gentleman from Microzoology held a small transparent vial with a piece of yellow meat inside. When Derek asked about it, he said it was the intestine of a hamster.

"Did it with microknives," he said proudly.

The Art for School Children lady had a large photo of several fair-haired children crashing their fists down upon a bulky computer. She was a plain, middle-aged woman, not the shapely person from the meeting whom Derek had hoped to see again, even in these bizarre circumstances. He couldn't imagine where they had found the photo; certainly he had witnessed no such scene on the Spitfire campus. Lastly, Bert Bangles tightly gripped his offering, his variorum McGonagall, as if it would explode if he dropped it.

Derek Rosenblum, who thought he presently resembled an actor in a sleepwear ad, was not happy. His mood was not what it had been only a few weeks earlier. And he was cold. His robe was thin, thinner than the others' were, and the month was December. When they could be inside somewhere, it was absurd to languish in the chill while Lozange led Thutcher, Denis, and some large and silent men in suits on a hasty tour of the grounds; but that was where the head and principal insisted they should stay. More importantly,

Derek simply disliked presenting the prime minister with a book that was the work of someone else, someone with whom he had long felt an unpleasant rivalry. He'd explained that to Lozange, but was told, effectively, to shut up.

Derek understood that both he and Bert were there to represent Spitfire Press, with English being a secondary consideration. It was clear to everyone, in fact, that Lozange's precious press was more important to him than anything else about the college. This annoyed people greatly, especially those in Com Science, whose department had been given no role in the proceedings.

Derek had thought old Bert a risky choice to represent anything. What if he were called upon to say something to their guests and got all jammed up the way he did? But when Lozange gave them the order to wait beside the door, he had mentioned that no one need worry about how to address such exalted personages.

"You aren't required to say anything. You merely take a knee."

"You mean kneel?" asked Derek.

"No, I didn't say that. Just bend your knee slightly."

He demonstrated. "Like so. See? Is that asking too much of you?"

What a change in the man!

Now Derek shivered and crossed his arms upon his chest. Clad in thicker robes, his three colleagues seemed not to feel the cold. It was apparent that Lozange had chosen wisely in their case. The microzoologist and the children's art lady plainly adored Thutcher, even though they still called her that, and Bert smiled broadly and prayerfully entwined his hands beneath his chin whenever he heard that precious name. And these three were hardly exceptional. Though in reality their emotions had been mixed, once all at the college had professed to hate her. But as the day of her appearance drew ever nearer, their collective mood regarding the prime minister had grown downright worshipful. Lozange never said anything bad about her anymore, and in his frequent memos to faculty her last name was always spelled correctly. He even capitalized "She" and "Her," no matter where they appeared in a sentence.

Dense clouds rolled in from the Channel. The chill entered Derek's bones. He wished he were in California.

"Oh," said the art lady, holding the kids-and-computer photo up before her face, "what if it rains? How will I dry it? I can't give her something wet to hold."

It was Derek's understanding that the gifts were to be handed to her husband, standing beside her, and he said so.

"No," she said. "I wish to touch her."

"Can you give it a smell?" This was the scientific member of their party, having removed the lid from his hamster intestine vial. "Doesn't have an odor, does it? Hard for me to tell, being in the lab night and day."

He proffered the lidless vial first to Derek, who politely sniffed and detected a hint of alcohol, not unpleasant, and then to the woman, who batted at it with her hand.

"Ugly thing!"

"I spent hours on that bit of intestine. How dare you! Let's have a look-see at *this*!" He grabbed at the photo, but she snatched it away. Thus behave the dunces in Pope's prophetic poem.

"No, no," gasped Bert Bangles, horrified at the prospect of an unseemly squabble with Mrs. Thutcher due momentarily at the pub. He interposed his shriveled body between the combatants, holding the McGonagall volume safely high above his head. The two subsided into a muttered conversation about being on the same side and not wanting to embarrass the college.

"She comes! She comes!" bellowed swift-striding Lozange, rounding the corner of the pub. He made rapid accordion-playing gestures with his hands, indicating that they were to form their line.

When Derek was slow to take his place at the end, Lozange admonished, "You too, Glick."

"I didn't know you were still here," remarked the microzoologist.

"I'm not," grumped Derek, resenting the principal's slip.

"Go, go!" ordered Lozange, as if they were paratroopers hesitating to dive. And so they entered the pub.

It had been cleared of its tables and benches, so that all were standing except the guest of honor. Several faded photos of Spitfires in flight had been glued to the walls with a sticky blue substance Derek had never seen in America. One, a shot of three Spits soaring wing tip to tip, drooped slightly at the upper right hand corner. The prime minister, garbed in blue, occupied what was presently the room's only piece of furniture, the throne. This was a large item, but she had easily filled it, being a bigger person than Derek had supposed, judging from her photos in the *Times* and her appearances on the television news. Her face was broader than average, he now perceived, and her blue eyes would have seemed outsized in most people's faces, though not in hers.

Derek was unsure of what he was feeling, awe or fear, or both emotions commingled. No longer did he resent having to take part in this alien ceremony; he hoped only to get through it without committing some awful disruptive blunder.

At Thutcher's left stood the man who must be Denis, gray-haired, bespectacled, with a bag of golf clubs at his feet. Had some Spitfire functionary already presented them to him or to her? But the college had no Phys Ed department or sports teams. They must be Denis's own clubs, a valuable set that he wished to keep an eye on.

The prime minister crossed her legs. Not bad. But it was wrong to think that way of her. It was rude, or worse. Like casting carnal glances at your mom, and now Derek thought for a moment about dear Mimi back in Malibu and how he loved her, even though she was a complete stupe. The feeling, the filial adoration, then transferred itself to the present time and place. Adoration. Adore. He loved her, Thutcher. No. What was he thinking? This woman certainly had a talent for inviting affection, but she wasn't his mother or at all like his mother.

Now she spoke and they listened in silence, the pub's motley collection of faculty, students, and assorted burly characters wearing paper hats whom Lozange had hired to impersonate pressmen, since he himself was the only real employee the press had.

Distracted by his varying responses to the prime, Derek was unable to make much sense out of what she was saying. It concerned Spitfires, he could guess that much. Indeed, her gestures tipped him off to that, as when she extended each arm stiffly to either side and made machine-gun noises with her lips. *putta putta putta* This elicited a great roar from the crowd, several of whose members extended their arms also and similarly sputtered. So Lozange was wrong. She really had come for the plane's fifty-first anniversary.

But then, "Boom! Boom!" the prime minister ejaculated, perhaps on to another war. The Falklands, he would guess. Back in '82. Naval guns. Hadn't she been a big hero in that one? Yes, he remembered that. She thought herself more important than the plane, apparently.

Did she talk about British taxpayers' money and how the college might be getting less of it? Derek hadn't picked up anything like that, but it wouldn't have dismayed her audience had she mentioning killing their every grant. Just a few weeks earlier everyone at the Spitfire College of Higher Education had blamed Thutcher for making the entire nation beastly. Now, though, Derek detected not the faintest hint of ill-feeling. They loved her. It was a pure love with nothing sexual about it, as there had been before she came. A religious sort of thing, Derek supposed, amazed. He didn't feel it. Something was holding him back from sharing in the otherwise universal adoration. He hoped that no one could tell.

Time for the Presentation of Gifts. Or past time, at least for Denis, who gazed longingly down at his bag of clubs. He gave his wife, who had finished making boom boom noises, a nudge, whereupon she summoned Lozange, who sprang to her side. He inclined his head. She bowed hers and whispered in his ear. Reeling dizzily, he waved at the suppliants, who stood in their line against the wall of the pub furthest from the prime.

Lozange had arranged them. Of the four, Derek stood last, behind old Bert. Unfortunately for decorum, the microzoologist and the children's artist each claimed the first position. They began again to struggle, he placing a clutching hand upon her shoulder, she raising and thrusting with a knee. Lozange sputtered, but they seemed not to hear him. Thutcher raised her hand. "Now, now," she sweetly said.

They quieted then and shyly approached her. Derek was astonished to see that they were holding hands. Would he have to clutch the withered paw of Bert Bangles? Then the two recent combatants bent their knees. It made a pretty picture. Now, that he would have to do. Should have practiced while waiting outside. Too late now.

The light in the pub was getting all fuzzy. It was hard to see. Derek blinked several times, but that made no difference. Had he been in other places with that same sickly light? He thought he remembered the light and a chair, too, like this, a throne, and another large lady. Or were there two other such ladies? But they were distractions, these memories, perilous ones. What if he missed his cue? That would be terrible. He concentrated on the present scene.

Thutcher had accepted the art lady's photo and the bit of meat from the microzoologist and now was passing them on to Denis, who slipped the hamster gut into the part of his golf bag that contained balls. The photo was too big to fit, so he tucked it under his arm. He looked at his watch. Derek looked down at Sheldon Glick's Eusden volume, making sure he still had it. He was next, after Bert, who stumbled toward the throne.

Bert took a knee; he did it pretty well. His left hand trembled as he raised the variorum McGonagall overhead. The prime minister took it from him and held it on her lap. She motioned first for Bert to rise, and then to Denis, to help when the old man struggled. Eventually he managed it without assistance. He then unfolded a sheet of paper he had been gripping, unnoticed, in his right hand and held it up before his eyes. Bert cleared his throat. The crowd murmured in excitement. Was he going to try to read something? Aloud? Could he do it? And what was it?

"O beautiful Falklands," he quavered, and stopped, then tried again. It was amazing, the quantity of words Bert Bangles then spoke.

> O beautiful Falklands where live British people
> To protect them Mother England was not feeble.
> For when invaded in 1982 by Argentina
> Our naval forces were far keener.
>
> It was then or never, with big winds coming,
> So the Pee Em called a War Cabinet into being,
> For swift decisions needed to be made,
> To show the enemy his plans were most ill laid.
>
> The war went on for two months and more,
> Until that country had its fill of war,
> At its end, 649 enemy were dead,
> And the Falklanders could lie safely in bed.
>
> Thus ever does Great Britain hold her own,
> Not ever do we sit and cry and moan.
> For the sad sailors of the foe we did butcher,
> Under the wise leadership of Margaret Thutcher.

Thutcher beamed. Even Denis seemed impressed. When Derek heard that final "Thutcher," he feared they might express displeasure at the alteration of their name, but obviously they had no problem with it. Maybe they liked it that way. Plainly they liked the poem, despite its close stylistic resemblance to "The Tay Bridge Disaster" and being almost as bad. That gave Derek confidence. Even Laurence Eusden's worst efforts were better than that, so he needn't be embarrassed by what he was to present to her. Not that it was his book, anyway.

A collective gasp from the crowd! Derek, lost in thought, looked up. Bert had fallen forward, so that his face now reposed in Thutcher's lap upon the McGonagall volume. Lozange scampered toward the throne, but the Pee Em held up a hand, and then, with the same hand, slipped the book away and handed it to Denis. She stroked Bert's gray head, which proceeded to thrust itself between her legs as if it were some species of burrowing animal.

"Now, now," she said again. "Mustn't, mustn't."

The big men in suits came forward and detached old Bert. They settled him in a corner of the pub and patted him on the back.

Surely what Bert had done was a glaring example of lèse majesté, but no one seemed upset, not even Lozange. In the corner, a faint glow seemed to emanate from the McGonagall scholar and epigone. His expression, with closed eyes and beatific smile, could have been either ecstatic or idiotic, depending on the eye of the beholder. Derek was unsure what kind of beholder he himself was. Had Bangles been ... what? Blessed? Is that what you get for rooting in the lap of Thutcher? Would it happen to him? Did he want it? He had a horrible suspicion that he did.

Now was his moment. Derek felt small. She was big. He hesitated. Lozange hissed at him. He stepped forward.

He knelt before her just as the others had and extended the Eusden volume with the correct hand. But Thutcher did not take it. He risked looking up at her. She was absorbed in Bert's moronic poem about the Falklands War. Her lips were moving. She read and reread.

While she busied herself with that, Derek crouched beneath the stern gaze of the crowd. As Bert had burrowed in Thutcher's lap, so did Derek, arm rigidly outstretched, now root within his own head and there found words, damnable words.

Oh She doesn't want it again She doesn't want ... yes signed off on the diss but with a stamp just wanted me to leave ... then She spurned the scroll mememe either love me or live me, okay ... HerHerHer just take it already, take the fucking book ... not even mine but the work of vile—

"Glick. Glick, old man."

"I'm not Glick." But Denis wasn't listening.

"Can't you see," continued the prime minister's husband, "that she doesn't give a toss for your little book? Give it here. I'll get rid of it for you."

Robotically, Derek handed the Eusden to Denis, who stowed it in his golf bag, which he then lifted and slung from his shoulder. Thutcher stepped down from her throne, which now appeared to be an ordinary large chair. Derek stood up, turned around, and walked through the pub to the door where he had waited before making his vain attempt to please her. Turning, he gazed at the crowd; they all looked mournful, he thought, as if something very sad had happened in front of them. He walked on for several paces, into the cold. The heavy pub door banged shut behind him. He held up then and placed his chin upon his right fist. What had just happened? What had happened in his head?

The *Dunciad!* That crazy poem with its reigning goddess. It was easy—nay, unavoidable, or he wouldn't be doing it—for Derek to think of the ritual just completed as a real-life allusion to that diabolical mock-epic. It also alluded to his dream in which the duplicitous Luteplucker had morphed into Dulness. And just then Thutcher had seemed to be beginning the same transformation. Derek felt the boundaries blurring between reality and dream and also between literature and reality, as if the old poem were insisting on being alive. The thought shocked him. Poems can't do that can they? All his academic training told him so. If they could, then no one could analyze them. You can't dissect something that keeps flopping around because it's not dead.

He resisted. Maybe Thutcher on her throne did resemble Dulness on hers as Pope describes her, and the dream had begun with a seated Luteplucker who became Dulness. But it was all an accident. Both prof and prime were merely mortal ladies with exceedingly forceful personalities. They were certainly not incarnations of the dimwitted goddess of the *Dunciad*. He had read it too many times so that it constantly slumbered in his brain. Now it had stirred, prodded by a coincidental real-life event. It didn't seem to matter that the parallel was inexact, for in both poem and dream there was a whole legion of squabbling suppliant dunces, not a line-up of just four.

Then, however, Derek looked about him and observed his Spitfire colleagues strolling from the pub, many glaring in his direction. It was because Thatcher (use her real name, she's just a regular human) had spurned his gift. They had all so much wanted to please her with their little college; they were quite manic about it, too. And the micro man and the art lady had been so competitive, like the dunces. Strange.

The rain, long threatening, finally began. Everybody hastened away from Derek. If he correctly remembered the plan for the day, the prime would now visit one or more of Bert Bangles' soporific classes. Rather than follow the crowd, which would not have welcomed him, he shuffled, draped in the sopping robe, to the corner where he could catch the bus.

Soon it arrived. He boarded and slopped into a seat. The lady next to him got up and pushed past his knees without his noticing. For some reason he was thinking about his recent use of "incarnations" to describe what Thatcher and Luteplucker weren't. Why had that word come to mind? He didn't like it, didn't like its religious, cultish sound. It was not needed. Forget it. Forget the prof. Forget the prime. Forget Dulness, who wasn't even a real person.

Indeed, it occurred to Derek that soon he would have something else to worry about. Since the iron lady had scorned the book that everyone thought was his, effectively scorning *him* as a representative of press and college, Lozange would not be happy. It wasn't fair, but the perceived threat to the college's grants had already made the principal half crazed. Besides that, Lozange now appeared practically to worship the prime and was liable to feel that anyone unpalatable to her was a pariah who must be expelled from the community.

So when the principal next deigned to speak to Derek, it was to fire him.

"You must go," said Lozange.

Since he went on to say that the college would pay for his flight back to the States, so eager was everyone to be rid of him, Derek did not strenuously object. Still, he felt obliged to defend himself.

"I did nothing wrong," Derek said. "I did what you told me. What did I do wrong? Tell me, Louis."

"Doesn't matter what you did," responded Lozange. "It's what you are. She knew. She saw."

"But it wasn't me she saw."

"Eh?"

"They thought I was Glick, " Derek pointed out. "That's what Denis said, because it was Glick's book. So *I* can't be blamed for anything. Can't you see?"

"Oh, that doesn't matter. You're *like* him. Lately that's become all too plain. Both of you think you're so clever. No wonder you haven't fitted in here."

He hadn't. That was true. He wasn't like the rest of them.

"I did my best," protested Derek, knowing how weak that sounded.

"Ah, but she knew," Lozange insisted.

Rather than begin a discussion of just what it was that she knew, Derek returned to the confusion between himself and the departed Sheldon Glick.

"But they thought I was another person. I wanted to tell them who I really was, but they wouldn't listen."

"Who *you* were? That would've been worse. You're the one who did that poem that hates England. "

Derek explained that "The Origin of the Knights of the Bath" wasn't exactly anti-England and that it wasn't his poem. He had only written an article about it, but nothing mattered to Lozange.

"You must go," he repeated. "Bert can teach your classes. She loves him, the dear lady. It remains to be seen how much graunt money you've cost us."

But before long, though after Derek had left the college, Lozange became much cheerier when it transpired that, in fact, there would be no reduction in government support. Indeed, at the close of the academic year, Spitfire's funding was actually increased, while that of other colleges of higher education was drastically cut. It was because Thatcher liked Bert's poem, as did the public when it was set to music by thrash metal rocker Ubik, with twelve other patriotic tunes. No one in Britain knows it anymore, but "Falklands Victory" is recited every Victory Day in Stanley, East Falkland.

Without further protest, Derek accepted the plane ticket Lozange offered. It wasn't as if he wanted to stay at Spitfire. They didn't like him anymore at the college, wouldn't talk to him. Even Simkin, his fellow American, would not. It was plainly unfair, since he hadn't done anything except once again not be good enough. Thatcher had ignored him. To be thought to be someone that one isn't is a powerful act of ignoring. Indeed, she had spurned him. That was the word for it, that was how he felt. Involuntarily he recalled his dream and how his gift, the scroll, had been rejected by the goddess.

Sitting in his Southampton house, he sought to control his thoughts. This was difficult at first. There were three different things to think about, poem, dream, and recent event. He couldn't help thinking about them. Nor could he readily separate them. He gave it a try.

Now, poem differs from dream (and encounter with Thatcher) because there the goddess accepts the gifts of her devotees and approves every suppliant as an absolute dunce. Indeed, Dulness adopts them. Derek looked up the relevant passage in Book 4 of the *Dunciad*, which he had checked out of the Southampton University library. (Spitfire College lacked a copy of the poem and had no video version.) He considered the couplets:

> Then blessing all, "Go Children of my care!
> To Practice now from Theory repair.
> All my commands are easy, short, and full:
> My Sons! Be proud, be selfish, and be dull."

She blesses all, while Thatcher hadn't even looked at him. That made two rejections, with the dream. Three times, if Luteplucker's job non-recommendations were included. *She* certainly didn't think of him as a son. It was hard to imagine her as anyone's mom, but she still reminded him of Dulness. Though he wished it wouldn't, his mind kept making these connections. It was all right to compare Thatcher to Luteplucker, for both were real. The big woman in the poem, the one in the dream—they were the problem. She was.

Derek took an apple from his little British fridge. Walking in a circle, he nibbled at the apple. He decided to go, as people used to say, with the flow. For the moment, for *a* moment, he would assume that the dream goddess and the poem goddess were the same person and that this individual was in some way real. In the dream while she accepted everyone else, she rejected him. What had he done to piss her off? Same question, more or less, he'd asked Lozange. He was always pissing people off. Nobody liked him. But Dulness in particular.

He didn't fit in. That's what Lozange had emphatically said. Could that be what the goddess didn't like about him, that he didn't fit into *her* world? That would make him a non-dunce, right? Or, anyway, a bad dunce. Well, he knew he was capable of sinking into duncehood. It attracted him, but he didn't stay in its swamp. That might be important. Back home he'd reveled in a brainless orgy of selling and seducing, but eventually he'd tired of it. And shortly after arriving at Spitfire College he'd fallen into a state of, well, dullness, but that hadn't lasted either. It had grown distasteful to him before Thatcher came, all knowing Thatcher. He would sink, but he wouldn't, or couldn't, stay sunk. She wouldn't like that. But she wasn't real. So, away with the thought experiment. It was getting him nowhere. Go away. Please.

He found himself shifting to a consideration of something unfortunately real, his sorry career, or non-career. Could that be why Spitfire wouldn't have him, why no college would? Because they wanted him to be a good dunce, even though they didn't think of it that way, and he wasn't? And did that mean, incidentally, that he was smart? But he had never felt smart, like his computer buds, although could be they weren't so smart now either. As for himself, he just liked to read a lot or had liked to. Average. That was Derek on Derek. Everyman.

Could that be why both Luteplucker and Thatcher had treated him so shamefully? Did his very averageness incite them? Whence this strange thought? Of course not. For there was nothing special about being not special. Okay? Enough. He took a finishing chomp of the apple.

Now he considered more mundane matters. Lozange had paid his airfare to Los Angeles, where else? It always would be his home, his fate, no matter how ill he fared there. But since the ticket was good for three months, Derek decided to do some traveling first. He had never been to Europe, besides England, and he could afford a little trip. Lozange had miscalculated his time-tic sheet, overpaying him by seven hundred pounds; it would take the principal at least a month to correct his mistake, by which time the money could all be spent.

At first Derek thought about France, just a hop across the Channel from Southampton. He could speak the language, probably; at least he had passed a qualifying French reading exam back at Heartland. In the end, though, he decided on Italy, Venice to be specific. The French are grumpy. That was an English vibe he picked up from his travel agent, who found a cheap hotel for him near St. Mark's and also a good deal on a one-way flight. From Venice, he would fly direct to L.A., when his money ran out.

"It's a good time to go," the agent said, "the weeks before Carnevale. Less tourists. The real Venice."

"I can speak some Italian," Derek told the man, warming to his proposal.

"Very useful, I'm sure," the agent said.

He'd passed the Italian exam, too, and now he memorized some handy expressions found in a travel guide. "Grazie." "Per favore." "Può portarmi una pulita forchetta."

On the day before his flight, Derek read the entire fourth book of the *Dunciad*. This required a constant struggle with his belief that the poem disturbed him too much and was best left alone. He wouldn't have read it had his interest been merely scholarly. It was, instead, medicinal.

His purpose in going through *Dunciad* 4 one last time was to vaccinate himself against it. With virtually every line he read he reminded himself that none of it was real. Dulness and her manic worshipers were only the creation of a clever little Englishman who had died in 1744. Oh, it was a spooky piece of work, to be sure, and quite possibly a prophetic one. There seemed to be an awful lot of stupidity in the world, at least in the parts that Derek knew. But it was just a poem, and Pope's Dulness only a personification. Matter from the *Dunciad* had leaked into his dream life, there being nothing strange about that, but it had no place in the waking world. So he insisted to himself.

He had discovered the goddess, this dismal deity, lurking in his dream, in the pub ceremony, and maybe in his last face-to-face with Professor Luteplucker, because he put her there. It was like reader-response criticism, Derek noted, only in reverse. There you bring what's in your head to the text so that you "find," say, the Battle of Culloden in a poem written 20 years before it was fought. In Derek's present case, however, it was the poem in in his head through which he had been reading the text of his own life. That must be how many people come to believe in all sorts of nonsense: it comes from books.

"Books are a load of crap," the poet said. Too true.

Derek returned the *Dunciad* to its library. That night it left no mark upon his dreams. This he took as a sign that his treatment had worked and that the poem was no longer in his head, shaping his vision. But he couldn't be sure. Maybe it was dead, but maybe it wasn't.

In the morning Derek took a shuttle to Gatwick and boarded his Venice-bound flight.

Realistic in Venice

Venice was cold and wet. The travel agent was right about the paucity of tourists. In fact, there was almost nobody out in the streets. Nonetheless, Derek often felt that he was being watched as he strolled and while eating in the cafés. It must have been because there were so few Americans around, or non-Italians of any stripe. He stood out. That explained it, but didn't make him more comfortable.

One morning, after leaving his hotel to visit Piazza San Marco, he realized that he had forgotten to put on a belt when dressing. Immediately he returned for it, lest his pants slip halfway down his flanks and expose his boxer shorts in the style of gangbangers in Venice, CA. Tautly belted, he resumed his walk, thinking now of that southern California beach town, with its surfers and pick-up bars. Not much culture. Not much of anything for someone whose mental age exceeded sixteen. The weather was better in that Venice than in this one. He would mention that if some Italian should ask where he came from. But no Italian had asked him anything, and when he'd tried simple phrases, even plain old "per favore," they had snickered or played dumb, as if he had made a nonsense noise.

Soon he would be back in the other Venice, or some other marginal spot in and around Los Angeles, doing ... doing what? Nothing he wanted to do. Working at his dad's store with Spero and the guys? That was a frightening prospect for a man not far from forty. While at Spitfire College, he hadn't thought about his future, hadn't thought much about anything. He hated thinking about his future now, but couldn't seem to help it. The months in Southampton, these days in frigid Venice were just holiday time, holidays from life. Soon he would be back in the real world, and so again he asked himself, doing what?

He might apply to the big insurance company, but now he was probably too old to be accepted as a trainee. He didn't want to sell insurance, anyhow, or silk ties and monogramed undershorts. Literature. He would like to sell that in a college classroom, even though he no longer possessed the enthusiasm of his youth. But maybe some of that would come back. But how? But where?

It may appear remarkable that Derek still wanted to teach after the Spitfire Experience, which would seem sufficient to sour him on the profession for the remainder of his days. It wasn't being unfairly dismissed by Lozange that was so bad. That was a special circumstance, with the prime minister visiting and disturbing everyone. But the college was such a dismal place. Now that he was away from it, Derek understood this very well. The students were incurably lazy and cynical, the staff incompetent and alcoholic, and Lozange, who ran everything, was probably insane.

And yet, despite his memory of the fog of dullness wetting the brows of all who labored in the shade cast by the granite fighter plane looming over mid-campus, he missed his life in the college. Italy made him realize that. Here he was uneasy, what with the Italians looking at him all the time and probably talking about him. At Spitfire one could relax; one could not not relax, in fact. It was the culture of the place. How nice if he were there now, sitting with his students, emitting every now and then a drowsy word. How nice to be hanging in the pub with his buds, even if they were a bunch of jerks. A little dull was okay, he assured himself, fixing on the ordinary sense of "dull," rather than the light-quenching force it becomes in the *Dunciad*. A little dull made for a nice casual feeling. It wasn't necessary to go all the way.

Spitfire College was over the top, of course. It was as if no one there could really think at all, which might be why they were all knocked sideways when Thatcher came. Most colleges weren't like that. They couldn't be and stay in business. But they were still restful places for faculty, once you had tenure taken care of. College teaching would strike many people as boring, Derek understood that, but it appealed to him. In fact, there was nothing else he would willingly do for the rest of his life. Where he would do it, that was the problem. So think about it. Solve it.

By the time he reached the Piazza, so engrossed was Derek in his thinking that he took note of no other persons as he strode rapidly around the square. Others noted him, especially when skipping out of his errant way, and they wondered at the large, rapidly striding American, for whom they seemed not to exist. Thus Europe saw him, but he did not see the Europeans. Such is the situation of a certain British tourist in the *Dunciad,* the poem that Derek hoped had lost its grip on his mental life. Indeed, he did not recall the pertinent lines.

Just wait, Derek.

Indeed, maybe the *Dunciad* was working on him already. Maybe it was partly or wholly responsible for what he decided then, just as he set his eyes upon the four horses of St. Mark stationed above the façade of the Basilica. They were a noble sight, and they seemed to inspire him. They carried him, so swiftly, to his decision.

He would go back to Heartland. He would make them hire him. It would be for composition, of course, probably remedial and certainly part-time. But it was a start, and that was all he needed.

It might not have mattered to Derek had some local character told him that the horses he was looking at were not the bronze originals, kept inside the Basilica, but copies for the tourists. His sensations were powerful. But he surely would have been less sanguine had he known that one day in the not so distant future he would vow to give up all ambition of entering, on any level, a profession that truly deserved its place in the *Dunciad.* Then something remarkable happened, as a result of which Derek turned into Professor Derek Rosenblum, Dept. of English, Enola Gay State University. That morning in Venice, of course, he foresaw nothing of this. Unlike the poet of the *Dunciad,* average guy Derek was no prophet.

Yes, he could start at Heartland, but he didn't have to stay there. He could—he would!—move up to someplace better. It didn't have to be a fancy one, as long as he got to teach a lit class now and then. Of course, no matter where he sought to work, fattening his bibliography would be necessary. At the moment it contained one item, the ancient "Laurence Eusden's Subversive Vision." He would have to write and publish some new criticism. No problem, really. It might be useful to read some theory—there were handbooks everywhere—so that he could stick in some hot French terms. He recited a few that he'd heard here and there. "Signifié." "Différance." (To him just a regular word quaintly spelled). "Jouiss—"

"Mi ha parlato?" inquired an elderly Venetian whose shoulder Derek had brushed in passing. He hadn't realized he had been speaking his thoughts.

"Faccia perdere," Derek replied, confusing it with "mi scusi," not realizing that this was perilously close to "fuck off." The man stood and stared, but Derek didn't notice. His caution reflex was kicking in. He had begun to think of what he might be letting himself in for if he continued in this optimistic vein.

Noticing a bench, he plumped down upon it, and called himself to order. Was he not doing a Derek? That is, conceiving of something as possible, even reasonably easy to obtain, when it might not be possible at all. Dating Tracy remained his most painful example, despite that flop having occurred almost twenty years ago; but hadn't his whole life been one big disappointment? That's what came of expecting too much.

They were watching him, the Italians in the piazza, and wondering. Was he dangerous, a crazy American cowboy packing a pistola? Why was he nodding his head like that? They couldn't know that he was complimenting himself for being realistic instead of aiming too high or expecting too much. It wouldn't be pleasant dragging himself back to Heartland and begging the English Department's director of composition to let him teach even the lowliest of the sub-sub-remedial courses. But he was their product, wasn't he? He had a right. After a few years of that, at $9.50 or something an hour, another, more advanced course might come his way. It would still be comp, of course, since universities don't hire their own Ph.D.'s to teach literature unless they were truly brilliant, and he wasn't. Didn't want to be, either. Always hated show-offs.

There were lots of students at Heartland who had to take remedial English, and so it was not unrealistic to angle for a job teaching them. At least that would get him onto a college campus. He shouldn't kid himself: it wouldn't be the same as at Spitfire College of Higher Education, so tranquil, well, too tranquil. Just as at any American university, the set-up at Heartland was strictly hierarchical. Not even the grad students would want to drink with a remedial teacher in the campus pub, if there was one. He couldn't remember. At Spitfire, he'd been accepted as one of the boys until the difficulty with Thatcher. Lozange had paid pretty well, too, and provided housing for free, and he had never slept so well as during those few months at Southampton.

Heartland would give a remedial comp teacher barely enough to live on. Moreover, since there wasn't the faintest possibility of such a lowly one gaining tenure there, he would always worry about losing his job, contemptible as it was. But at least he could tell prospective university employers seeking an eighteenth-century guy that he was experienced in the classroom. He might even call himself a Heartland professor in the cover letters to the articles he would submit for publication, employing the term in a non-technical sense.

It was up to him whether he stayed on his old campus or not. If he got into a couple of journals, people might remember the Rosenblum Thesis, which had made quite a splash in its day. That would surely help. He nodded a final nod.

Suddenly Derek became aware that he was cold. He looked around and noticed several warmly dressed Venetians staring at him. He attempted a scowl, but they kept on staring. His belt was too tight, and he felt like taking it off. Let them see his red and blue striped boxers! He was proud of himself for having made that day such important and reasonable decisions.

Oh, wait. Lucia Luteplucker. He didn't want any part of her, and Heartland was where she lurked. She might torpedo his application to teach there, but since she hadn't objected to his teaching comp when a grad student, that didn't seem likely. Probably she wouldn't even know about it or know about him. The campus was huge and hugely populated, easy to hide in. She wasn't so much anyway. Just a weird woman was all.

So, having looked reality square in its noncommittal face, Derek rose from the bench and returned to his hotel. There he got on the phone and changed his flight's destination from Los Angeles to Chicago. From there he would travel by Grayhound to Heartland.

Now that Derek had made a firm decision about what to do with his life, he believed it was his to control. He was wrong, for the poem was a part of him, and at last, after much struggle, he would choose to be a part of the poem. For Derek did become Professor Rosenblum. One of Pope's dullest dunces is a professor, who proudly claims, "Words we teach alone," no meaning required. In Derek's time, he would teach a great many words in just that way.

An Old Acquaintance

But that great offloading lay in Derek's future. Now we return to the Veneto of early 1988, and his chilly hotel room in early morning. Rising from bed, he wonders how to pass the current day of the three that remain before he will fly off to resume real life. He consults his British guidebook. Padua is an easy train ride away. "Padua" is what it says in the book, and anglicized "Padua" is what he insists on saying to himself instead of the proper "Padova," because he dislikes the Italians for staring at him. In past centuries, they'd had better things to do than rudely gaze at harmless tourists. For example, in the early fourteenth century Giotto di Bondone decorated a church in Padua known as the Scrovegni Chapel, after the wealthy banker who paid for it, and that is what Derek will travel to Padua to see.

And he saw it; that is, he saw what people go to the chapel to see: Giotto's frescoes inside it, depicting the lives of the Virgin and the Son. It was important artistically, his guidebook said, that these well-known persons looked like regular people. Derek agreed that they did. That was his only response. Mother and Son meant nothing to him in a religious sense, though not because he was a Jew. Of mythic creations it was his lot to believe only in monsters, and none dwelt in the chapel.

Exiting thus unaffected, Derek encountered Sheldon Glick. Glick, who was heading into the chapel, recognized him, not he Glick.

"Rosenblum!"

Such enthusiasm! It left Derek speechless.

"It's me, Sheldon! Sheldon Glick?"

Yes, it was, although his appearance had altered perceptibly since the first time—it was the only time, but had made a sizable impression—Derek had seen him, clad in his jammies in a Tenderloin hotel. He had a hairpiece now and seemed taller, was taller because here he had on shoes, and perhaps they were elevator shoes. Glick was staring at him, the way the Italians often did. Why must everybody do that?

"You look different," observed Glick.

"Oh, not so much." Derek felt uncertain in saying this. He'd gained about fifteen pounds since his grad student days, but when he looked in the mirror he didn't think they showed. His hair couldn't be described as thinning, for that would mean making visible little patches of head skin. But since now he could feel the bristles scratching his scalp when he applied a hairbrush, perhaps the individual strands had gotten finer, if no fewer in number. Could this be detected with the eye? Well, at least his hair was still black, and it was his.

"*You* look different," he said. "Sort of."

Sheldon did not respond to that.

"Hey, Rosenblum," he almost shouted. "Let's go for coffee, okay? I wanna talk to you."

"But you're going into the chapel."

"Yeah, but I've been there already. Maybe later we could go. Now I want coffee."

Derek surprised himself. He wanted to go with Sheldon, pushy Sheldon. "All right," he said.

"And," Sheldon added, " there's something you don't know that I should tell you about."

"That's what you said last time, more or less."

"I did? In San Francisco? What did I mean? Anyway, let's go. Andate!"

"Andiamo," corrected Derek. He thought that was right.

"Hey, fuck you," Glick said, laughing.

They found a place on Via 8 Febbraio and sat at an inside table.

It turned out that what Derek didn't know and Glick for some reason wanted to tell him was what led to his leaving Spitfire College so abruptly, soon after the fall term had begun. Though Lozange announced that the American had quit of his own accord, that wasn't true.

"I didn't quit. He fired me."

"Me, too," Derek said. "Just did."

"Yeah? What happened?"

"The prime minister ... no, I can't explain it. Just tell me what happened to you. "

"The prime minister? Really? Well, Lozange agreed to say that I'd quit if only I left in a hurry. He thought I was infecting the place."

With what disease? Derek might have asked him, but Glick hadn't paused for breath.

"He even wrote me a letter saying I'd quit for personal reasons and that I'd done a good job as a teacher. But how could anyone do a good job at Spitfire? Anyway, if anyone there asked me why I was leaving, I just said, 'Greener pastures.' Oh, I don't care about being fired out of that dump, but I don't want it getting around."

Derek thought about that. Lozange had offered him no such letter, but so what? He was going home, where no one had ever heard of pipsqueak Spitfire College. Could Glick have done something truly awful?

He continued. "So I don't talk about how I was really fired, except with you. Because we have a thing going."

"A thing going? A thing? What thing?"

The waiter brought the cappuccinos they had ordered. He had certainly taken his time. "Grazie," Derek said, thinking to impress Glick with his accent, which surely did not impress the waiter.

"What? What you say?" Smiling broadly, Signore Cameriere then addressed the entire room in English: "What he say, huh? What the Americano say?" He then produced a gargling sound from deep in his throat that Derek, who could not remember the Italian words for days of the week, registered as a *sghignazzata,* or scornful laugh. Many sghignazzate were then vented by the café's customers, hands shielding mouths. This activity seemed not to affect Glick, placidly sipping his drink. Derek tried to ignore it.

"This 'thing'?" he inquired again.

Glick grimaced, as if Derek's ignorance annoyed him. "Our special relationship. You don't see it?"

At Spitfire various people had connected Derek Rosenblum with Sheldon Glick. Some, like the prime and her husband, thought Derek *was* Glick, and he hadn't cared for that. Oh, certainly they were alike in obvious ways, including their shared involvement with a certain obscure English poet and now being hired and fired by Lozange. But Glick's "thing," or "special relationship," would seem to go deeper than that. A question popped out of Derek's mouth.

"Did she come to you?"

As soon as he had spoken, he realized that he had asked Glick about a being he knew not to exist, but was still somehow present in his head. He had hoped she had left him. Thus he regretted his question, but felt nonetheless faintly disappointed with Glick's non-answer.

"She? Who?" But didn't a shadow pass over Glick's face? Maybe, but if it had, it was gone in an instant.

"Nobody," Derek told him. "I was thinking of something else. Look, I've got to go. To catch the train."

"Then they'll think, you know, they drove you out. These Dagos. You want that?"

Derek shook his head. In fact, he really didn't want to leave, being curious about Glick's clash with Lozange. "All right then, tell me," he said. "What happened? Lozange fired you. All right. Why? What did you do? Make it quick, Glick."

"It's very simple, and I want to tell you about it, so you'll know what kind of a guy I am. You think I'm an asshole, but I'm not. We can be rivals, but friendly rivals. Okay?"

He paused. Derek said nothing. Glick slumped a bit, then drew himself up.

"I told the truth," he said. "That was my big crime. It was in the pub. I told Bert Bangles that McGonagall was the worst poet in the language. That's a universally accepted fact except at Spitfire College, Then I told that creep from New Jersey that Ambrose Philips's pastorals stank of fertilizer. My own guy— your guy, too, but I was first—"

"Hell if you were."

"All right, you can be the big pioneer in Eusden Studies, if it makes you happy. I said old Laurence was mediocre."

"No kidding."

"Well, Bangles just grinned the way he always does and I'm sure he didn't grasp what I was saying, and neither did Gentle Simkin, because he was drunk and kept dropping his head on the table. They weren't at all pissed off, but Lozange was crouching behind the bar and later he accused me of bad-mouthing his press. According to him, he's unearthing obscure masterpieces, so he won't tolerate anyone speaking the truth about them. Oh, and I was a monster of ingratitude, since he'd published that Eusden collection I did, which would seem to make me *the* Eusden man, not that I give a damn."

"Think I do?" But they both did, a little. Academics are competitive, even on such matters as who was first with a poet whose only distinction was to be the most mediocre British laureate in three centuries. Anything for the bibliography.

"Tell me," Derek asked, as if he cared, and perhaps he did, "why did you say those things?"

What he really wanted to know was too complex to ask about in a noisy café: how had Sheldon Glick been able, not merely to think those things about the Spitfire Press authors (whose worthlessness was plain to see) or even to say them, but to *care* about them as much as he evidently had? For there was something about setting foot on the Spitfire campus that made you stop caring. You stopped making judgments. It had happened to him. Evidently Glick had been more resistant to the college's dulling atmosphere than he had been.

"Why did I say them?" echoed Glick. "Because they were true. I do enjoy pissing people off. I figure that goes with being a professor, as long as what you say is true. So it cost me my job. I didn't care. Last thing I'd ever want to do is hang around the campus there. They're all half-asleep, bored me to death. Lozange gave me a ticket to Kansas City, good for a couple of months. He screwed up my stipend money, too, gave me too much, and I knew it'd be weeks before he caught the error. So I hit the road for Italy."

Glick wanted Derek, with whom he shared a "thing" of some kind, to know what kind of guy he was. That was what he'd said. And that kind, evidently, was the truth-telling kind. Maybe he was tired of being taken for a Brooklyn smarty-pants.

Certainly he had told the truth in San Francisco about Luteplucker's non-recommendations. And it was true what he had just said about the Spitfire College of Higher Education. It was profoundly dull, Derek agreed. But at times, loitering in Venice, he'd sometimes caught himself thinking fondly of the college.

He asked Glick, "Do you ever miss it at all?"

"Miss it? Spitfire College? Ever? Do I?" Sheldon seemed uncertain, surely not a customary mood for him. "Could be I do, could be, now and then. It was, you know, restful there, particularly in the pub. I don't care for bars as a rule, but you could spend hours in there, sitting, drinking, sitting, drinking. Ah, shit."

He looked disconsolately at his stubby cappuccino, perhaps wishing it were a full mug of Spitfire's darkest brew. He then resumed.

"You know, if he hadn't fired me, I just might have gotten used to the place. I was fitting in, yeah. One day something got into me. I just got this urge to speak, and I opened my mouth. Wrong place, the pub. But I'm glad it happened, or I might be there yet."

"What about the classes?" Derek asked. "The kids?"

"The kids. Well, you know they won't read anything more than a few pages in that pathetic anthology they have, so there's nothing you can do in class even if they show up. At first this made me uncomfortable, but after a while I figured it out, the routine. You sit, you wait, you mumble occasionally, and it's over. There's absolutely no excitement, but there wasn't much of that at Enola Gay. And you know, Derek, I never slept so well as I did when I was at Spitfire College of Higher Education. But it's no good, no good."

Derek declined to mention that until the end of his stay at the college he had relished the quiescence of the pub and the seminar rooms and that he too had slept well there at night and almost as well in the day. And yes, it was no good, though Glick seemed to feel more strongly about that than he did himself. The time seemed right to change the subject.

"So you left."

"So I left."

"For Italy," Derek said, struck by the consistent parallel between Glick's career and his own. Some day he would ask him if he had ever sold overpriced men's togs and accessories.

Glick shrugged. "Yeah. First Rome. Nice place if not for the Italians. Spent the last week here in Padua, reading and thinking, reading and thinking."

He sighed. "Have to."

"Have to what?"

"What, you don't know? Knock out an article, a bunch of articles, a book! What else? The Eusden edition impressed no one, that's for sure."

"Sounds like you're shooting for tenure, " Derek said. "But I thought you had it already. Aren't you a full professor?"

"Yeah, but where? Kansas, that's where. They have hurricanes in Kansas. They scare the piss out of me. Someday all the lights will go out. And Enola Gay's almost as dead as Spitfire College. The whole damn profession's going that way, seems to me. Even so, I have to move on."

Spitfire wasn't so dead when the Thatchers came, Derek thought. Glick missed that. Then everybody in the college went from dull to flat-out crazy, with nothing in between. He wondered what the place was like now. Maybe it was even deader after all the commotion. Something like that happens in the *Dunciad* with Pope's dunces. First lethargy, in the first three books, then frantic struggle, then blackout as the *Dunciad* ends and the world ends with it.

Damn *Dunciad*. He hadn't meant to think of it. It snuck up on him.

Glick pulled his coat collar up around his neck. He blew on his hands. "It's cold in here," he complained. "This is Italy? Sunny what-the-fuck?"

He waved, made a v- sign with his fingers to indicate they wanted two more coffees, called out "Hey, signore."

"Ooh," exclaimed the waiter. "Sig-noray. Molto bene." Giggles burbled from his patrons. Derek stared at the table. Glick acted as if he hadn't heard a thing. The man could not be embarrassed.

Derek was still interested. "So you're going to write. Got a subject?"

"Pope's *Dunciad*."

"Oh."

"Oh? Is there a reason I shouldn't? No, don't tell me. You're working on it, too?"

"Hell, no." That was true. He wasn't, wouldn't. Not in the sense that Sheldon meant, anyway.

"Haven't even read it in years," Derek added. A lie. "Or thought about it," he added. Not exactly a lie. It was more a case of it thinking him, poking into his head without an invitation.

Why was Glick staring at him?

The waiter arrived bearing two little cups and a shit-eating grin. He looked a lot like George Rosenblum's ace salesman, Spero. Better to think even of the store than that poem. The dunces, the goddess. He feared he would see them if he closed his eyes, which he resisted doing. This required some effort, and it told on him.

Sheldon seemed concerned. "You okay, Derek?" he asked. "You look pale all of a sudden. Drink your coffee, son. That's why the boy brought it."

That was good advice. Derek sipped and thought he was okay. Glick had a question. He had a little trouble getting it out.

"Uh, Derek. What you asked me before, did she come to me? So I'm wondering, who? Who's she?"

"Nobody. I—. Nobody."

"Let me guess. Someone we both might know, right? Or anyway know about?"

"Forget it. Just forget it." Derek got up from his chair. "So long, Sheldon," he said.

"Woe, woe," cried Glick.

"What?"

"Whoa. Slow down. I should go, too. It's colder in here than outside."

They paid at the bar and left. The waiter said something Derek didn't get that incited a collective gust of downright belly laughter. It propelled them out the door. A cold wind blowing down their necks, they proceeded down 8 Febbraio. It proved to be colder there than inside. Sheldon hadn't told the truth about that.

"My ass," he grumbled, a comment on Italy's deceptive reputation for temperate weather. Derek didn't respond. He'd had enough of Sheldon Glick for the day. Without preamble, he mentioned that he was heading for the station. What Glick said then surprised him.

"The trains run all the time. I'm going back to the Scrovegni Chapel. Why don't you come too?"

"Well, I just saw it, the Giotto fresco cycle. You saw me coming out. Wait, didn't you say—"

"Right. I've been there before, but now I want to see it again. Wouldn't hurt you either, Big D."

Derek couldn't see the point of it. So they looked like ordinary people, the Mother and the Son. He could see ordinary people every day of the year. A mirror would do the job just fine.

Then Glick stopped walking and made Derek stop, too, by seizing his right shoulder, having to stretch to do it. What he uttered then had the air of a confession that he was being forced to make. Maybe he had a compulsion to tell the truth as he saw it, no matter how unpleasant it was.

"Listen to me, dammit! I don't *like* our profession. I wish I could change it. Oh, it matters so goddam much if you're at some major place, if you get the pubs, the grants. And now this French stuff just so we can have new words to say. Don't like to hear this, do you? Cause you want to be a player in the game. Well, so do I. There's nothing else. Because I gotta move on. Greener pastures. Yeah."

Derek glanced at Glick's hand on his shoulder. Glick removed it, then thrust both hands into the pockets of the long coat he was wearing and resumed.

"You know I'm right. There was a time. There was." He fell silent and looked down at the cobblestones.

Derek heard a crackling sound coming from his pockets.

Glick shrugged. "Paper for my ideas about the *Dunciad*. I use little pieces, old envelopes and stuff. They get all scrunched up. Got some promising leads."

He withdrew his hands and glanced around him. His expression was not that of a man with promising leads.

Now Derek was the one who had to speak. "There was a time?"

"When it meant something. Literature. When it lifted you up or dropped you down. But either way, it made you think, and you wanted to pass it on. Know what I'm talking about?"

He did, but he said nothing.

"Come on," Sheldon said. "Come into the chapel with me."

"What? Why? I just said."

"I can't explain why. You have to feel it."

But Derek had felt nothing special on his visit to the chapel earlier that day. A revisit a few hours later shouldn't be any different. Those pocketed notes made him suspicious; maybe Glick just wanted to hold on to him and pick his brain about the *Dunciad,* which he didn't want to talk about. Derek stared at the sky, then held his palm aloft.

"Looks like rain," he said. "Better get to the station before it starts."

"Rain?" Glick held his palm up, too, mocking him. "It'll be a while. But hey, if you want to go, go. Ciao, Derek. Gee, did I say that right?"

Always the wise guy. Smarty-pants. Notes in his pockets. At least he'd correctly pronounced "ciao."

"Ciao, Sheldon." Derek turned toward the station. The train was filling when he got there. He was lucky to find a seat. Staring at, rather than through, a grimy window, he considered what Glick had said about their profession, English.

It wasn't *that* bad, surely. It was like most other lines of work. You scrambled to get ahead, went as far as you could or wanted to and then settled for whatever you had. Maybe thinking that way was a little cynical, but so what? It was funny about Glick, though. Today he hadn't seemed very much like the cynical Sheldon of the Tenderloin hotel, especially at the end of their time together; and he seemed so set on telling the truth about everything and shaking people up.

What, exactly, was Sheldon's truth? That reading was an emotional experience that also made you think? As simple as that? It wouldn't get you a job. You couldn't sell this truth to a scholarly journal. You couldn't talk to students about it. They'd laugh at you for offering them kid stuff. It wasn't even wise to reflect privately on your own readerly innocence, for that could make the academic present seem even more of a grind. Evidently Sheldon remembered his quite well, for all the good it did him.

And there was this "thing" that Glick claimed they had together. Derek couldn't absolutely deny that it existed. At the very moment he sneered at the entreating hand on his shoulder, he'd felt that the Brooklyn sharpie meant to help him. That was why he had said that about what literature was really for and also why he'd suggested a return visit to the Scrovegni chapel. Now Derek wished he hadn't turned Glick down. They might not have talked about the *Dunciad.* But what, then, was the purpose of Glick's request?

* * *

If Sheldon and Derek had entered the chapel together and looked at the scenes depicted there, could they have been transformed—if only for a moment—into the innocent readers both had once been? That's another of those knotty questions I mentioned when first shouldering my way to the surface of this story, just before Derek arrived at his parents' place in Malibu. Remember me, Fame the trumpeter? Course you do.

So, again. Would those two have regained the fresh vision of their early years? Possibly, although Derek might have hoped that the effect wouldn't be permanent, as that could screw up his job prospects. But it might not have been altogether beyond him, inspired somehow by truthful Sheldon, to read Giotto's virgin and her singular son as counterfigures to Pope's monstrous female and her numerous squabbling brood. Mary is the important person here, as I'll explain in a moment. But first consider this Glick, his function, his mission. And not just him.

Later, back in the States, Derek sometimes thought about Glick with his insistence on their "special relationship," not anticipating that this would eventually be tested under the severest of conditions. He was rarely mindful of Ace Goldman, the video producer who looked and sounded so much like Sheldon that Derek had asked if they were kin. When Sheldon said of literature that once it had lifted him up, dropped him down, Derek might have recalled that Ace had said essentially the same thing. He said, "I got high when I read, or sometimes low." He remembered, and that was something. Derek might well have returned to Gold Man Productions, hung around a bit, learned something.

Two wise guys, both willing to give him counsel he hadn't asked for, what did they matter? Well, if you can believe it possible that Lucia Luteplucker and Margaret Thatcher, too, had a kind of relationship with a monstrous poetic creation that actually existed in some unknowable way—and Derek could not entirely disbelieve this, try as he might—why not think along parallel lines of Sheldon and even of Ace? Damaged and distorted, made small by the same worldly conditions that fattened Lucia and Margaret into immensity, perhaps they too were bound to a power, one made more palpable within the Scrovegni Chapel.

Call this power the Muse. Read Giotto's Virgin as the Muse. What's stopping you? She came to Giotto, didn't she? Once she came to many minds and hands, but now, diminished along with her agents and lacking in computer smarts, she must make do with uncreative Derek Rosenblum. She could do worse. Oh, Derek is no creator, but he is something equally indispensible. Derek is the Reader. If she loses him, if he defects, then all is lost.

Derek the Reader. Nothing else could make him such a prize that Dulness always kept her eye on him, a guy who always insisted he was nothing special. But why not simply claim him for her own, wherever he kept himself? A professorship almost anywhere would have done it; but something about him prevented her. Derek was more special than he believed he was. And he wasn't alone. He had allies, even if they too didn't seem like much. Think about it.

Big league academic and potent politico vs. Sheldon and (perhaps) Ace, bush league prof and (maybe) animal video guy. The contest hardly seems equal, but don't forget the belle of Sam Yorty High, Tracy Chatham. Team her up with the lady in the chapel. Don't both oppose the darkness and promise light and life? And there might be others, potential allies. If one such appears in your life, as Sheldon Glick had in Derek's, don't deem it a coincidence. If only he had gone into the chapel with Sheldon!

Even so, there's a chance. Yes. Think about it.

* * *

Derek didn't, but on the night before his return to America he dreamed the dream again. First he saw an ordinary chair with a mortal woman in it, but too briefly to see which mortal it was. For in an instant, the chair became a lofty throne; there Dulness towered, while Derek stood still upon the dim and featureless plain, lost amid a multitude of dunces brandishing their crappy prizes. As they dashed by him, they sneered. It was just as before, except that he himself held no prize, no weighty scroll. He had only himself, evidently a prize of little worth. This caused him great concern, especially since he was much closer to the throne than previously. Sensing that she was about to note his empty hands, he was both intensely curious and considerably alarmed about what would happen then. This time, beholding the chubby, balding fool sprawled in the divine lap, Derek felt that he was about to recognize him, and that prospect, too, held great significance.

He woke up, sweating, before either of these things came to pass. He was both glad and somehow disappointed. Both feelings were disturbingly intense, so it was good that he was leaving Europe that very day. Back in the stolid, sensible Midwest, far from either Venice, such dreams would not assail him.

True, he was heading toward the stomping grounds of Luteplucker, for only Heartland would have him. But its campus spread far across the prairie. If he took care, she would never find him. He wondered, though, if she still looked as he remembered, spookily, sinisterly sexy, especially when viewed from the rear. Perhaps he could glimpse her from hiding.

He also gave some thought to Sheldon Glick, hoping he'd seen the last of him. He was basically a good guy, but Derek felt he was better off without Glick hanging around talking of a special relationship and begging him to visit churches. He had been careful not to tell Glick about his plan to return to Heartland.

All Derek wanted was to work, to bury himself in work and forget everything else. He couldn't wait to get started teaching, reading, writing. He couldn't wait to get to Heartland, and he couldn't wait to leave it for someplace better.

On the plane, though crammed into a tiny, economy-class seat, he slept deep and dreamless and counted that a good thing. He forgot that sometimes dreams are warnings.

From Chicago he took a bus to Heartland. He settled in there. Nearly two years passed.

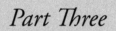

Part Three

Higher Education in the Midwest

Derek was late for his ESL class. Walking swiftly across the Heartland campus, he caught up with two large, buzz-cut fellows and briefly tuned in to their conversation.

" Yo, Cletus," said one.

"Yo, Byron."

"Hey asshole, you go beer bust Theta house?"

"Yuh! You?"

"Get fucked up! Yuh!"

He passed them yoing and yuhing at each other.

The guys had to be football players. Any large male person on campus was likely to be that in a university where most students were neither large nor small. In appearance they were remarkably average in every way, except for the jocks, who had their own generic looks, depending on the sport. There were more of these than there had been in Derek's student days, for after moving up the NCAA ladder from Division 3 to Division 2, Heartland had begun recruiting athletes from other states. The big boys Derek had overheard sounded like Texans. It hadn't helped. The teams kept losing; though big, the Heartland jocks were also slow and dumb. The university had also busied itself recruiting students from another population, foreigners; hence the sixty English as a Second Language sections. The jocks got paid, the foreigners paid; they paid a lot.

It was Derek's impression that the classes at Heartland had grown considerably easier since he had studied there. Perhaps the increased number of ESL students had led the faculty to ease up. The same might be said regarding the jocks. There was heavy grade inflation. Derek knew that the average grade in all subjects was now A-, and he'd read in the student newspaper of complaints filed against professors who dared to hand out B's. Even admitted plagiarists complained about B's. He gave A's to everyone in his classes. Another sign of easing standards was that the English Department, which had made Derek pass three rather simple reading exams in French, Italian, and Latin, now required only American Sign Language for the Ph.D. If you saw two people madly waving at each other in the Humanities Division Refectory, you could bet they were in English, practicing. Most of the other programs had dropped language requirements altogether. Fewer courses were required, too.

Everything was easier for those interested in literature or history or philosophy. Nonetheless, Sports Management Science was the hottest major on campus, while enrollments in literature courses, as in the other non-business subjects, were in steady decline. That meant less money from the state, and *that* meant hiring loads of low-salaried, untenured part-timers to teach in every humanities department, but particularly in English, given the high demand for ESL and remedial composition. Other public universities were in the same fix, bad news for anyone who wanted a regular, old-fashioned, tenure-track job teaching literature.

Bad news for Derek when he thought about it, as he was presently doing while he walked. He was glad he had a class to teach, to take his mind off it.

He entered his classroom. Thumbtacked next to the door was a 4 by 6 card informing anyone who cared to read it that the class about to begin was ESL 1 and that the instructor was Derek Rosenblum, Ph.D. Derek smiled at his students, opened the big Twick and read aloud:

> Men, some to Bus'ness, some to Pleasure take;
> But ev'ry Woman is at heart a Rake;
> Men, some to Quiet, some to public Strife;
> But ev'ry Lady would be Queen for life.

As Derek recited these lines, he took care to pronounce every syllable with maximum precision. "Queen for life," he concluded, and then looked out at the faces before him, ivory pale, and eyes dark and sparkless. His students came from different parts of Asia. Occasionally their faces reddened and they spat insults at one another in what must have been some kind of lingua franca. What fueled these arguments? Ethnic strife? Religious hatreds? Who knew? Who cared? Not Derek Rosenblum, Ph.D., carrying out his educative function by expelling little bits of traditional Western culture in exchange for the big bucks out-of-nation tuition that came to the university, not to him.

This wasn't what he was supposed to be doing. The Director of Composition had thrown him a beginning ESL class ("to get you out of my office"), but hadn't told him how to teach it. He hadn't learned or tried to learn. Despite having been in the program for five consecutive semesters, including one in the summer, he had no idea what was expected of him as an ESL teacher. There was a program "mission statement"; he hadn't read it. Monthly meetings were held for the sixty ESL teachers; he never went and was never missed.

He thought it best to recite the four lines again. His students didn't seem to be responding in any way. He read, and then he closed the book.

"Alexander Pope," Derek told the ESL class. "'Epistle to a Lady,' 1735. Fine English poem."

"At least short," remarked his best English speaker, Mister Feng.

"Oh, that's just a little bit of it," Derek said, cheerfully. "It's about 300 lines in all."

"Fuck all," snorted Mister Feng. An engineering student in his forties, he considered the compulsory ESL class a waste of time. This after the Cultural Revolution had interrupted his university education in China by sending him off to harvest maize in Jijin province.

Feng was right about the class, as Derek would have cheerfully admitted to anyone not in a position to fire him. For the students it was surely a waste. At every class meeting he gave them a small chunk of Alexander Pope. He tried to get them to talk, hoping for something useful—for him. What Derek was attempting, of course, was to generate raw material for journal articles, as an Asian perspective would be a likely seller in this multicultural age. For he needed pubs if he was ever to get a tenure-track job somewhere, anywhere, teaching literature. So besides reading Pope nightly in the big Twick, he carried on in class, hoping that some student's comment would start his mind to working and his hand to typing. None had so far. It was getting a little tiresome.

"Well now," Derek said, addressing the class. "How about it? Do *you* think every woman is at heart a rake?"

A girl in the class, one who always wanted to please teacher, leaned sideways in her seat and made raking motions with her arms.

"Oh, yeah," said Derek. "I should have told you. In the poem a rake is a libertine."

"Latrine?" inquired Feng, with a giggle. He then addressed the class.

"What's he talking about, hey? You understand? No me!"

The class giggled. Derek was reminded of the mocking waiter in the café in Padua, but he didn't let it throw him. This was his country they were in. He noticed that the girl was still raking.

"No," he said to her, "not that kind of rake, but it's very good that you know that. This kind of rake, a libertine, is, well, a big screw-up."

Feng: "Ha! Like you!"

Teacher and student laughed together. The fall semester was just three weeks old, but they were already real pals. Feng liked Derek. Derek liked Feng, whom he wished to keep in good temper so that he wouldn't complain about time wasted to the Director of Composition.

"Is true about ladies," Feng said. "Always wanting to be queens."

The girl who had raked was now swirling her hands above her head. "Crown," she said, smiling beseechingly at Dr. Rosenblum. "Queen wears crown?"

"Well, not literally," commented Derek, "but very good. Excellent! Anybody else want to add something?"

Feng got upset. "Queen! Like Mao's wife, bitch Jiang Qing. Send me to fields!"

Another student spat something poisonous at Feng, who spat back. They might all get into it in another minute, and since the hour was almost spent, Derek dismissed them.

He'd decided to concentrate on Pope, whom he'd always liked best of all the eighteenth-century writers. It went beyond liking: at times, when reading him, he thought he could hear Alexander's voice. It was rather shrill, as Pope was a little guy. "An Epistle to a Lady" was a poem of medium rank and thus an exception for Derek. Usually he chose to study and to give to the ESL kids the poet's minor pieces, those thought minor, that is, and generally ignored. Obscurity had paid off with "Laurence Eusden's Subversive Vision," and while the laureate of the first two Georges had soon reverted to ultra-minor status, that fate could hardly befall something by Pope.

Occasionally Derek referred to the major poems, but not to the *Dunciad*, which he had resolved never to reread, let alone introduce to his ESL class. He followed this rule because it was good for his head. Since coming back to Heartland he'd had no repeat of his *Dunciad* dream.

Nor, during his first year back on his former campus, did he worry over much about Professor Luteplucker. It did trouble him that occasionally he felt drawn, almost physically pulled, toward his former adviser. He would even take a few steps toward wherever he thought she might possibly be. Almost instantly, however, an opposing force would rise up within him and bear him off in the opposite direction.

One afternoon this force slackened so that he found himself standing in front of what he thought to be her office door. After a troubled moment's hesitation and a deep breath, he briskly knocked.

"We're not here," he heard a woman say, not Luteplucker. He pushed the door open, to reveal four small women rapidly grading student papers at four small desks awkwardly pushed together. The women were part-time comp instructors, adjuncts. He could tell by their pinched faces.

"Oh, no you don't," one said, accurately taking him for a fellow wage slave but inaccurately assuming that he was looking for a quiet place to grade *his* papers. "No room here. Go to the tents."

In fact, Derek had been assigned a tent in which to hold his office hours, but he had never held any. Nor had he any papers to grade, because his ESL students could write only in their own languages, which he had no desire to learn.

That Luteplucker was not in her former office made him feel relieved and yet faintly frustrated at the same time. Maybe she had gone off to another university and he could forget about her, could try to. It might be possible, but perhaps not. He wasn't sure he wanted to forget *all* about her. She was important to him in some uncertain way. Curious, Derek asked about her at the English Department and was told that Professor Luteplucker was taking some time off from teaching. She was now a dean. The office secretaries referred to her as Dean, rather than Professor, Luteplucker, but, strangely, claimed neither to know what she did as a dean or where on campus she was. Derek didn't press them. If he didn't know her location, he wouldn't be afflicted by a perverse need to go there. That's what happened.

As he never encountered her on campus or anywhere else, Derek thought about Luteplucker less and less. This freed his mind to concentrate on Pope's minor poems, which he read and reread almost every evening. He tried to write, too, of course, but produced very little. He would get ideas, but when he settled down before his Selectric, they seemed impossibly trivial. Accordingly, he could only write brief notes, and the few he'd managed to complete impressed him so little when he read them that he chose not to send them out. Though he stuffed them with every fashionable theory term he could think of, these served only to make the little he'd written unintelligible. That wasn't really a drawback, he knew, given the present state of literary criticism, but somehow he just wasn't satisfied.

If only he could write and then publish a real essay, not a skimpy note. That would at least have the benefit of showing Sheldon Glick who was the superior eighteenth-century specialist. For what did Sheldon have, after all his big talk in Padua about the *Dunciad*? A note, even if it was in the sacred pages of *Poetics Now*, guessing at the real-life identity of one of Pope's minor dunces. Since Derek was reluctant to delve into the *Dunciad* to find out just what Pope had written about this unimportant person, he didn't know if Glick's note was brilliant or otherwise. It contained none of the current theory words, not a good sign.

The issue of *Poetics Now* with his note, imbedded within a cluster of other brief notes, had come from Enola Gay State. So Glick had his old job back, and Derek remembered how much his Eusden rival, pockets stuffed with scraps of paper, had counted on a prospective *Dunciad* essay to deliver him from hurricane-swept Kansas. That wasn't going to happen, not on the strength of two pages. But Sheldon had a job, a real job, not a part-time gig teaching ESL. That Derek couldn't work up any resentment over this inequality surprised him. He didn't know how he felt about his rival, or friend, and he chose not to write to say he had read his note.

How had Glick known he'd returned to Heartland? Derek was sure he hadn't said where he was headed, and he knew people couldn't be talking about him. He was too obscure, too unpublished, for that. It was just a case of trusting to chance, so that wise-guy Glick might signal, "Here's my pub, bub. So where's yours?" Or maybe Glick only meant, "This is what I've done. What do you think?"

The one thing Derek had finished about the poet was a brief syllabus for his class. It said that Alexander Pope (1688-1744) divided his time and talent between (1) attacking the evils of the world and (2) denying they existed. Consider (requested the syllabus) the famous last line of the first epistle of Pope's didactic *Essay on Man*: "One truth is clear, 'Whatever IS, is RIGHT.'" This was because nice God is in charge of all events so that everything turns out for the best, no matter how awful something might seem to us limited-vision mortals. This was also the philosophy of the detestable Soame Jenyns, annihilated by Johnson but unmentioned in the syllabus, and of Gottfried Leibniz (1646-1716), whose name did appear there. Derek knew that no one in his class would know who Leibniz was and had mentioned him only to remind himself to read *Essais de Théodicée*, which he never did. Eventually he forgot who Leibniz was.

But also consider (continued the syllabus) that in the same decade, the 1730s, as the *Essay on Man*, Pope also wrote powerful satires attacking a variety of contemporary ills. This strongly suggests that he never convinced himself about the rightness of everything or, perhaps, of anything. In 1743, the year before his death, Pope published the final version of the *Dunciad*, in which Dulness triumphs and therefore civilization crashes. He seemed to have found this amusing, which, Derek speculated but did not write in the syllabus, might be the intelligent way to respond to such an event. Feng, having lived through the crash of his own civilization, might not have agreed.

The class had never given any sign that they understood a single word of the syllabus. Derek occasionally reread it to remind himself of what he actually thought about Pope; when he wrote with publication in mind, he seemed to turn into another person who said things Derek didn't find interesting or even believable. Of course he couldn't send the syllabus anywhere. It was just for his class.

So he had nothing to submit to the journals, and that meant remaining at Heartland and pretending to teach ESL until someone caught on to what he was actually doing. Until then, it wasn't a bad life. No serious demands were made upon him, and he was surely better off here than doing janitor duty on the Third Street Promenade. His existence was quite bearable, he told himself, until something better came along.

But it would end, for eventually they would catch and fire him, and sometimes he wished they would hurry up and do it. A bearable existence. How was that different from a boring, or futile one? There were no signs of anything better coming his way, and with every passing week, his routine weighed more heavily upon him. It was frustrating. It was dull. Sometimes he felt just as he had during his last days at Spitfire.

Derek ordered himself to be realistic about his future, but while making that selfsame vow in Venice had enlivened him with purpose, to contemplate it here filled him with dismay. If he lost his little ESL job, what would he do? Nothing occurred to him. To work for his father was impossible. He knew that much, and he knew one other thing, also negative. He didn't want to be a cop for the rest of his life. For when he wasn't jesting with Feng, that's what he was. His official title was Campus Security Officer, but it was the same as being an ordinary cop.

Security

Toward the end of his first year as a pretend ESL instructor, tiring of the struggle to make his meager ESL salary cover both rent and food, Derek read in the university employees' bulletin that Campus Security was looking for recruits. Two of their officers, Davis and McGilvray, had been dismissed, with no reason being given. He applied, and once qualified in both shooting (expert) and driving (barely passing), they took his fingerprints and issued him two pairs of blue twill trousers, two blue shirts, and an absurd London bobby-style helmet. Donning this gear in the unit's locker room, he reported for his first Friday afternoon inspection. The sergeant told him to wedge himself between two troopers in the third rank.

And there, without at all expecting it, Derek encountered Lucia Luteplucker, Dean of University Facilities; for along with her other duties, she occupied the position of Campus Security Commander. After being loudly greeted by her officers, she proceeded to troop the line, inspecting each man from helmet to shoe tip. Derek's feelings as she neared him were both intense and strongly opposed.

Soon, in a moment, they would be eye to eye, and half of him wanted that. He wanted her to see him, own him. Simultaneously, remembering her power to magnify herself and diminish others, he feared that she might blast him, wither him. He fought down a desire to flee from the formation. Suddenly she stood before him.

After she moved on to the next man, Derek was again assailed by opposed sensations, but different ones. He was relieved, he was pissed off. His professor, his adviser, his nightmare lady, had not given the faintest indication that she knew who he was. Nor did she bother to ask.

"You have no name badge?" she said.

"Not issued yet," he gulped. It was true.

"Get," she said and moved on down the line.

Had she really seen him? Standing beneath her imponderable gaze, locked out by her red-lensed specs, Derek couldn't glimpse her eyes. They might have been closed. They might have been seeing something other than himself, though he stood right before her. He *felt* unseen and he felt her power. But it wasn't overwhelming. She had made him shrink an inch or two. That was all.

On the next day—as a new officer, Derek had to patrol on the weekend—the company sergeant rushed upon him with his name badge. She must have spoken to him. Dutifully Derek pinned it on and wore it when out in the field, but not at inspection time. There the dean continued not to know him, or seemed not to. A good thing, decided Derek. Better to be ignored than undermined, as when she'd forced Eusden on him and sent him off to interviews with mocking recruiters. He also felt that if she chose to recognize him that might revive his *Dunciad* dream, in which she'd figured, at least in the first one. And *that* would surely distract him from his self-appointed task of calmly going through Pope's minor poems, one after the other, and writing publishable things about them. Which didn't seem to be happening.

But he didn't dream. Moreover, while he couldn't help mentally picturing Pope's Dulness after confronting Dean Luteplucker on Friday, the image faded away over the weekend. As long as he didn't read that damned poem, he could keep his imagination under control and focus on the poet's lesser works.

At inspections he alternated between presenting himself as either Officer Davis or Officer McGilvray, whose name badges he had confiscated after spotting them on the sergeant's desk. Eventually he learned that these two had not only been dismissed from Campus Security but were also barred, at Luteplucker's insistence, from university employment of any kind. When he asked a fellow trooper what offense had merited such a penalty, the answer was that "they got out of line." He and Derek were in the locker room, both half-dressed.

"Well, what?" Derek asked. How bad could it be? He hadn't heard that Davis and McGilvray were in jail or had been executed.

"Uh-uh," replied the officer, who pointed first at the ceiling and then at his own ears. There was no camera up there, but the gesture reminded Derek of Lewis Lozange in Heathrow pointing at a wall-mounted camera and saying, "She tapes everything, she knows everything." Meaning Thatcher, of course. Luteplucker apparently didn't need mechanical devices to know everything.

Even after learning that the departed officers' guilt was too horrendous to be spoken, Derek continued to wear their badges on Fridays. In time, after several months of service, he came to consider this semi-masquerade an act of masculine defiance and thought it essential in maintaining his self-respect. Surely the dean knew who Davis and McGilvray were and that he was neither. Why didn't she say something? He was virtually daring her. In fact, he was almost positive that she knew very well that he was Derek Rosenblum and was simply choosing to ignore him. Did she despise him that much? All right, it was good to be ignored by the dean; but it made him think of how he was scorned in his dreams and by Thatcher and Tracy Chatham and Lozange, and, well, everybody, with the possible exception of Sheldon Glick.

Dean Luteplucker called him neither by his real name nor his false ones. Friday after Friday she called him nothing, which was highly aggravating. But it was also safe, as he kept telling himself, and it wasn't hard to fit his Campus Security duties in with his teaching and Pope reading, as long as he didn't do anything else. Derek's problem with this routine was that, in his sixth semester at Heartland, it was plainly getting him nowhere. Often he asked himself if he would be doing the same things ten years from now. Even getting promoted to ESL 2 or Campus Security corporal seemed unlikely. Should he leave before he became incapable of ever leaving? But without a teaching job elsewhere, that would mean giving up his goal of becoming a real professor. He wasn't ready for that decision and might never be, for he could not imagine being anything else.

Nothing in his life, he felt, he feared, would ever change, but one Friday something did. Though it had begun like any other day and would continue in that mode during the daylight hours, it ended differently.

Insecurity

That morning he'd tried his class on bits from Pope's "The Three Gentle Shepherds," "Lines on Mr. Hatton's Clocks," and "On a Lady who P——st at the Tragedy of *Cato*." No Popean Derek knew of had ever said anything about this trio, and the third one was a definite possibility. Few knew the poem, but it was common knowledge that Pope heartily disliked Joseph Addison, author of the *Spectator Papers* and also of *Cato*, a boring tragedy set in ancient Rome. He could make something out of that. Of course, his students were no help. Their only response to Derek's recitation of "On a Lady" was embarrassment. He let them go early. He was doing that more and more.

As Derek ambled from the classroom to Campus Security headquarters, he wondered who the pissing person was. The big Twick's note didn't tell him. Maybe Sheldon Glick would know, but he didn't want to start up with Glick.

Entering the locker room, Derek put away his teaching clothes, cords and an ancient sport coat from his dad's store, and donned his blue uniform pants and shirt. As always, the room was eerily quiet, even though other officers were also changing and opening and closing the metal lockers. There was none of the towel snapping and general foolery that was traditional American locker room behavior. Of course, most of the men on the force (all the officers were male) were unemployed humanities Ph.D.'s, and so might have been too intellectual to indulge in such horseplay. That made sense, but their degrees didn't explain why they said practically nothing to one another at any time and stumbled about like sleepwalkers. Maybe they were simply depressed by their common failure to find academic jobs, or perhaps it was mostly their commander's influence—as Derek had latterly begun to think. She cowed them.

He attached a name badge to his shirt, exactly one half-inch above the left-side breast pocket. Today he would be Davis. Plopping on his bobby helmet, required headgear when otherwise outfitted for duty, he trotted to the assembly room.

There he fell in, after the order from the sergeant. Third man, second rank. He assumed the position of parade rest, but flicked his eyes to the right, toward the door through which their commanding officer would enter. In a moment she did.

"Gentlemen," she barked. "Good afternoon."

"Good afternoon, Dean," they dutifully chorused.

Luteplucker's face was the most unexpressive of all the faces Derek had ever seen. Anyone would have thought her thoroughly bizarre; in fact, everyone did. Yet she was also compellingly attractive. At least she was so to Derek. Plainly in awe of their commander, his fellow troopers would turn their eyes away from the bomb-shaped breasts thrusting out the thin material of her blue blouse. Derek boldly stared. By now he was used to them, but they still had power to arouse. She wore no name badge above her left bomb-shape. Everyone knew who she was.

If only she would just pause for a second, look him in the face, and say ... say anything, but not much. Ah, here she came, striding down the line. She paused. Casting a brief glance toward his genital region, she said, "Gig line" and swiftly marched on. Derek looked down.

Yes, it was true. The line down the middle of his shirt where the buttons were was twisted just where it led into his Brasso-polished belt buckle. But her eyes had not descended further. She stood before the next man.

"Good afternoon, Officer Greenberg."

"Afternoon, Dean."

She knew Greenberg; she knew all of them and addressed them by name, for which boon all were pathetically grateful. It angered Derek no end to be so overtly spurned, deliberately unrecognized, the only one without a name, anyone's name. Never good enough, his life story.

After inspection, Luteplucker departed, presumably to get out of her uniform and perform some other task delegated to the Office of University Facilities. She was probably managing the entire university while also controlling the agenda of the Modern Language Association. The sergeant distributed assignments. Derek got headquarters duty for the rest of the afternoon, meaning, essentially, that he was backup. If the brother officers covering the campus were engaged and someone needed a cop, then Sarge might send him out. Usually that meant rescuing a foreign student who had gotten lost on Heartland's large, flat campus with its large, flat buildings. They were always grateful and he'd received a few cash tips from the oil- rich Middle Eastern kids, but he detested the dead time spent waiting in the office. He wasn't alone, they were a force of four or five, sitting before a table; but no one wanted to talk.

Instead, they took brief naps, heads on desks. The dean had forbidden reading matter and radios. Derek suspected that when not on duty the other Ph.D. cops were doing what he was doing: searching in their disciplines for material to write about. Maybe they were actually finishing notes and articles and even books, which was more than he could say for himself.

Derek tried to nap, but was too fretful to settle. It was often this way on Friday, bringing Luteplucker back into his life and with her the one poem of all the world's poems that he had vowed never again to read. Oh, by Monday he would be free of it; but then he always had the following Friday to look forward to, and this one was even worse than usual, because he couldn't stroll about the campus on foot patrol and look at things and distract himself.

The police work itself was hardly a distraction. If they ever had a real crime to deal with, he and the other cops might have found their jobs more interesting, but nothing like that had occurred since the capture of the last four ABD gangsters a few years before Derek's return to Heartland. A library clerk discovered them, crouching together in a washroom toilet stall. All well into middle age, they didn't put up a fight. They had their sympathizers, and for a short time graffiti were painted on the walls of campus buildings. "Free the ABD Four" and "ABD will win." The slogan-croaking protesters, it turned out, were also old, relics from the sixties. No one else cared.

Derek lifted his head from the table and gazed at his half-slumbering colleagues. They were always that way, just as the faculty at Spitfire College had slumped and sometimes snored in both pub and seminar room, until the boundlessly energetic Lozange had keyed them up for Thatcher's visit. What would it take to awaken these guys? A little crime wouldn't do it. They needed a Ted Bundy copycat, at the least.

He felt a need to put himself in motion. Arising, he picked up an empty paper cup from the table and tossed it toward a trash can by the door. It hit the side of the can. He bent over, grabbed it, and tossed it in. By Campus Security standards this was a burst of activity, and everyone in the room breathed more easily when he left and started roaming the halls. (Officers on HQ duty were forbidden to go outside except on official business.) Several times he paced all through the building, hands clasped behind his back, and still, despite himself, he thought. So at least he tried to be realistic in his thoughts.

He considered Luteplucker. He got a dose of her every Friday, so now, even if he resigned from Campus Security, which he couldn't afford to do, she would still be lodged in his brain for an indefinite period. Even if he were able somehow to quit the campus, that wouldn't make any difference. For if he went elsewhere but remained in English, as he hoped to, she could always find him. There were Luteplucker epigones all over the country, and they would be her spies. When he'd lived in Britain, Thatcher had taken her place, and he'd been drawn to her. But that was there and then, and Thatcher, who thought he was Glick, hadn't cared about him in the least. It was different with Luteplucker.

Was this a realistic thought? It wasn't, but he couldn't help thinking it.

Despite her show of not recognizing him, he sensed a message for him in her uttering every trooper's name but his. What? Was he supposed to *earn* his name through some dumb ritual, like the one he'd screwed up in the pub at Spitfire? He didn't know what she wanted from him, but for some reason he mattered to her ever since she'd made him write about Laurence Eusden. But he couldn't imagine what the reason might be, being sure that he was just an ordinary fellow.

So it was not a realistic thought, that she cared about him. She liked exerting her power, that was all, and he was a convenient target. He tried to dismiss the thought, and it submerged.

Derek's ordinariness was an old conviction of his, nurtured ever since certain experiences in high school. It was correct, too, regarding intelligence and talent. But what Derek didn't grasp and that signified how really extraordinary he was, in one particular sense, was how few in his profession were willing to think of themselves as ordinary. Perhaps no one was thus willing besides himself. Some might claim to be satisfied with a junior college gig, as long as it was full-time, but secretly they considered themselves unjustly condemned to keep their brilliance under wraps. What all really sought was to attain such an exalted post—at Yale, say—that they need not actually think to be held in high esteem. It was so easy to not think, too, thanks to the new theory that encouraged the importing and inventing of words without requiring them to mean anything. Simply to spout them sufficed.

To rise in the profession allowed you to fall from the ranks of thinking beings. This was the common pattern. This was the subtlety of Dulness. I know about these things, for I am Fame.

Derek did not aspire to spout at Yale. High places held no attraction for him. After all, he was used to obscurity, for who could be more obscure than a Laurence Eusden specialist who was also one of sixty ESL part-timers at a populous state university? All he wanted was a break from ESL and comp and a chance to teach the writers he liked. But fate and the goddess would summon him from his lowly station to the very center of things.

Oh, Derek is special, you can be sure about that. And Professor Luteplucker has taken a special interest in him; count on that as well. But what accounts for that interest? And what makes *her* so special, anyway? And is this story I'm telling important, and if so, why? These questions will reappear on the final exam, if there is one. Now, please read on.

Do I want to be like them? This was Derek's present concern as he paced in a circle through the building. He had principally in mind his brother cops, but also, even though dimly, the dunces of Spitfire and those in the poem. No. He did not want that. He did not want to be a dunce. However, just as soon as Derek had decided on that, honesty forced him to concede that at times he enjoyed what he hoped were mere temporary downslides into duncehood. In his ESL class, for example, he particularly relished the moments when the students, utterly baffled by a tidbit of minor-league Pope, fell silent, even the gabby Mr. Feng. At such blessed intervals, he recalled his Spitfire Experience among the dunces of Great Britain. Such tranquility, until Lozange had made them all scurry. And as much as he disliked the down time in HQ, so did he looked forward to reposing on his bench in the quiet locker room. So what if Luteplucker knew what was going on there? Nothing was, so why would she care?

Tonight, however, he was seriously antsy. He continued to pace.

"Davis. Yo, Davis."

The several officers with whom he had been sitting were now approaching him in a body, headed for the lockers. It was six o'clock, shift change time. Now for Derek a modest thawed dinner at home and a little brainstorming about the lady who pissed herself at a performance of *Cato*. What fun.

"Davis. Hey."

He realized that one of the guys was trying to get his attention.

"What?"

"Sarge wants to see you."

"Yuh."

Odd that on the few occasions when they did talk to one another, the Ph.D.'s of Campus Security used virtually the same vocabulary as the oversized jocks recruited from places south and west.

Sarge told Derek he would be on driving patrol that evening. It was an order, not a request, even though he'd already completed his required duty hours, but Derek didn't mind. Maybe something interesting would happen. He'd never driven before. Campus Security had only one vehicle, a ten-year old jeep of the kind favored by dictators in Latin America.

Though the sergeant usually gave his orders without explaining why he gave them, now he chose to account for this sudden assignment. Officer Mason, that evening's scheduled driver, was sick, said the sergeant, shaking his head as if poor Mason had just hours to live. This seemed strange to Derek, who had seen his fellow trooper, a corporal, standing smartly at attention and appearing perfectly well. It wasn't worth talking about, though he almost asked "Why me?" out of simple curiosity: why him to drive, of all those the sergeant might have called on? For while in qualifying on the pistol range he had shot a brilliant score, he'd barely passed the driving test. The six-speed gearshift, the two overdrives—they had flustered him.

During the test, the sergeant, sitting next to Derek and muttering to himself, had made him more nervous still. Now, alone, he encountered fewer difficulties. After a brief cruise around the campus, he ventured into the city just beyond its borders for a Big Mac and Coke. He saw nothing anywhere that warranted investigating. Had he the big Twick, he might have risked parking in some quiet spot, flicking on the dome light, and prospecting for nuggets. But since the book lay on his desk at home, he drove and drove, experimenting with the six gears and occasionally grinding them—until the order came.

The vehicle's radio coughed and delivered itself of a word. The word was "Rosenblum." The voice seemed to be that of a woman. Commander Luteplucker? That would be strange. He couldn't be sure. The radio exerted a depersonalizing effect, and the hard-sprung jeep clattered so much that it was hard to understand what he was then told to do, though he thought he had it right. If it was Luteplucker, what had led her to address him and to use his real name? Could there be another woman in Campus Security that he didn't know about? But there was no time to ponder these questions. He could do only as the voice instructed: drive to Temporary Housing Unit 14A and speak with a female in a state of upset, having reason to believe that in her absence someone had invaded her THU and might still be there. After pausing for a moment to digest this message, Derek stomped the clutch, yanked the shift lever down into what he thought was second gear and stalled the jeep. He restarted the engine and got under way.

The Temporary Housing Units had been thrown up during World War II to accommodate the families of employees in a former clothing factory that had been switched over to producing the army tents called shelter halves. After the war these boxes for living, still designated temporary, were donated to the university, which reserved them for GI Bill student couples and families. Later married junior faculty and grad students were allowed to live in the THUs, as was still the case. Derek would have tried to finagle one for himself—the rent was lower than anywhere else—had he a wife.

They were double-deckers, one metal-sided rectangle on top of another, with the A's on the bottom, B's on top. 14A's door, he noted, was halfway open. The doorway and visible windows were dark. Sitting in the jeep, Derek scanned the area. No one was in sight. His radio buzzed.

"Where are you, Officer?" This voice he recognized. It was male, that of the sergeant. Derek felt simultaneously relieved and disappointed. Now he wasn't sure if the previous voice had been a woman's at all.

"I'm in front of THU 14A," Derek said. "Where's this woman supposed to be?"

"In 12B, with friends. Go there."

After parking in front of 12B, he mounted the external stairs, which creaked. They must have heard him coming: the door was open when he got to it and was recognized as an officer.

He found two adult women and three children. The kids kept moving around so that it took him a moment to count them. He was supposed to write down such things and put them into a detailed report, but he had nothing with which to write in his little book and thought it would diminish his authority to ask to borrow a pencil. The woman who lived in THU 14A explained that when she had returned home from having dinner with her friend in 12B, she had found her door ajar and thought she heard someone moving around inside. She immediately returned to the friend's place and called Campus Security. But now she wondered if she might have just neglected to close the door behind her upon going out earlier. She had trouble with the concept.

"I can't believe I did that," the woman said. "I never do that."

"Well, we all," Derek began, but she cut him off.

"Maybe I shouldn't have called you guys."

She was a small woman, small and cute. A nice change from Commander Luteplucker. Her big dark eyes were unobstructed by tinted glass.

"No, no," protested Officer Derek. "Always best to play it safe. Can you think of anyone who might be legitimately in your place?"

"Legitimately?" she repeated. "No. No one has a key except me," she said.

She was cute. He was curious. Was she faculty or a grad student?

"Grad," she told him, when he asked. "For my report," he said. He wiggled his fingers, miming the act of writing.

She had a faint musical accent that Derek tentatively identified as Indian. There were lots of Indian students at Heartland, most of them in engineering. She didn't strike him as the engineering type. Had she a husband? You were supposed to be married to qualify for these units, but she'd said no one except her had a key. That could mean the guy was out of the picture. The three kids couldn't be hers. She was too young, and they were all blonds anyway, like the other woman in the room.

"You're on your own here at the university?" he asked.

"Yes. I'm alone."

Interesting.

Derek knew no women. He knew no one. Between his two jobs and his constant reading of Pope and struggles to write, he lacked time for anything resembling a social life. It would be such a pleasure just to sit down and chat with someone besides somnolent, monosyllabic campus cops and his ESL students with their incomprehensible antagonisms. Certainly she would not be one of those; her English was far too good. He wondered. What if she were a grad student in English? Uninvited, he sat down on a couch. It was very low, a children's couch, so that his knees stuck up almost level with his head. It occurred to him that neither radio voice had mentioned the caller's name, and now he asked her. Couldn't write it down, but he should be able to remember it.

"Jackson," she said. "Priya Jackson."

Indian all right, but Jackson? The husband, presumably an ex-husband.

"What are you studying, uh, Ms. Jackson?"

"English," she said.

"Oh, is that so? I—"

"Officer Davis?"

Instead of responding, Derek cursed himself mentally. Usually when away from Security HQ he wore the name badge with his real name, but this time he'd forgotten to change. This was awkward. Well, he could tell her his real name later, though that would be awkward, too.

"English, huh?" he said. "What's your period?" Meaning Medieval, Renaissance, etc. Then, remembering that the younger people mostly did theory, or theorists, rather than literary periods, "Who're you reading, now Derrida? De Man?"

At that moment, he couldn't think of any names besides the two Ds, and Ms. Jackson seemed to be waiting for more. Wasn't there an L-person somewhere? "Le" something. He offered "Lemaitre." It sounded right.

"Officer Davis," she said again. "Please. They need to go to bed." She waved at the children; racing around, they hardly seemed ready for bed.

"Yours?" he asked, just to be sure.

"No, mine," said the occupant of 12B, a large Nordic-looking woman, addressing him for the first and only time. "And it's getting late."

"I'm on it," Derek said, heaving himself up from the little folks couch.

"Take care," said Ms. Jackson.

"Where's your gun?" asked the oldest kid, maybe six, who had a wise-ass look to him.

Ignoring the question, Derek descended the stairs, conscious of the mom, the children, Priya, all clustered on the landing above, waiting to see what he would do.

The wise-ass kid called after him, "You don't have one. I bet!"

Little fart! No, he did not have one. Campus Security's ancient Army .45 was reserved for qualifying on the range. Only the commanding officer toted a gun, a small, shiny pistol Luteplucker wore holstered at her side on inspection Fridays. The weapon issued to officers on duty was a spray canister of a chemical called Postman's Pal.

Derek doubted that anyone was lurking in Ms. Jackson's apartment, but as he walked from 12B to 14A he pulled the Postman's Pal from its place on his belt and gave it a squeeze. Dead, juiceless, even though he had never used it. He stepped warily into THU 14A. No one was there, and nothing seemed out of place. From a campus security perspective there was nothing to be concerned about. As a scholar, however, one item he discovered on the premises interested him considerably.

It had taken almost no time to check out the unit, which was scrupulously neat. There were two small bedrooms; one contained a bed, the other a desk with a computer set on it, along with a small, tidy stack of pages. Derek glanced at the topmost one and was startled by the title he found there.

Versions of Female Nature in John Gay's *Fan*

Below that was her name, Priya Jackson. In the upper right-hand corner was a grade, in green ink: A++!! Since John Gay was an eighteenth-century writer, Derek instantly ceased thinking about the cuteness and aloneness of Ms. Jackson. She was competition, and it disturbed him that while she had written on Gay's *Fan* and received a high grade, he had never even read it.

At least he was aware that it existed, which couldn't be said of everyone in the field. Traditionally considered a lightweight, Gay was currently less respected than ever; not even the *Beggar's Opera* was getting significant ink in the journals. All Derek knew about the *Fan* was that it was a mock-epic, like the *Dunciad* but much shorter, that it told a concocted myth about the creation of the first fan, and that it was and always had been generally despised. He'd read somewhere that Samuel Johnson thought it worthless, and that a major contemporary critic had pronounced it "unutterably trivial." So, what had this Priya (forget the "Jackson," which simply didn't fit) found to say in the neat pile on the desk before him? The *Fan* could not have been unutterably trivial to her.

But this was his sort of thing, defending the virtue of the ill-regarded, like poor Laurence Eusden. She was infringing on his territory. He had to see what she had done.

Derek settled himself in Priya's chair, which creaked under his weight, augmented by all the police crap dangling from his belt. He didn't know what most of it was for. With his Postman's Pal wedged uncomfortably between the chair's back and his own, he read the essay's initial page and found it cogent, clear, and jargon-free. After mentioning that Gay had written two quite different endings for the *Fan*, Priya promised to discover meaning in this fact, this real difference, rather than (Derek mentally provided the phrase) a foggy, froggy *différance*.

And her essay was different. It was readable. It engaged him and made him want to read on, no matter what the critics thought of its subject. He compared it to his own boring and vague essays of the last two years and immediately felt stupid. Anger, as always, was better. Grasping a pen from a little bowl holding several pens, he scrawled at the top of the page, "This is shit."

Instantly he regretted his action, because it wasn't true. Maybe his work was shit, but not hers. And she was so cute, and he might like her, and she would not at all like his impromptu comment. Perhaps there was some of that Wite-Out stuff. He worked his fingers among the pens in the bowl, but found only paper clips and rubber bands. Stupid! With a computer, she wouldn't need Wite-Out.

"Officer Davis."

She was standing behind him. He hadn't heard her enter. For a moment he wondered why she was calling him by another man's name.

"My friend had to get her kids ready for bed. What are you doing?"

Now he stood and leaned over the desk, blocking her view. Using both hands, he rearranged the pages of her paper so that the first of them was now somewhere in the pile's middle. After he moved aside, she wouldn't be able to see it and the dubious judgment he had scrawled upon it. But that hadn't been smart of him, to hide the page. He should have just taken it. Eventually— soon, in fact—she would see it and despise him then, unless he could find it again and sneak away with it when leaving the THU.

"Let me meet you outside," Derek said. "I need a few more minutes to check out some things. Best if I do it alone."

"I've been outside, waiting." Now she was glancing over his shoulder. "Were you looking at my *Fan* paper?"

"Just checking for prints and such, but nobody's been here."

That last was to reassure her and seem masterful, but he was sorry later: he could have blamed his comment on a supposed intruder. Too bad the ABD gangsters were all in prison.

"So there was nobody here," Priya observed. "I guess I just forgot to close the door. But you weren't checking for prints or anything. You were reading my paper. I saw you."

She smiled. Though her teeth were straight and white, her smile was slightly off-center, betokening to Derek an ironic way of looking at life. He liked that. Hadn't Tracy Chatham smiled in that same enticing way? He thought he remembered. How odd that he was thinking of Tracy at this moment, since Priya and she were so opposite in appearance (except for the smile), one fair and the other dark. And John Gay's *Fan* was the last thing that would ever interest the cheerleader.

"Did you like it?" Priya asked. Oh, that smile.

He rose from the chair, turned, and stood with his back to the table. If he could only get her to leave, it would take just a few seconds to find and seize the altered page, but telling her to meet him outside hadn't worked. She seemed inclined to tease him. What was this, flirtation? How stupid to have written "This is shit"! Maybe he should just confess, but it would take so much explaining.

"I wasn't really reading it," he said.

"Oh, yes you were. But who is this Lemaitre you asked me about? I don't think he's in here."

As she turned toward a nearby shelf, he snatched up a random page, which he crumbled and thrust into a pocket. He gazed at the little book she was now holding up before him. It was a hot-selling short guide to contemporary literary theory. Every grad student had one. He'd been planning to buy a copy. No Lemaitre, huh?

"He's new." It was all he could think of to say. It was stupid.

They couldn't go on like this. It was either leave or start telling the truth, at least about his real identity. He pointed his thumb at the name badge on his shirt.

"I'm not Davis. Davis is just my Campus Security name. My real name is Derek Rosenblum, and I teach ESL and I do the eighteenth century."

"Like me," he hoped she would reply, thus forming a bond between them.

Instead, she said, "Hm," and then, "I think I've heard of you."

"Oh?"

"You did a dissertation with Professor Lucia Luteplucker, didn't you? About a poet no one ever heard of. Little known? Least known?"

"'Laureate Little Known.' Yeah. Laurence Eusden."

"Who?"

"Eusden. Poet Laureate, 1718-1730. Mediocre."

He was never in a mood to chat about Eusden. Now he wanted to leave THU 14A, rumble away in the jeep and forget about "This is shit." He was also sorry about inventing Lemaitre. Priya could easily find out that no such person existed. He'd blown it with her. But she wouldn't let him go.

"Professor Luteplucker. Tell me about her. I think people think she's nuts, but no one ever says anything definite."

"Oh, I don't know if she is or not." It made him anxious to hear her spoken of in such a cavalier fashion. This was dangerous ground. She knows things, hears things.

"Derek—you said Derek?—why are you pointing at your ears?" asked Priya.

He lowered his hands. Priya continued. "I've only talked with her once, for about five minutes. She just sort of appeared. There's a conference someplace, and she's chairing a section. She wants me to write a paper for it. We're going to talk about that next week. And even though she's now a dean of some kind, she's going to be my dissertation director. I don't seem to have a say in the matter."

Only talked with her once, Priya said. Then she probably wasn't the one who gave Priya an A++!! Couldn't have been, not with that show of enthusiasm, a quality Luteplucker had never displayed.

"You're going to write about the *Fan?*" Derek asked. "In the dissertation?"

The conversation was getting interesting, but it was also unnerving, like anything to do with Professor Luteplucker. Besides that, it was time he got back on patrol. Sarge had probably buzzed his radio three times by now, or the woman had, if that first voice had been female. But Priya's answer to his question made him delay.

""I was," she said. "I was supposed to, but the professor I wrote the *Fan* paper for, who was going to advise me on the dissertation, he. . ."

She hesitated, gently bit a nicely formed lower lip.

" ... he's gone."

"He is? Where did he go?"

"No one will tell me. They just freeze up when I ask. He was new. That's all I know. So it's Luteplucker now, and she hasn't said what she wants me to write about. Just that it can't be the *Fan,* which she says is unutterably trivial. You know her. What do you think? Is she really crazy or just scary?"

Time to go. Definitely.

"I don't really know her. Look, I gotta—"

"She mumbled something about eighteenth-century dog breeding. Have you ever heard of lurchers? They're a kind of dog. When I asked if that was for the conference paper she'd mentioned, she shook her head. Does that mean I have to have dogs in my dissertation?"

Now Derek mumbled. "Could be some angle, I guess."

Why tell her? Why burden her? If dog breeding, which might be interesting for all he knew, did find its way into Priya's dissertation, Luteplucker would take it out and claim it as her own. Sooner or later would appear another Luteplucker note.

Priya walked him to her door. He mounted the jeep. Driving toward the center of campus, he clashed the gears, not caring that he clashed them. He imagined her at that moment ordering the scattered pages of "Versions of Female Nature in John Gay's *Fan*" and discovering the one he had written on. Unless, that is, he was lucky and that was the page he'd snatched up and had thrust into his pocket. Pulling up behind the former Men's, now Persons', Gym, he uncrinkled the page and saw it was the last one, not the first. He read the closing paragraph.

> If an active sexuality is natural and even attractive in women,
> passivity, the eighteenth-century feminine ideal, may not be.

This implicit bit of reasoning lies, like a seismic fault, at the center of Gay's *Fan* and keeps it in an unsettled state. The mock-epic machinery works, even though its product, the debate on female nature, is not smoothly finished, for the debate is never resolved. In fact, the machinery works all the better for that reason. In the end, Gay isn't sure about female nature. Unwilling or unable to accept fully the mythical ideal of passive womanhood, he rose above the smooth certainties of his time and created a poem that remains alive.

Now Derek chose to judge this sample with the keen eye of a modern editor. It was certainly clear. Given what he remembered from the first page about the poem's two endings, he imagined that that was where the "debate" lay. But "Gay isn't sure about female nature"? Wasn't that *too* clear, too simple? Her professor should have cautioned her about that sort of thing. The man should have known better; no wonder he was gone.

At the least Priya could have written "is unable to adjudicate" or, better yet, "is incapacitated to adjudicate the ... uh ... signifying différance." One thing for sure, she could never get this essay published anywhere if the whole thing was like that, in ordinary English. It didn't matter that it would be a pleasure to read.

But it should, he thought, it should matter. Something wrong here.

His radio buzzed. The sergeant, righteously pissed. Where had he been? How dare he not check back in? Come in now! He was done for the night. Any wandering wogs would have to find their way across campus unassisted.

But for a few minutes more Derek remained motionless behind the gym, assailed by questions he didn't know how to answer. Had Luteplucker sent him to Priya? Was that voice hers? She could easily have originated the order that he, a barely qualifying driver, take out the sergeant's precious jeep. A flunky could have been sent to pry open Priya's door. Luteplucker never had trouble getting others to do what she wanted done. She didn't need the powers of a goddess. Now, why did he think that?

She was interested in Priya, as she was in him. Or should that be as she *had* been interested in him? Was he now to be merely her instrument? Had she enlisted him as a dunce, with a dunce's combative nature, so that he would play the hostile critic to discourage Priya and lead her to corrupt her lucid writing style? He didn't like thinking he might have been used in that way.

Again the radio interrupted his thoughts, Sarge, waxing wroth.

Derek started the jeep and turned onto the main campus road. It was ill-paved, and the bumps served to stimulate his brain. He understood that, like Pope's goddess, Luteplucker preferred her admirers dull. She had rendered all of Campus Security that way. For whatever reason, he hadn't been affected as strongly as the others, or so he hoped. He had resisted her influence with his false names and by daring to gaze at her bomb-shapes. Didn't seem like much of a resistance, actually.

She dulled the cops. She dulled her students, too, and she had lots of them. Then, after she'd finished her work, off they went to other campuses to do unto their students as had been done to them. These were her dunces. That hadn't happened to him. And so he wondered: could it be that he had not been dull *enough* for this mission? Could his dissertation on Eusden not have been dull enough? Maybe its ruling premise, that mediocrity deserved serious critical attention, was suitably empty; but he hadn't tried to hide its emptiness beneath a blanket of words severed from sense. He had dared to use plain English. Now if Luteplucker had simply rejected 'Laureate Little Known,' that would have made him an ABD and forever unemployable. But she seemed not to want that, even though she had made sure that he was offered no job at the convention in San Francisco.

Who could figure out Luteplucker? What about his stupidity with Priya's paper, writing what he had? That was certainly dull of him, but at least he regretted it. Even when he wrote it, he knew it wasn't true.

Bomp! Half of a front tire dove into a hole, the violent drop shaking out another thought. He was sick of his pretentious notes, the dreary criticism he was writing. Maybe it was publishable—it was fashionably word-heavy—but somehow he was unwilling to see it in print. Suppose he took to writing as clearly as Priya had in her essay on the *Fan*? He could read his own work then without feeling dismay and, acute boredom. It was the other kind of writing, the muddy kind, that made the writer dull. But to write otherwise made publication chancy,

Derek turned in the jeep at headquarters, ignoring Sarge's hostile glare. As he walked to his apartment, he fancied that someone was there at that very moment writing scathing comments on the slips of paper scattered on his table, abortive births of notes for *Poetics Now*. Of course no one was there. He collected the slips and put them into the kitchen trash, then covered them with the morning's coffee grounds.

What had happened tonight? He'd met an attractive woman and screwed up with her, but something had passed between Priya and himself. He'd felt it. And, oh yes, Luteplucker may have spoken to him, but why should that matter? He didn't have to do what she wanted him to do. On that thought he fell asleep in his chair and did not dream.

An Unexpected Invitation

On the following Monday Derek taught his ESL students, dumbfounded as usual by his latest Popean snippet, and then set off for Campus Security. On the way he encountered Priya Jackson, who said nothing in response to his hello. Having seen him earlier only in his uniform rather than his teacher clothes, perhaps she thought him a bumptious stranger. Or if she did recognize him, she may have wanted to avoid starting a conversation with one who had so harshly judged (misjudged) her work. But she had smiled her lovely off-centered smile, he was almost sure she had; so maybe Priya was being a good sport and wasn't really angry.

In the Campus Security locker room he dressed for duty—rather sloppily since there was no inspection on Mondays—and reported to Sarge. The commander wanted to see him, said Sarge, in her office. Now. Go! Derek asked where the office was and was given directions. "Nice serving with you," said the old noncom over his shoulder, retreating from Derek as if from one unclean.

He had been waiting for this to happen. It wasn't just the possibility that it had been her voice on the jeep's radio. He had always suspected she knew who he was. Finally she had chosen to admit it. Maybe she had another use for him, if, indeed, she had intended him to belittle Priya's essay. Well, he wouldn't do it, whatever it might be. That went double if the use involved Priya. She liked him, possibly. Even if she didn't, he was on her side. He told himself that she had lent him strength, and he felt ready for the dean and commander.

Derek was nonetheless disconcerted, as he stood in the doorway to her office, by the perfectly circular globes displayed upon her desk. Opening the door in response to the dean's rather muffled "Come in," he had beheld her thus, leaning across the desk's top with her rear end facing him while she searched in its long central drawer amid pencils and paper clips for he knew not what.

As she fumbled, her buttocks, tautly sheathed by her customary black leather, twitched muscularly and seemed to grow slightly apart from each other with each twitch. Twitching in sympathy, Derek grew large. He took a step forward, then, shocked at the madness of his intention, stepped back into the hall. He considered fleeing, but that would surely anger her. He concealed his erection— bad boy, down!—with the only thing he had large enough do the job, the can of Postman's Pal, positioning it before his groin. When the dean suddenly pulled herself half-upright and turned her broad face toward him, he pressed the can's little button, knowing it was empty. It made a faint hiss, but nothing came out.

"Just testing," Derek said.

Straightening herself completely, Dean Luteplucker ambled, hips swiveling, around to the desk's other side. If she'd found what she was searching for in the drawer, Derek couldn't see what it was. She lowered herself into her metal chair and placed her coupled hands upon the desktop. Derek let himself be drawn into the room, but it was safe. He was no longer aroused, not that. Pal was back in his belt, and he felt ... he wasn't sure what he was feeling, but he'd felt it once before.

In the dean's office were two chairs. She had taken one, he found himself occupying the other. She said nothing. He didn't know what to say. Dean and ESL instructor, commander and cop, they faced each other across the narrow territory of the desk. Though Derek was taller when both stood, they were approximately the same height sitting down. He felt her eyes, behind her red-tinted lenses, peering directly into his. Yes, in height they were equal; why, then, did he feel small when with her? Something popped in his ears, or his head. The light dimmed.

Now it seemed to Derek that he had grown yet smaller until becoming a mere speck in her field of vision; it was the same experience, he now recalled, into which he'd been plunged years ago when telling her of his failure to obtain a job. Then the whole Midwest had lain open to Luteplucker; now her purview seemed to extend to either coast and across the seas. This time he sensed other individuals beside himself as the objects of her focus. Sheldon Glick, back at Enola Gay, was there, only one state distant. But Derek could also feel the presence of Lewis Lozange in Southampton and knew somehow that Lucia Luteplucker favored the tiny Briton over him and that Lozange would be a ranking officer in her army of dunces, while he ... stop! She was not ... She, she was not. ... She had not become—

Luteplucker spoke. "Rosenblum." It was a summons.

"Mama," he replied, or maybe it was just a moan.

"Rosenblum," she said again, but this time she carried on for several sentences, like a normal person. The global vision burst like a soap bubble. Derek regained his normal stature and drew back from the brink of supposing the impossible. Determined not to be overcome again, he focused on her words, but could find nothing suspect in them.

The American Association for Eighteenth-Century Studies, Literature Branch, was holding its annual meeting in October of the current year, 1989. The convention city would be San Francisco, just as when he'd attended eight years earlier, though held then in the spring. She was chairing a section, one of nearly 500 such little groupings. Its subject was mock-epic poetry. Derek Rosenblum was to speak for fifteen minutes on the *Scribleriad*.

She sat back in her chair. That was that. She glanced at the door. It was time to leave. But Derek had never heard of the *Scribleriad*, doubtlessly another unknown or much scorned work.

"I'm not familiar with that one," he admitted. He was surprised by how easy it was to talk to her. Shit. She was no goddess.

"Richard Owen Cambridge," she announced. Must be the author of this mock-epic. Nor had Derek ever heard of him.

"Aha," he said, nonetheless, as if recalling the name.

"October seventeenth," she said.

"Yes?"

"When the convention is. When you present the paper."

"Oh." Starting from nowhere he had to do this thing in a month? He really didn't have to, he could say no. But it would be madness to pass up an opportunity to address a gathering of fellow scholars. Anything he could do to make himself known was good. She dismissed him with a nod, and Derek left her and the building.

Luteplucker had spoken to Priya about writing a paper to be delivered at a section in a convention somewhere, probably the same one for which she had just recruited him. Briefly he followed the campus path leading to the THUs, but soon turned back: he was in uniform, and he didn't want her to think of him as a cop. Returning to HQ, he changed back into civvies and got out before the sergeant saw him and gave him some chore. Then, however, Derek changed his mind about visiting Priya, who was, after all, competition, and went to the library instead. What was this *Scribleriad* about?

The Heartland library lacked a copy, and Derek could only learn that it was a mock-epic, which he already knew, and that it was in some way about science. There was a bit more about the poet, Richard Owen Cambridge.

He was born in 1717 and spent most of his life in Twickenham, Middlesex, where Pope had also lived. He would have been somewhat less obscure, and Derek just might have heard of him, had he been a member of Pope's circle of friends. It was possible that they had never even met, since Pope had become a semi-invalid by the time Cambridge reached adulthood.

He had a reputation for being a nice guy. People liked him, and some also liked his *Scribleriad* when it was published in 1751; but by the time of Cambridge's death in 1802 the poem had become virtually unknown. It did not fit into the new century at all and had never regained its place since then. Familiar territory for Derek, uplifter of literature's lost and lowly ones. He had given Eusden a few minutes in the sun, and would gladly do the same for Cambridge. If only someone would do as much for him! Well, perhaps someone was, at last; but trusting her would not come easily.

Indeed, it may seem less than likely that Derek would accept anything offered by Lucia Luteplucker, in view of his long held stock of doubts and worries regarding her and her treatment of him. But he had wanted to be an English professor since his high school days and now, pushing forty, was still unable to conceive of practicing another occupation. So while he continued to harbor suspicions, which sometimes seemed to him preposterous, regarding his former adviser, her offer was opportunity knocking, the only one he had.

Had he thought a little harder, he might have had an inkling of the role she meant for him to play.

The next day, entering his ESL classroom Derek found a short Asian man addressing the students in the lingua franca they used among themselves. Whatever he was saying, it made them hold their breaths and hearken to every word he uttered or rather, so it seemed to Derek, snarled.

"May I ask," Derek began, but was not allowed to finish.

"I'm working here now," the man said, without a trace of accent. "English wants to see you. Now. Do not delay, Rosenthal."

"Blum."

"No!" shouted Mr. Feng, addressing him. "You no go! Please!"

He pointed at the new teacher. "Bad man! Bad man!"

The bad man placed his hand on Rosenblum's shoulder and pushed him toward the door. He proceeded to English, just down the hall.

The secretaries there acted as if they had been waiting for him. He'd been awarded a departmental grant, they said, in an amount equal to his teaching salary. It was to support him so that he wouldn't have to teach while working on his new project. Greatly excited, they beamed at him.

Where did the department find these little women? Two peas in a pod. They finished each other's sentences. He didn't trust them. He trusted no one, excepting perhaps Sheldon Glick, who scorned to lie.

"Wait," said one secretary.

"We almost forgot to tell you," continued the other.

And then the first again: "You're an assistant professor now! Professor Rosenthal!"

"Blum," he snapped.

Two years of dealing with these people, and they didn't know his name. As for his new title of assistant professor, that was surely Luteplucker's doing, and he didn't like it. It was just to make him seem a bit less unimportant to the audience for her section. *She* thought he was unimportant, obviously. He would revert to being a Heartland ESL Lecturer 1 as soon as this big do in San Francisco was over.

Soon, however, he got over his upset. He wouldn't allow anyone to address him as either Professor Rosenthal or Professor Rosenblum. Screw that. But money, money was different. He was being paid without having to work, just as if he were a real professor. Couldn't complain about that or about having extra time to spend on the paper that, if it impressed the right people, might take him to a campus where, unlike Heartland, he could have a fair shot at tenure. He was mindful of his old weakness, expecting good things that never came to pass, but what he wanted was nothing fancy, just a permanent job. In any case, what could he do but try? "Hope springs eternal in the human breast," wrote Pope.

What about Luteplucker, her interests? One thing he was sure he knew about her was that she had no interest in advancing his career. (He was wrong, actually.) She just needed one more person for her section on mock-epic, a traditional and therefore unattractive topic. Eight years ago, she had screwed him at this very same convention, setting him up for interviews with college representatives who didn't want him. This time *he* would schedule his interviews, with people impressed by his paper. How could she screw him then? If she even still wanted to.

And if no one was impressed? That was possible, no matter how good his paper was. Or if someone was impressed, why suppose this person's department would have any openings? Well then, back to bearable Heartland. But Derek had a feeling about this convention. Something would happen there for him. A job, he hoped that meant, but that wouldn't be all. Rapport with Priya? He hoped that, too, but he couldn't be sure about anything.

He ordered the *Scribleriad* from a Florida library that specialized in eighteenth-century texts other libraries had thrown out. It would take a week to arrive. While waiting for it, Derek could have done some reading on eighteenth-century science, the poem's subject, but that didn't attract him. What did was the genre to which both the *Scribleriad* and the *Dunciad* belonged: that of mock-epic. Rather than read what the critics had to say, he simply compared the examples he knew. The result was fresh ideas, so absorbing to Derek that he forgot to report to Campus Security one duty day and was chewed out by Sarge later in the week.

Derek had always accepted the handbook definition of mock-epic: i.e., a mean-minded poem that satirizes the poet's contemporary world by alluding to the distinguishing features of the ancient epics: decades-long battles, perilous sea voyages, foundings of nations, pokings out of giants' eyeballs, and so on. And gods and goddesses, of course; thus, instead of Zeus or Hera, in the *Dunciad* Pope gives us Dulness. Imported by these allusions, the heroic ancient world serves as a positive norm, contrasted to which the present, the satiric poet's target, looks even dirtier, stupider, and uglier than if the epic allusions weren't present. Usually excepted from this description is Pope's *Rape of the Lock*, whose present-day world seems kind of pretty; for which reason the poem's admirers have done their best to deliver it altogether from the low rent neighborhood of mock-epic.

But now Derek conjectured that sometimes the satire could flow the other way, with the ugly present lowering and staining the no longer pristine past. He recalled a passage in the *Dunciad's* second book that depicts Jove squatting on an eighteenth-century commode. Which does that lower, the gabinetto or the god? Derek also supposed that the classical allusions may occasionally lend dignity or even beauty to some aspect of the poet's present-day world. Does this not happen in the *Rape of the Lock*, a mock-epic, after all?

Derek was thinking for himself. He found this exercise invigorating. One byproduct was a strengthened determination to be unafraid of Lucia Luteplucker or to care about her in any way.

Though he no longer taught, he still had to stand inspection before the commander on the several Fridays preceding the conference in San Francisco. Since he could now be sure she knew who he was, he showed up for inspection wearing his own badge instead of that of Davis or McGilvray. In ranks Luteplucker looked him up and down, but still did not say his name. Irked, he stared at her breasts more overtly than ever. When she turned from him to Greenberg, he lowered his head and followed her rotating buttocks. He let his uniform grow wrinkled by not hanging it up and his gig line twisted, to express his resentment at having to spend twelve hours a week playing cop when he had something much more important to do.

But there was time enough, certainly, especially since he'd decided to give himself a break from reading the minor works of Pope. There would even be sufficient time, once he'd finished the paper, to practice delivering it clearly and loudly; for he imagined himself reading in a large, scholar-crammed lecture hall. He felt confident. His ideas about mock-epic were revolutionary. It was only necessary to get them down on paper in connection with Cambridge's *Scribleriad.*

A Wandering Dunce

When, however, the *Scribleriad* arrived, it proved to be an awkward sort of thing, chronicling the adventures of a wandering dunce named Martinus Scriblerus. Just explaining what the poem was about—to an audience, however scholarly, that had probably never heard of it or of its author—would take time, and Derek had only fifteen minutes. How would he find room for his recent insights about the genre?

In the poem, Cambridge attempts to criticize the coldly impersonal approach he thought typical of scientists. That was interesting, or could have been. Unfortunately, most of the *Scribleriad* was a dull parade of allusions to classical epic with scant reference to anything happening when it was written, so that it was only occasionally satirical of contemporary science or of anything else.

Eventually, however, Derek came across a passage that he liked. It was not satiric. Having survived a series of goofy adventures, the brainless Scriblerus visits a strange land whose queen falls in love with him. When he sneaks away, she kills herself, an act uplifted into genuine tragedy, rather than being lowered in some way, by the unmistakable allusion to Vergil's tale of Aeneas's desertion of Dido, who then kills herself. Derek was moved, he felt sorrow. This surprised him. It had been a long time since any poem, except for the dangerous *Dunciad*, had mattered to him other than as a possible subject for a two-page note.

Despite the fantastic setting, Derek read the queen as one victimized by the anti-human scientific temper of Cambridge's real place and time. For besides being thwarted in love, the queen is gravely ill, but callous scientists, fascinated by her medical problems, think of her only as a specimen. One such problem is the hideous Plica.

> Her head th'inextricable Plica grac'd,
> Whose folds descending, veil'd her beauteous waist,
> Then length'ning downwards, form'd a regal train,
> And swept, with awful majesty, the plain.

What was this Plica? In a note, for Cambridge imitated Pope's practice in the *Dunciad* of writing pseudo-scholarly footnotes, he explains that "Plica Polonica" is a "matting together of hair" upon the ill-groomed heads of the rural poor, a condition "epidemical in Poland."

Her grotesque disfigurement? To the scientists, fascinating. Her broken heart? Who cares? This was the perspective loathed by Cambridge. Derek found himself in agreement. In his paper he devoted a few sentences to the Plica.

At this time Sarge told Derek to go to Luteplucker's office and take his paper with him, as much as he had written. He brought it in the next morning and waited as she glanced through it. As she read, she frowned. Intent on clearly expressing his ideas, he hadn't thought to use the current critical jargon with which he had larded his abortive notes on Pope. Perhaps this omission displeased her,

However, the dean said nothing about his un-hip style. Her only direction was that he do some research and write more, much more, on the fascinating Plica Polonica. He knew this would be a waste of his time. That the Plica was a big, stinky mess was all his hearers would need to know. Moreover, he was quite sure that Luteplucker would eventually have him delete all mention of the Plica, reserving it as material for one of her little notes. All right, she could have it. Surely he would need to spend less time in the library on Plica Polonica than he had regarding the famous Admiral Vernon and the Battle of Porto Bello. There was less to be known.

In his brief discussion with the dean there was none of the creepy vision across the planet stuff that he recalled from their earlier session. Whatever odd power she had, it wasn't working that day, not on him.

Leaving the office, Derek found Priya Jackson waiting in the hall. Though he'd always looked for her on campus, he hadn't seen her and wondered if she was avoiding him.

"Hello there," he said. "You're doing this mock-epic thing, too, huh?"

Priya nodded, but said not a word. She entered Luteplucker's office with remarkable speed, as if she were gliding on wheels. He might have supposed she was rushing to get away from him, but just as she whisked through the door, she turned her dark eyes upon him. They seemed sad rather than scornful, and they made Derek feel sad, too. He remained in the hall for several minutes, but Priya didn't emerge. So he went to the library. He didn't see Priya again on campus that day or later.

Derek found the Plica not uninteresting, if thoroughly disgusting. Plica Polonica, aka Polish Plait, results from never washing or combing one's hair, which becomes matted, stinky, and encrusted. Lice get in there, too, and party hearty. So what you've got is a tangled mass glued together by a hard-drying cement made of pus, blood, dirt, and deceased lice. It was especially common among peasants, but the upper classes were hardly spared. Even a king had it, Christian IV of Denmark (1577-1648), who had his portrait painted with a long, goopy plait dangling down on the left side of his head. His courtiers all grew plaits, too, making Copenhagen the Plica capital of seventeenth-century Europe.

The connection with Poland is that it was considered good luck there to have a plait and bad luck to cut one off. Therefore the plaits of Poles achieved astonishing lengths. Samuel Johnson's intimate, Hester Thrale, visiting Dresden, saw one (separated from its host, a Polish woman who had died) that was fourteen feet long and so could easily have "swept, with awful majesty, the plain." Though his audience at the convention wouldn't know who Cambridge was, they would all know of Mrs. Thrale. Should he put her and the lengthy plait in his paper? Why bother? Luteplucker would seize that too.

And as Derek expected, one week before lift-off for San Francisco, Sarge ordered him to leave the paper for her at the English Department and to return for it on the following day. When he did so, he found a paper-clipped note instructing him to remove all Plica references and to resubmit the paper thus trimmed.

He obeyed. The paper he finally left for her contained not a solitary mention of Plica Polonica. He was determined, however, to stick at least one back in when he delivered it, the quotation about the queen's "inextricable Plica." It was his prime example of science's chill perspective. More importantly it was part of Cambridge's story of Martinus and the queen, with its allusion to that of Aeneas and Dido. As such it was, he thought, a superb example of the power of epic allusion to elevate the most unpromising material. That was one of his major ideas about the mock-epic genre. Perhaps a new Rosenblum Thesis? He would see how it was received.

If mentioning the Plica in the paper when he delivered it made Luteplucker unhappy, too bad for the dean. He no longer particularly cared for her approval. Though he had stopped shining his shoes and belt buckle, he himself wasn't dull. Perhaps he had been at times, but not now. Wait till they heard his paper.

Departure

Their plane, bound for San Francisco's neighboring city of Oakland, left from a nearby airport. While Lucia Luteplucker lounged in first class, Derek flew tourist. So did Priya. When Derek saw her, he forgot about the awkwardness between them and headed for the empty seat next to hers. Quickly she threw her arm across it. Staring straight before her, she refused to acknowledge him. He found a place next to a drunken shoe salesman. His big convention had just concluded. Derek's lay ahead.

After all this time, it seemed small of Priya not to forgive him for what he had scrawled. It was such a little thing, really, just three short words that didn't at all express his true opinion of her *Fan* paper. In fact, her essay's lucid style had been a model for his own in his work on the *Scribleriad*. Now, that was a serious compliment, one she would hardly be able to resist, if she would only let him talk to her. Eventually she would. Being in Luteplucker's section with Priya might be uncomfortable at first, but she could hardly refuse to allow him to explain about "this is shit." A pleasant, adult conversation—that's what he needed. He warmed up for pleasantness by practicing his smile. The salesman thought Derek liked him and proceeded to share his copy of *Penthouse*.

Arrival

They paused first in Salt Lake City, where the salesman staggered off the plane, then in Las Vegas. In each location, they sat on the tarmac a while and were forbidden to use the rest rooms. Inconvenient, but Heartland was picking up the tab for the flight. Reaching Oakland at 1:00 a.m., two hours behind schedule, all were bade good night and good luck by hostesses too tired to smile. Derek watched Professor Luteplucker and Priya get into a limo, obviously prearranged, which purred smoothly away, headed for the Bay Bridge and San Francisco. Buddies now?

Derek needed to go to the Green Lantern Lodge, on Capp Street in San Francisco's Mission District. The university had declined to pay for his hotel, and the Green Lantern was the cheapest place on the official list of places where convention attendees might stay. The convention itself was being held at a far ritzier establishment, the Sir Walter Raleigh Inn, that he couldn't possibly afford. When making his reservation, he'd asked how to get to the Green Lantern from OAK and was given instructions as follows: (1) from airport take minibus to nearby Bay Area Rapid Transit station; (2) take BART train to 16th and Mission Street station in San Francisco; (3) get a cab if one is waiting by the station; if not, walk one block south to Capp Street, turn left and look for address; (4) while walking, guard valuables.

These instructions would have been easy to follow, but since both minibus and BART had stopped running at midnight, Derek was obliged to take a cab all the way to San Francisco. This wiped out a large portion of his funds. Having recognized Derek as an academic (cord jacket, khakis), the driver mentioned that he had a Comp Lit degree from UC Berkeley. Busy figuring how much money he would have left after paying the fare, Derek ignored this inducement to literary chat. The driver, obviously miffed, insisted there was no such place as the Green Lantern Lodge, and when they reached Capp Street made Derek get out of his cab.

Despite the lateness of the hour, Capp was heavily trafficked, and as Derek walked eastward he was accosted by two local entrepreneurs offering "blow" and a suspiciously tall and deep-voiced prostitute in a miniskirt. Trailing his wheeled suitcase behind him, he stopped twice to touch his inside jacket pockets, the left containing his wallet and the right his paper, folded lengthwise, "Richard Owen Cambridge: Low-Spirited Loyalist."

Luteplucker had insisted on the title. It was misleading, for Cambridge was neither a loyalist in any political sense nor a low-spirited person in his social life. He was a jolly fellow. If anyone was curious, Derek had prepared himself to say that the author of the *Scribleriad* was loyal, in fact too loyal, to the conventions of epic and was low-spirited about the relentless advance of science. He could hardly say what he really thought: that the dean must have a thing about double ells, as in *Lucia Luteplucker*. She had also insisted on the 'Laureate Little Known' in his dissertation's title; that this made sense considering Eusden's negligible career could have been an accident.

Double ells. Lewis Lozange. Recently in Luteplucker's office Derek had conceived the notion, without any evidence that she knew he existed, that the little Briton was one of her favorites. And had Lodwick Lvov, the deceased big shot of *Poetics Now*, been one too? Ridiculous. Still, it was odd, those two with their ells.

After a twenty-minute walk, Derek saw ahead of him a cluster of white males, all pounding on the ponderous front door of what he took to be the Green Lantern Lodge. There was no lantern of any color, but the address was right. Just as he reached the hotel, its door was opened by an employee, rubbing his eyes. Derek trundled in his case, waited in line, was eventually given a plastic card that admitted him to a small, but clean room. He showered, then sat naked on the bed and began to read his paper aloud. After three pages, the party in the next room banged heavily on the wall for silence and he finished in a whisper. He'd timed himself. Almost seventeen minutes, when he was allotted only fifteen. Back at Heartland his record was 15:09, so what was making the difference?

He must be tired after the long trip, and that was making him slow. Though he didn't feel tired, he nonetheless got between the sheets after calling the desk and asking for an early morning wake-up call. He would walk to the convention. No more budget busting taxis if he could help it.

He tossed a bit and then slept poorly. In the morning he knew that he had dreamed, but he couldn't remember about what. Once, waking in the night, he heard a blaring sort of noise that might have been produced by an unskilled musician trifling with a large horn. It seemed to come from a place near him, and Derek considered banging on the wall and telling the guy in the next room to knock off the tuba practice, but the sound soon died away. Perhaps that had been a dream.

No, Derek. It was real.

Welcome, Scholars

For in the morning, waiting at the convention hotel for a session to begin, Derek heard others in the audience talking about the strange sound they'd heard in the night. Everyone was curious. It could well have been that every meeting room in the posh Sir Walter, fully booked for the week by the Association, was the scene of a similar discussion.

"It went like this," asserted one silver-haired gent, addressing another who also claimed to have heard it. "Like this: *blaat*. If you really heard it, you'll know what I mean."

"Well," said the other, who resented being put on the spot. "Certainly I heard it. It woke me up, didn't it? But it had more of a 't' sound, like this: "*tuuut.*"

"*Blaat*. Not *tuuut.*"

"No. *Tuuut* is correct," claimed a Professor Secker of Charles University in Prague. "But before *tuuut* is also *ka* or perhaps *fa*. Is obvious."

The *blaat* man walked out in a huff.

Had anyone asked Derek to judge, he would have ruled for the prof from Prague as coming closest. *Ka* or *fa* + *tuuut*. Or possibly *ka* + *zoot*.

Yeah, *kazoot*.

But nobody asked him, and if someone had he might not have been capable of responding intelligibly, so startled was he by the presence of Spitfire College's Lewis Lozange, perched on a chair in a corner of the room. What was he, an ambassador from Thatcher to Luteplucker, from one dark queen to the other? From one incarnation to the other? Chilling thought, quickly dismissed. Derek focused on the college principal, whom he had strong reason to dislike.

"What are you doing here?" he demanded, assuming his part-time persona as a Campus Security trooper. The little publisher of ill-regarded texts was utterly unfazed.

"Graunt," he boomed. "Big one for travel. She loves us, thanks to old Bert. No thanks to you, Glick."

"Not Glick!"

To keep from committing violence upon him, Derek turned from Lozange without another word and seated himself across the room from his former head and principal. Soon every chair was taken, as the section scheduled for this, the nine o'clock hour, promised to be an interesting one. Of greater interest, for the moment, was the mysterious early morning sound. The scholars debated and fluttered their lips.

The four paper-deliverers who then entered and took their seats behind the table at the front were understandably confounded by the noise, misinterpreting it as a symphony of Bronx cheers directed at them before they had even begun to speak. Their section leader, who would not himself read a paper, slammed both fists on the table. That quelled the racket, which had been drawing curious stares from hotel staff passing in the corridor.

The name of this section, "Titling the Century," had appealed to Derek. While it could mean a lot of things, it had a nice, relaxed sound to it and contained no French words or made-up French words. Moreover, while many of the other sections at the annual meeting featured papers by job-seeking new Ph.D.'s and even mere grad students, the line up for "Titling the Century" boasted established scholars: Sibs Schwarz of Pasture State Agricultural and Industrial, Carla Little Falcon of Harvard, Sung Pong U of Lower Iowa Valley, and Simon "Hot Dog" Acres of the University of California, Surf City. Derek hoped to engage at least one of them after the session for coffee or a beer and conversation about vacancies in their departments.

In the event, he walked out after just two of the papers, which turned out to be about the titles of books rather than the century. The first, Professor Schwarz's, dealt with two famous poems of the period, Samuel Johnson's *The Vanity of Human Wishes* and Oliver Goldsmith's *The Deserted Village*. Derek guessed correctly that the paper's title, "Signifying V," referred to the V's in the title of either book. But when the lady from Pasture State insisted that the V's signified not only "vagina" (this was apparently a given) but also "void" and "valorize," Derek had trouble following her argument. In fact, he detected no argument at all and was tempted to ask why signifying V couldn't stand just as well for "vanity" or "vapid." Perhaps the paper would have made more sense to him if Prof Schwarz had not distracted him by constantly giggling at her own wordplay.

Derek was aware that critics now had license to be "playful," for why should only the writers, Joyce and Nabokov and their ilk, be so privileged? Too bad his own paper was damnably serious, especially in comparing the Plica-stricken queen to Vergil's Dido. But it was too late to revise, and he didn't think he could titter in the delivery without something funny to titter at.

While the audience had laughed along with Schwarz and called out, "Go, Sibs!" they fell abruptly silent when the next panelist, Simon Acres from UCSC, approached the podium. He was a man, a white man. So were three quarters of those he was about to address, but they looked on him with suspicion nonetheless. He would have to prove his bona fides. The book he'd chosen to talk about made a pretty good start.

His title was "OR or OO or NOKO? " referring to the constituent parts of the title of Aphra Behn's *Oroonoko*, first published in 1688. This book may be a novel and, if so, it would be the first novel. That no one can be sure about these points, because no one can say exactly what a novel is, did not detract from the present popularity of *Oroonoko*.

Behn's story centers on a slave insurrection in South America led by the title character, an enslaved African prince. In the late 1980s everyone was teaching it in both social science and English courses, and there were four different paperback editions and tons of criticism. It had everything: a female author, an African-American hero (sort of), evil white slavers and colonists, and shortness, under a hundred pages in every edition. Much of interest could be said about *Oroonoko*, but though Derek tried, he simply could not become involved in Professor Acres's discussion of three alternative pronunciations of the title and the hero's name, depending on which syllable was stressed. It seemed that underlying questions of hierarchy were involved. Jacques Derrida was invoked to settle the case, but succeeded only in muddling it further. This was a good thing, all felt.

Acres was not playful and the discussion that followed his paper was dull; there were no cries of "Go, Hot Dog!" But at least the group forgave him his whiteness and maleness. Derek made for the door. Whatever the others found exciting or even just interesting was not apparent to him. He wasn't sure it was all his fault, but this didn't make him feel any better. Since he had never become fluent in the theory-language these big shots spoke, he would only make a fool of himself if he tried chatting them up. Nor could he realistically expect to impress anyone with his plainly written paper on behalf of the unknown Richard Owen Cambridge and the pathetic queen. But he was here. He would read it.

Lucia Luteplucker's mock-epic section met at two that afternoon in a conference room much smaller than the large hall Derek had envisioned. Its title, "The English Mock-Epic, 1657-1782," lacked excitement and the dates signified nothing. Small wonder that at five minutes past the hour only three people had shown up to hear the three papers, Priya's, Derek's, and one written by a woman whose name he never caught. Chairperson Luteplucker was not yet present.

Cute little Priya, seated next to Derek, was considerably upset.

"This is shit!" she declared, seeming to speak to the nearly vacant room rather than to him. It was nonetheless an opportunity to set things straight.

"Look, I'm sorry about that," Derek said. "It was an act of impulse." He wanted to say more, much more. But when she took no notice of his apology, he realized she was referring to the present moment.

"How dare they?" Priya continued, referring, of course, to the abundance of non-attendees. Evidently an apology from him was not required, and her anger didn't affect her cuteness. It was quite amusing, this little woman snorting with rage, dark eyes aflame. It gave Derek a good feeling.

"Just wait till she shows up," Priya said grimly. This, however, gave Derek a bad feeling, as he knew who "she" was. The papers he had listened to that morning had diminished his confidence in his own work, and he was no longer so ready to face Luteplucker.

And at that very moment she entered the room, driving before her a platoon of cringing male professors. No retro section title could curb the power of the dean! Simon Acres was among them, still paying his dues. Presumably they all were. But how came a child to be present, caught up in the rout? Ah, no child, but Lozange, trying to keep up. They took their seats. The room was now entirely full.

"Hi, Lucia," Priya called, waving to the dean, who waved back, startling Derek. It was such a human gesture. Luteplucker ignored him, as he'd expected. He hoped that Lozange would ignore him too, rather than asking hostile questions after he read his paper and confusing him with Sheldon Glick. The group before him, distinguished scholars all, sat slumped in their chairs. Luteplucker had taken the spirit out of them. For Derek it was like being back at Spitfire. Briefly there descended upon him the same mental haze that hovered over the college named after a fighter plane. It passed as he watched the dean settle herself in her chair; now he simply felt uneasy.

He reached for his *Scribleriad* paper but felt in the pocket on the wrong side of his jacket and came out with his wallet instead. Distracted, he examined the photo of himself on his driver's license. What a goon! *This* is what they'd all be looking at while he read his paper? He looked frazzled in the photo, and he had less hair in front than he used to. His goony smile—who smiles for a DMV photo?—seemed that of a drug-addled person. He shoved the wallet back where it came from. The paper, where was the paper? Hoping that the now sizable audience before him hadn't noticed how he was pawing at himself, he yanked "Low-Spirited Loyalist" from the other pocket. It was badly creased, but he had it.

He proceeded to read it silently one final time, fearing that despite all his revisions he had committed some dreadful fuckup that would make everyone in the room convulse with scornful laughter. Priya nudged him with her elbow: it was rude being so obviously self-absorbed while the first panelist was speaking. Derek sat up straight. For a minute or two he was engaged by her subject.

This was the exceedingly minor eighteenth-century satirist Paul Whitehead. Perhaps he had written a few mock-epics. Derek didn't know. But if he had, the woman never mentioned them. She characterized this third-rater as a "lyrical libertine," and indeed her paper's title was "Paul Whitehead: Lyrical Libertine." Derek had never encountered the reader at Heartland, but undoubtedly she was a Luteplucker protégé.

As a libertine, Whitehead was interesting in a pathetic sort of way. He was associated with the Hellfire Club, Sir Francis Dashwood's gang of balling, blaspheming boozers, but as a servant rather than a full-fledged member. Grateful to Dashwood for keeping him around to observe the fun and occasionally to partake of it, the grateful poet repaid his patron by willing him his heart. This organ was kept in a jar eventually stolen by a thief who didn't know what was in it.

Interesting, yes, in its bizarre fashion, and Derek might have profited from hearing more about this man's pitiable life. Underemployed academics aren't the only ones to have it tough. But soon the woman reading began to busy herself "teasing out" the "trace" left by Wordsworth's "It is a Beauteous Evening, Calm and Free" in one of Whitehead's satires. That Whitehead had died when Wordsworth was only four and not yet published proved no obstacle to the paper's author, who perhaps was only seeking justification for calling the libertine lyrical. But it seemed senseless to Derek, forgetting that he himself had transcended mere chronology in his old essay, "Eusden's Subversive Vision," and he couldn't help tuning out. While he appeared to be listening, he perceived the woman's words only as a faint hum easily ignored, a harbinger of the teaching style he perfected in the fullness of his career.

Eventually the humming ceased and was followed by a few perfunctory claps. All eyes turned toward Priya, whose turn it was.

Her subject was the mock-epic *Lousiad*, written by the eighteenth-century mental case John Wolcot, better known by his pen name. Peter Pindar. While Derek hadn't read the *Lousiad*, he knew of it as the tale of an adventurous louse, modeled on the heroic Odysseus. Sounded like fun. But Priya delivered a paper so clogged with poststructuralist critical jargon that the poem supposedly its subject completely disappeared. In everything that mattered, "Liminal *Lousiad*" was several dimensions removed from the unmarketable clarity and plain sense of Priya's essay on Gay's *Fan*.

Consequently, it was about nothing. Her paper was only a collection of exotic-seeming names and other words and had Derek not been so nonplussed by this development in one who had seemed resistant to such infection, he might have recalled the boast of Pope's mind-destroying schoolmaster in *Dunciad*, Book 4, "Words we teach alone."

Instead of the stipulated fifteen minutes, Priya's paper took up almost half an hour. Toward its end Derek began to worry about having enough time to deliver "Low-Spirited Loyalist." The section's chairperson, the dean, who had not spoken a single word thus far, made no gestures urging Priya to hasten.

Finally she finished. Derek prepared to rise, but the audience, recovered from their initial lethargy, wouldn't let Priya go. Instead they burst into tumultuous applause, and several raised their hands. When called upon, they offered praise rather than questions.

Like Professor Acres, Priya had neglected to be playful, but she had far outdone the man from Surf City in importing theory and theorists. Though Derek had worried about being too serious in "Low-Spirited Loyalist," now he saw where his real problem lay. He had not poled through the swamp of signified and signifier, of Derrida and de Man, that Priya had evidently probed to its murky bottom. She had even referred to the celebrated "postfeminist" Lemaitre, now given the Christian name of Claudette, a person Derek believed he had invented.

Obviously, in neglecting to salt his paper with the magic words the group before him would expect to hear, he had committed a fatal error and, since he came right after Priya, his lack of professionalism would be even more apparent. To stop fretting about what couldn't be changed, he mentally rehearsed the series of actions he would soon be required to perform: rise up on feet, circle table, take place at podium. And read. Read what he had and sit back down. Then leave this place, where he didn't belong among these people. That was becoming clearer every minute. He could be sure now that he and Priya had no future together, and that saddened him. What she had done to herself made him sadder.

Derek sensed, however dimly, that Priya had made a choice. She had chosen to become dull, which she was not by nature. It was as if she had enrolled herself among the dunces who thronged the goddess's darkling plain, Surely Luteplucker had worked on her, tempted her, but she had given way. True, the dean had entered academe before the Gallic wave had crashed upon our shores, and her own specialty was writing skimpy notes stolen from students' forced researches. But it was evident from her protégé's performance that Luteplucker understood what "theory" could do.

It could do quite a lot. For dullness has compensations in this world, such as, for some, splendid careers in English. Though Derek regretted that Priya was no longer the person he had met that evening in the THUs, he could hardly criticize. She wanted what he, too, would like to have, a comfy professorship, but that would never happen for him. Nevertheless, he intended to read his paper, and as Priya continued to hold the floor, their section ran ever lower on time. He would have considerably less than fifteen minutes, requiring him to jabber like a monkey to get everything in.

Suddenly the room fell silent, for Luteplucker had risen from her chair. With all eyes upon her, she turned toward Priya and spoke her first words of the afternoon.

"Great job."

More applause followed. Priya nodded her gratitude. While Derek had been sad, now he was pissed. So his little paper would be different, not what they wanted. So let them sit there as he threw his plain words at their faces. Let them hate "Low-Spirited Loyalist"; he hoped they would. He stood up, pushed back his chair, and started around the table toward the podium. Priya still lingered there, drinking in the love; but when she saw him coming, grim-faced, she hurried to her seat.

Because of later events at the Sir Walter Raleigh Inn, what happened next in the meeting room left no lasting residue of resentment in Derek, even though he was understandably upset at the time.

For Luteplucker spoke again. "Thank you," she said, then turned and headed for the door. She swept the audience with her, along with the Whitehead panelist and Priya. Derek stood forlorn, leaning on the podium, gazing at the swiftly emptying room. It was a set-up. It was—ah, it was just what she always did. Now the anger in Derek gave way to despair. Again she had seemed to accept, almost to encourage, but in the end she rejected and humiliated him. She hadn't treated Priya that way, quite the reverse. What about him was different?

The answer was simple enough: as of that day's date he hadn't made Priya's choice, and that the goddess must have. But this was something Derek had never fully understood. Almost, but not quite.

Someone spoke. "Goodbye, Glick." Lozange, damn him.

And there Lozange was, passing through the door en route to the hotel bar, where a grant would pay for his martinis. But the person to whom the little Briton had bade farewell was the real Sheldon Glick, who must have entered the room singly, after the entrance of the Luteplucker-driven herd. Now only he and Derek remained.

Erect, frozen, Derek continued to hold the undelivered paper in his right hand. Finally he tossed its pages down. They scattered on the floor. Let them lie there! He would never offer that woman, any of them, another thing. But even as he swore this to himself, he felt the bitter sting of rejection and wished for a moment, without actually articulating the word to himself, to be a dunce and join their jolly party. Now he heard excited shouts as might be uttered by hyperactive morons vying for the attention of a presiding deity. The cries were merely those of scholars in a nearby room, happily hashing up some old book, but the difference was not easy to discern.

"Good opener," said Sheldon, having gathered up Derek's pages and read the first of them. That was nice. It was nice to be praised, even if the praise was premature. He should read the rest of it before he said anything more.

"Okay if I read the whole thing?" Sheldon asked.

"Now? Read if you must."

So his audience for "Richard Owen Cambridge: Low-Spirited Loyalist" would consist entirely of Sheldon Glick. It must be true that they had a special relationship, as Glick had kept on insisting in Padua. Well, it was better than having no relationships at all. He certainly hadn't one with Priya.

They entered one of the Sir Walter's three coffee shops, and found a vacant table. Glick read. When finished, he pronounced the paper good, very good. Derek was pleased, though he tried not to show it. To be grateful for such a little thing.

"Submit it," Glick advised. "*Poetics Now*, maybe. They like our stuff. But try using a more, uh, current vocab. Or play with the words a little. Like that Sibs Schwarz character."

"Oh, you were there this morning? Didn't see you."

"She read today? No. But she's got the rep. No, I was catching Chatham's thing."

"What? What thing? *Whose* thing?"

"Chatham's, at noon. Her big address. I was surprised not to see you. I'd thought you and I would be the only ones who would know what she was talking about, besides Lozange. I guess I was wrong. Packed house. But is it possible you don't know about it? It's the talk of the convention."

What was that name? Derek cast his eyes upward. Upon the ceiling appeared the outline of a perfectly formed female leg. To his ears came the distant strains of the Yorty High pep song.

Glick went on.

"It was about McGonagall, old Bert's guy. Remember? Worst poet in the language?"

"It can't be," Derek protested.

Sheldon thought he was referring to McGonagall as a subject.

"Oh yeah it can. I didn't understand everything she said, but it was basically a defense of awfulness. See, awfulness is going to be so important that the Association didn't care about McGonagall not being an eighteenth-century person. It's important because without something that's extremely bad, how can anything be really good? For the *différance*, you know, and there's gotta be a "trace," like they say. So she found traces of "The Tay Bridge Disaster" in Shakespeare, Keats, Wallace Stevens—"

"Stop! Stop!" Derek jumped to his feet, startling Sheldon, who spilled his coffee.

"Hey, easy," Sheldon said, dabbing at the table with a paper napkin. "So it's totally crazy? It's all a game, right? Next year it'll be something else."

Cynical Sheldon. But had Derek not been so distracted by what he had just heard, he might have noticed how Glick's lips had narrowed as he spoke.

"First name," demanded Derek. "What's the first name?"

Sheldon misunderstood. "You know," he said. "William. William Topaz."

"*Her* name. Who read the paper. Chatham's. You said Chatham?"

"Right, yeah, I did. First name? Oh, one of those California last name-first name jobs. Kelly. Taylor, Madison. Something. I can't think with you breathing on top of me like this. No, wait. I know."

They said it together. "Tracy."

"Yeah, that's it."

"Gotta walk," Derek said.

He left the room and slowly paced the corridor. Oddly, his immediate response was to realize, with no little envy, how rapturously Tracy's McGonagall paper would be received nationwide after its appearance in some distinguished journal. As the ultimate reputation repair job—*his* forte he'd thought—it would dazzle all of English with its grand scope and make every critic grateful. Think of all the poets, whenever they lived, who were thought good and got in all the anthologies only because they had unconsciously loaded their poems with McGonagall allusions for professors to unpack. Derek now realized that others in the coffee shop had been talking about the paper. Its author would surely be one of the stars of the convention, along with Priya Jackson.

Yes, it was his Chatham, cheerleader Tracy, high-kicking belle of the b-ball court. Given how screwed-up his life was, it *had* to be. Thinking of her, he felt then a sense of loss, which seemed to him to make no sense. It was not as if he'd ever had her.

But high school crushes can last a lifetime, and Derek's memories of Tracy, painful as they were, had helped to keep him in the realm of flesh, which has its own warm light. Priya might have helped him there, too. Now, in a few hours' time, he had lost them both to the dark other of academe, dusty shelves, nodding heads, endless wordy foolery. Sad to say, that dull world still tempted Derek, despite his experiences that day. It might have been otherwise had he entered the chapel with Sheldon, but who knows? Indeed, by the time he had nearly circled the floor, he was thinking of how best to approach either woman, so that they might assist him in his academic career.

Rather heroically, he caught himself. He remembered. Maybe he didn't want a career in academe. No, surely he didn't. The papers he'd made himself listen to that day had each worked against what had drawn him to literature as a boy. He could still respond in that way, too. The death of the queen in the *Scribleriad* had moved him, hadn't it? He was still capable of registering feelings. They couldn't, those others. Words were all that they could register.

Idly, he wondered what had happened to Tracy to put her on the fast track to academic stardom. The girl he remembered from Yorty High couldn't have gone straight from cheering to literary theory, and she had been an unwilling reader, anyway. Was this the work of Dean Luteplucker? Was Tracy one of her products? If she had been at Heartland he would have known, would have sensed her; but a Luteplucker disciple or a disciple of a disciple might easily have laid hold of Tracy. Derek knew there were many such rooted in English departments across the land, rivaling in number the dunces of Pope's creation. Perhaps one of them had infected Tracy, vampire-like, in an intro to lit class at Santa Monica City College. If that was the case, no wonder he'd never encountered her in his Venice barhopping days. She was holed up someplace reading theory, forgetful of her remarkable physical gifts. Somewhere she had learned of William Topaz McGonagall, and then had followed her invention of what would soon be known to all as the Chatham Thesis.

So now she was dull. So was Priya dull. And everybody thought they were wonderful. How could such things happen without someone or something behind them? Dulness lived. No doubt she took on different forms for different persons, places, times. Because of his own lengthy acquaintance with the *Dunciad*, he saw her in his imagination and his dreams as Pope had in the poem. Maybe she had a basic, fundamental shape. Or shapelessness. He hoped he never got to see it.

Why did she do it, make dunces out of people, some quite intelligent before she got to them? Easy question. Like any other deity, she wanted worshipers. Harder question. Derek considered it for only a moment. What would happen if everyone in English, from top to bottom, from Yale to the tiniest community college, became a dunce? Would the machinery keep on running, turning out stupefied students and gobs of nonsensical criticism forever and ever? Or would something drastic and sudden take place? Did she want that, too?

He had a feeling that the *Dunciad* held the answer, but he wasn't going to look. Why should the fate of English matter to him? He was getting out. He would be no dunce. No, Ma'am.

When Derek returned to the coffee shop, he found that Glick had changed his mind about "Low-Spirited Loyalist."

"No," Sheldon said. "Don't change anything. I like it the way it is. You don't need all that junk."

But this time he didn't say to send it to *Poetics Now*. He knew, they both did, that the fancy review would never take it. It was irremediably unfancy. Years later Derek did send the paper out, because he wanted to be promoted to full professor. Despite its unfashionable simplicity of statement, it was accepted by a journal little regarded but good enough for Enola Gay State. But then as he sat with Glick, styro cup of coffee cooling in his hand, publication and promotion meant nothing to Derek. He had other things on his mind.

Indeed, he was experiencing something quite unusual for him, a fit of introspection. First, he considered his relationship with his friend, Sheldon

Glick. He fully understood for the first time, having been misled till then by his fellow scholar's Brooklyn smarty-pants act, that Sheldon really was his friend. He was being sincere in praising the *Scribleriad* paper, rather than just trying to buck him up. But he was doing that, too. Sheldon was definitely on his side. Why had he detested him?

It was all of a piece, Derek felt now, with the stupidity of his life. The goddess was real (it simplified everything to premise that), and he had spent too many years attempting to please her, most recently by scrawling jargon-filled notes. That English as a whole was doing the same thing made his personal situation no less dire. It was, however, different. He'd had his periods of dullness, had indeed enjoyed them. But in time something welled up inside him that said "no." Was that why he had nothing to show for a lifetime spent as either a student or a teacher? Certainly there could be no greater contrast with his present hapless plight than Priya's reward for becoming a spouter of gobbledygook: "Great job" and, inevitably, a great job. Tracy, of course, in exchange for having given the profession a brand new way to analyze every text in the language, could go anywhere she liked.

If advancement in English meant submitting to the goddess, as Priya had, someone who couldn't submit or stay submitted, like himself, would never get anywhere. But what if that voice within him fell forever silent? He had no guarantees that it wouldn't. If that should happen, though he might qualify for a job, he wouldn't be himself. Not that he was much. But still.

He would give up English altogether. She would leave him alone then, he hoped. He couldn't be sure, for he had never understood her interest in him. The old question. Why me?

Oh, by the way. If not English, what? He doubted he was smart enough to do things with computers, but maybe his old friends could teach him, if they remembered who he was. Worry about it later.

Something was weighing down one of his jacket pockets. Inserting his hand, he felt the wrinkled pages of his undelivered paper. He'd picked it up after Sheldon's editorial verdict and stowed it away without thinking. He left it there. He saw that his friend was studying a little yellow card.

"Big speech tonight," Sheldon said, raising his head. "Not going, are you?"

"No," Derek said. That was what his friend expected him to say, but since he didn't know what he was saying no to, his tone betrayed a lack of certainty. What big speech?

Sheldon was unsatisfied, therefore. "You're not?"

"Not? Not what?"

"Wake up, Derek! Why do I always have to tell you things? Not going to the plenary address, the big fucking deal. And it's Luteplucker! Sure dissed you today, killing the section before you said a word."

"Now wait. *She's* giving the plenary address? She's not in the program. It's a man."

"This is new. See this card?" Sheldon waved it at him. "Just printed. She got hold of the guy who was supposed to speak and ten minutes later he'd packed his bags and left. Big shot, but she had something on him. You know, she hears things, knows things."

"I know, Sheldon. I know about that. Hey, you think I'd go to see Luteplucker after what she did to me? I never want to see her again as long as I live."

Never? So important in his life, and now never to be seen again? The thought upset him, which he knew was crazy, considering how she'd mistreated him.

"Maybe we should diss her back," Sheldon said. "Maybe we should go and make noises like all those guys were doing this morning imitating that sound they say they heard. Well, I didn't hear it."

"Well, I did." But Derek wasn't interested in the sound.

"I get it," he said. "She gets rid of the scheduled speaker. She makes the big speech."

Sheldon nodded energetically. "Yeah," he said, "Yeah. About little, meaningless shit, I have no doubt. I've read a few of those notes she does. The one on Admiral Vernon wasn't too bad."

"That was mine," Derek informed him. "She took it."

"Yeah? Anyway, I don't care what she talks about. I'm not interested in anything she says."

"Well, I'm going home, tonight. Change my ticket."

"Tonight? You pissed off at the whole convention?"

"I'm pissed off at English, the whole fucking industry."

Sheldon said only, "Well, *I'm* not going tonight."

As if Sheldon thought he, Derek, still might.

"I'm certainly not," Derek said.

But they didn't exchange home addresses or phone numbers, as if they knew they would be seeing each other again soon.

Part Four

The Convention Rocks

A nd so that evening at seven o'clock Derek was one of hundreds in the Sir Walter's capacious 49er Room. Though he was curious regarding the subject of Luteplucker's address, that wasn't nearly enough to prevent his intended departure. It was that old gravity of her, her power to attract. During the recent weeks at Heartland he'd thought her influence on him had declined, and perhaps it had. It may be that the events of the day, including the defection of Priya and the startling news about Tracy, had restored it. In any case, here he sat, where he'd assured Sheldon he wouldn't be.

The audience was here, but the plenary speaker wasn't. No doubt she was cruising the halls, seeking additional eighteenth-century scholars to corral for her address. Derek looked over his surroundings. Rather than memorabilia of the Gold Rush of 1849, the walls of the 49er Room were tastefully decorated with team photos of the great Frisco 49ers football teams of the 80s and portraits in oil of their star players. Derek noticed Lozange standing rapt, head held back, beneath the life-size likeness of 320-pound offensive lineman Bubba Paris. Above them all dangled a huge chandelier in the shape of a football.

Again a clattering of hooves. Derek was surprised not to see Luteplucker at the rear of the company, driving them on, but perhaps she planned a delayed entrance for dramatic effect. Observing that a few of the new arrivals hadn't found seats, he briefly considered giving his to some aged professor and clearing out. He couldn't; she held him. Maybe if Sheldon were there, they could have left together, but Derek hadn't picked him out in the crowd. Nor had he noticed Priya, who would certainly attend a lecture given by her patroness. Tracy too, probably. He was sure he would recognize the former cheerleader, and just as sure that she would have no idea who he was.

Suddenly Luteplucker stood before them clad in her black trousers, jacket, boots: her usual costume except on inspection days at Heartland when she donned Campus Security blue and affixed a little pistol to her belt. If she had the firearm with her now, it was concealed. The 49er Room contained a stage occupied by a wooden podium and a large chair upon which she now seated herself. This chair, strongly resembling the queenly prop Lozange had found for Thatcher at Spitfire, seemed to interest Lozange. After leaping upon the stage, he examined it closely while all others in the room sat in rigid silence. When he spoke to Luteplucker, she nodded in response. He handed her a slip of paper, which she tucked away in some corner of her costume. Derek suspected a Bert Bangles poem of praise.

Whatever some dunce had to give her, she was happy to accept, but she wanted nothing from him, not really. Nor had Thatcher. Probably because he had just seen Lozange in action, he thought of her. He had come within inches of that great lady, and then was thrust away. For a moment the two mortal women merged for him into the gigantic figure of the poem and of his dreams. He shook his head, where this vision was, and made it leave him.

They didn't want him. She didn't want him. So he thought. He was mistaken. She did, she did want him, but first he must want her, permanently. You understand? How could you not? Though torn, he had resisted just enough. His was a special case. He meant something. Something depends on him. Am I boring you? I almost hope I am. I've given a sufficiency of hints. Even slow Derek, almost gets it.

What would you do without me? Without me to tell Derek's story, Derek's struggle, there would be nothing for you to read. And that time is coming. Listen for my posterior trumpet's final blast. Listen carefully. So many now are deaf. Now, back to the 49er Room.

Lozange skipped from the stage. Rising majestically from her ornate chair, Luteplucker strode to the podium, a sheaf of papers in her hand.

"Plica Polonica," she began.

The dean paused then in her speech and fingered an invisible button. Behind her a huge screen, previously undetectable, sprang brightly into view. Niner quarterback Joe Montana faded back to throw long. Luteplucker jabbed at the button again, morphing clean-cut Joe, whose hair was concealed by his helmet, into Christian IV of Denmark, he with the long, gooey lock drooping down on the left side of his face. Derek felt only mild surprise.

She was welcome to it. Why should he care? This was his last time with her. How ridiculous she was, with her black clothes and her air of mystery! He wondered how many among this sizable audience were even listening to her, distracted as they must have been by the succession of disgusting Plica cases flashed on the screen. The condition being prevalent even today in some shampoo-deprived regions, Professor Luteplucker had some striking contemporary headshots as well as eighteenth-century examples. For a while it seemed that she had left the period altogether.

She returned to it, but here Derek began to have trouble understanding what she was saying. There was some theory mixed up in it, the fashionable terms and theorists' names, but he also recognized some of his own plain words from the paper he hadn't been allowed to give—now he knew why—but they issued from her mouth in a monotone so deadly that she must have wanted to kill them. As a result they meant nothing, even to Derek, their author, as did the fancy terms and names. Words alone, drifting down from the podium.

Settling under them, Derek found a kind of peace. To really listen, respond, think—she made these actions almost impossible, but it was pleasant not to do them, soothing to do nothing except breathe. He looked about him. Though their eyes remained fixed upon the flickering screen, the others in the 49er Room might have been asleep or even dead, for all the animation they showed. In no other line of work could one obtain such a comfy blanket of words. To leave this world forever—ah, not so easy.

Then Derek dozed. Then all did. Luteplucker droned. Suddenly she ceased. The sleepers woke but remained half lying in their chairs, faintly stirring. Now Derek felt a certain irritation. No one cared that she had stolen from him and committed murder upon his prose. He would stand. He would call her to account. No, he dared not.

The screen was blank and white, the room dead silent. Luteplucker had reseated herself. It appeared that the plenary session had ended with neither a speaker's traditional fond farewell nor a round of applause from grateful hearers. There was, nonetheless, some activity among them, but of a peculiar kind. Why were they tilting their heads back, why stretch their necks? Now Derek heard faint exclamations of dismay. He, too, looked up. High above them the giant football-shaped chandelier swayed gently fore and aft. The motion appeared to hypnotize everyone below.

Derek lowered his eyes. For a moment he closed them in order to concentrate on his breathing. Something was sucking up the air. He tried not to gasp. Opening his eyes, he glanced this time at Luteplucker on her throne. He observed her mouth, gaping in a monstrous yawn far outdoing the capacities of even the mammoth football players peering down from on high. Her gaping mouth, that was where the air was going. At least it seemed so to Derek.

More she had spoke, but yawn'd—All Nature nods:
What Mortal can resist the Yawn of Gods?

Caught up in what was clearly becoming a scene of great peril, Derek did not recall these lines from the *Dunciad*, not that it would have changed anything.

He stood up—it wasn't easy—seeking air to breathe. Luteplucker's mouth snapped shut. The air came back, too much of it, squeezing Derek back into his chair. Hearing a creaking sound above him, he lifted his head and saw the football chandelier jerking strongly up and down, first one end and then the other. The same motion was going on beneath him. The floor was doing it. Suddenly his chair sharply tilted, and he almost fell from it. Somewhere an immense child was shaking a rattle. For a lengthy moment the sound filled the room. The disastrous Bay Area quake of 1989, the Loma Prieta, had begun.

Then all was utterly silent. Bits of glass flew at Derek from the blown-out windows on either side of the room. The towering video screen leaned toward Professor Luteplucker, who struggled to stand as the stage bounced beneath her. Even now she drew him to her, even as he told himself it was for the last time. Stumbling forward, he collided with others making for the doors. Lozange, damn him, was also rushing to help, and Derek quickened his pace. Both were too late. As the huge room rocked like a dinghy in rough surf, the screen collapsed on Luteplucker, concealing her from view.

Now Derek could hear. He heard the screams of those slashed by dagger sharp fragments of glass, though he himself was spared. He heard the thuds of combat as scholars of all sexes kicked and punched one another, each individual struggling to reach the doors before the rapidly swaying chandelier came crashing down. Time to go, Derek knew, but not there, into the melee. Was there another way? He considered the spaces where the windows had been. Too bad he was on the tenth floor.

He checked his pocket. The *Scribleriad* paper was still there. He regarded the fallen screen, which occupied most of the stage. It must have weighed several tons. Goodbye, Lucia. All he felt concerning her, in the moment he could spare before fixing on his own welfare, was relief. Why had he raced Lozange to rescue her? She had never been his friend, and now, after stealing his research and his very words, she was gone. His life would be different without her, though in what way he could not imagine.

But now it was only necessary to take care of himself in what was surely a major earthquake, to act quickly before even greater danger loomed. Nonetheless, he remained unwilling to penetrate the struggling mob at the doors, even though many were old and weak—some fat, some thin—and he could easily have bulled his way through them. But their behavior shocked him. That scholars should act like savages!

"Help me, Glick!"

Lozange, of course. For just when the screen had fallen upon Luteplucker, the full-length portrait of offensive tackle Bubba had flown from the wall and landed upon the head of the principal. Now his bloodied face protruded above the 49er's monstrous trunk.

"Help me, Glick!" he bellowed again.

Derek didn't now mind being mistaken for Glick, but Lozange was clearly beyond help, his blood having dripped as far as Bubba's number 77. It was best to aid those who had a chance of survival, such as himself. Nonetheless, he felt no little sorrow for his former boss, despite his being a pompous jerk, who was dying now upon a foreign shore. Was it any consolation to him to know that for a moment or two he'd had a body big enough to match his booming voice?

Lozange's would be the first remains extracted from the rubble of the hotel on the day following the quake, before being bagged up and air freighted to his grieving (hah!) subordinates at the Spitfire College of Higher Education.

"Goodbye, Lewis," Derek whispered, at the very moment the football-shaped chandelier finally dropped. It was the end of the principal. Several senior professors were also crushed to death. An additional score, though maimed and unable to walk, kept moving bravely forward at a crawl. They formed a slowly flowing streamlet of broken bodies, on top of which limped and hopped those colleagues who still possessed the faculty of bipedal motion.

Derek, heard cries of "Professor, you're standing on my head," and "Well then, move your fucking head." For his part, he did his best to avoid all heads and other organs as he wended his way toward the salvation represented by the tenth floor elevators. Then an aftershock hit the room, knocking Derek down upon the intertwined forms of two elderly scholars, male and female. Rolling off them, he noticed that the male's pants were down, the woman's dress up. Immediately they began to hump, becoming one throbbing eight-limbed organism. It amazed Derek that they could do this during a killer quake, that they had even found space in which to do it amidst the piles of plaster and glass, mountains of overturned chairs. Rudely, he stared at them, provoking their wrath.

"Leave us be," ordered the woman.

"Yah," added the man.

Derek thought he knew who the man was, a renowned Austrian scholar, author of a brilliant analysis of Gray's *Elegy* according to the hermeneutics of Hans-Georg Gadamer.

"Yah, leave!" the eminence commanded. "We are consummating a life-long love."

"Better get a move on," advised Derek, trying to be helpful and kneeling so that they could hear him more easily. "Aftershocks, you know."

"Go!" they gasped together just as one hit, raining debris upon the couple, who ceased to throb. Derek stood up, noting his own miraculously undamaged condition; as far as he could see, his was the only living form left in the crumbling 49er Room, among many dead ones. He congratulated himself on his good fortune but thought it time to take his own advice. Yes, better get a move on.

In the hall outside the room Derek saw a crowd of convention attendees massed before a bank of four elevators. They pounded on the doors and thrust at the buttons while also pushing, hitting, and biting one another. Others had gone to ground, sitting and kneeling beneath three wide tables that lined the wall opposite the elevators and were sturdy enough not to be upended by the quake or its aftershocks. Closely jammed together, the professors there fought on by thrusting with their feet.

No one cared about anyone else. Each shriek of pain was followed by a roar or grunt of triumph. These ladies and gents, all career-long students of the English language as wielded by the great wits of their chosen century, now howled with the wordless tongues of beasts. Derek was amazed by the unflagging energy with which all either defended their own cramped spaces or clawed to gain an additional inch of territory. Contemplating the tumult, he thought of how exhausted all would be in the morning, those who survived.

Something jabbed his ankle. The elevator combatants had extended their range to his relatively distant corner of the hall, and a woman lying supine had kicked him with her high-heeled shoe. He trod on her thigh, trying to be gentle. She stretched up her other leg and thrust at his groin. He grasped her foot and twisted it. Her scream dismayed him, but he knew she was beyond reason.

Simon Acres, he of UC Surf City, appeared, treading on the massed forms. Suddenly he was pulled down into the ruck. Snaps and crunches followed.

"Duuude," pled he, with his final expiring breath. Nor was poor Hot Dog the only one to die as Derek looked on, horror-struck. Dreadful was the carnage. It would engulf him too. How could he escape?

If only she could arise and make them all be still and quiet, as in her seminars. That was her power. But the dean lay crushed beneath the screen, dead or dying, and he had been almost glad of it. How wrong of him! How greatly she was needed now.

There came a voice, but not hers.

"You will see," the voice began. The accent was that of Brooklyn, not quite "youse," but close enough for Derek to realize who was speaking. Of course, Sheldon Glick, come to help. Had he been in the 49er Room? Never mind that. But where was his friend? He could be heard but not seen, so dense was the crush in the hall.

"You will see," Sheldon repeated. Somehow these words held them, so that they ceased to struggle. He carried on.

"That is, if you will end this show of barbarism and look about you, you will see an inscription next to one or more of the elevator doors that says, approximately, 'In event of fire or other emergency, take the stairs.' Are the elevators even working? I don't think so. Well, I know I'm not at all important compared to most of you. I teach at Enola Gay State—go ahead, laugh— where I must do Armenian diaspora free verse and similar things. Here in San Francisco, I'm staying in a cheap hotel with sex workers, though not the one I've been searching for. But all this is by the bye. If you'll countenance a suggestion from one so lowly as I, why not take the stairs?"

All but Derek charged for the stairs, crashing through the heavy swinging doors that slowly closed behind the crippled last of them. The clamor of their passage gradually subsided as they worked their way down, headed for the lobby, if it still existed, ten floors below. Would they arrive or was part of the staircase now missing? How many would fall along the way? To obtain passage from floor to floor, would they need to pay such tolls as a chair's promise of promotion to a tenure-seeking, flowerpot wielding junior professor? Terrible things did, in fact, occur, too horrific to record.

Now they were alone, on the tenth floor, Sheldon and Derek.

"So," said Sheldon. "Okay, seeing as we've got a little sanity up here, let's go down."

He advanced to an elevator and pressed the appropriate button. Smoothly the door slid open. Derek followed him inside. He closed his eyes, having never liked elevators and almost wishing he too had taken the stairs. But Glick had seemed so sure. The door slid shut with a firm clunk.

As if reading Derek's mind, Sheldon said. "Hey, the worst that can happen is we get stuck for a few minutes. They make the cables strong on these babies. Relax, okay? We don't want any part of those guys."

He waved in the direction of the stairs. "Uh-uh."

Now Sheldon pressed the button marked 1. The elevator descended silently, but only for a short time before coming to a sudden stop. It started again, just as suddenly, but jerked violently up and then down. This frightened Derek, who fought not to show it. Sheldon kept his cool. How far they had moved in either direction was impossible to tell. When the elevator settled, its ceiling light blinked for a second or two and then went out.

"Well," Sheldon said in the darkness. "Looks like this is it."

What did he mean by that? Derek would have felt stupid asking, so he didn't.

Ten hours passed while they remained trapped inside their steel box, suspended between floors nine and ten. Occasionally the elevator, and therefore they, shuddered in a disturbing fashion, but this eventually became a welcome relief from simply hanging there. Many more hours than ten seemed to pass while Derek and Sheldon remained in the elevator. Later, recollecting their experience, they couldn't believe it had been that long.

For most of the time, whatever that amounted to in their mental clocks, the two eighteenth-century scholars, pioneering rivals in the infertile field of Eusden studies, sat or squatted on the elevator's chilly floor. Every now and then they would struggle to stand, edging up a wall backside first and leaning there until their legs grew tired, whereupon they slid back down. Eventually it became hard for either to tell at any moment whether he was sitting or standing or lying down. Occasionally one would become convinced that both were outside, suspended in the midst of a particularly dark night. In the real outside, the skies lightened and the morning came, but not for them.

At times they spoke, but rarely to each other. What each needed was his own intermittent babble, to assure the babbler that he still existed, even if unable to see his own hand or any other bodily part. Even when they touched themselves, they couldn't be sure it was human flesh they felt or, indeed, any substance at all. Neither made the faintest effort to listen to the other, but Derek later recalled Sheldon saying something about bullies in his high school roughing him up and his crime boss dad issuing some awful retribution. "You shunta done it, Pop," moaned Sheldon, betraying the fundamental decency that underlay his wise-guy persona.

And poor Derek, with his sad stories of imagined success and resulting failure, imagined profit and shattering loss! He talked and talked. Even rapt in his own stupor, Sheldon, poor Sheldon, begged him to shut up. Basketball demotion, Ivy League rejection, perennial underemployment. (Tracy's senior ball treachery, however, was not mentioned.) To this sorry list he added Mrs. Thatcher's indifference and this very afternoon the refusal of Lucia Luteplucker to let him read his paper, from which she had plagiarized.

Where was Luteplucker, anyway? Oh, she was dead, that's right. Probably she was.

But wait. It was bad that she was dead, if she were. What had been wrong with him to accept it so casually? He hadn't had a chance to think, that was all. Too much going on. Nonetheless, he felt shame. He also felt blessed. For he was safe, while so many others were not. He had survived chaos without a single scratch. It was a miracle, and it was her doing. He couldn't think of anything else. Somehow, in some way, she had preserved him once again, just as she'd kept him going for years and years. Which meant she had plans for him. Which meant she was alive. For what could kill her?

Of what did her plans for him consist? What was his destiny? She'd let him know when it suited her. There was no point in thinking about these things. And it was worse to complain or protest. Now he regretted griping about not getting to read his paper and being plagiarized.

"I'm sorry," Derek said.

"Oh," said Sheldon. "Did you do something?" But, of course, he was not the one addressed. For a moment Derek had forgotten that his friend was there in the elevator with him, but when Sheldon made a noise, a gasping noise. Derek felt alarm. He inhaled deeply to prove to himself that he could still breathe. He fought off panic. Oh, where are you?

kazoot kazoot

Was that Sheldon? Or was that himself, Derek? Someone fetch a cork.

Their iron cell expanded with a soundless pop. Now there was light, sickly and yellow, but it illumined nothing that belonged in an elevator, the bare walls, the panel of buttons. What Derek saw, instead, was a writhing mob surrounding Sheldon and himself, and so for a moment he believed that the conventioneers fleeing from the 49er Room had somehow invaded their fastness. Now they would run out of air for sure. But college professors entrust their little bids for fame—the books, the articles—to the mail, whether snail or electronic, and the persons in this crowd were waving their offerings above their heads. Nor were they articles and books.

"A Nest, a Toad, a Fungus, or a Flow'r!"

Then Derek knew where he was, *Dunciad,* Book 4: the audience of Dulness, the convention of raging suppliants. And as in his second dream, he had no present for her. Oh, he still had his *Scribleriad* paper, safe in his pocket, but he could hardly give her that simple, pathetic thing. Where was she, anyway? Late again.

Sheldon Glick had hold of his arm and was pulling on it. Derek tried shaking him loose, but Glick held tight.

"We should go now," he pled. "We want no part of this."

He had a point. Here they were, part of the horde, with nothing to offer Her Who is Dull—except themselves. Yes, they should go.

But too late.

First came the ornate throne, smacking down out of the dim and gloomy skies. An instant later, with such a blast as might be made by a hundred tubas, she appeared and filled it. She, Dulness, this great woman, this goddess. Free of the husk of a mortal female, at last she appeared her truest self. Her flowing robe was the utter blackness of deep space. Across her broad face lay a dense barrier of commingled fog and cloud. This was reality, crashing through. This moment, he knew, would announce his true destiny, for she was here for him.

"Leggo my arm," he ordered Sheldon, who retreated in despair.

Derek gazed at the scrambling mob, the summoned nations. There had always been a mob, and everyone in it had always gotten ahead of him. They got what they wanted, he never did. Now, finally, he was able to see the picture whole. It was because he hadn't loved her enough, because his foolish obstinacy had kept him from recognizing how precious was the gift she had for him. But for that very reason, his final capitulation would be all the sweeter to her. How fortunate he was never to have rejected her entirely, not in his heart.

Thus did he dismiss the instinct that had caused him to resist her in the past. Thus did he give Dulness total victory. Already he felt the calm confidence she brought to those she loved most.

As the dunces continued to battle for the attention of the goddess, who saluted first one and then another, the sight caused Derek to wonder what was happening back in the hotel. Were the big shot professors still engaged in their combat, each against each? Eventually they would tire, if they didn't all perish amid the rubble. He was very lucky, Derek knew, he who deserved most just damnation. For she had forgiven him and come for him just when he had grown almost completely sick of a life that was one long scene of wasted effort. He had had nothing left and required absolute rest, but that was exactly what she had to give him. Sweet terminal repose. I am the One, Derek told himself. I am the Chosen One. I need no scholar's scroll. Just me.

All he had to do was say, "Take me, Goddess." So he said it.

Hearing this (at last!), she drew him toward her. Sheldon also felt the pull but resisted and cried out from the shadows, "No, no, Big D! Don't go. Do you really want to be dull?"

Readying himself for lift-off, Derek glanced at his friend.

"Yes," he said. "Yes. I do."

It would solve all his problems. To be accepted by Her. To be wrapped in her dark draperies and find the place of endless ease. In the past (oh, so long ago!) he had been in a fever to read books, talk about them, perhaps even write about what they meant to him. Now he knew that was the wrong approach. Finally wised up, he knew the secret of happiness. Pretend to read, talk, write, but don't actually do any of those things. Just focus on the words, signifying nothing. Think nothing. Wait. Then she will come.

And so he scrambled aboard the capacious welcoming lap. Supine he rested, contentedly he drowsed. The others in the gang far below gazed up at him with envy leavened with incomprehension. What was so hot about this guy? Just another feckless, word-mongering Ph.D. Plump and balding, and check out that stupid, global smirk. Poor fellows. They just didn't get it.

Hey, Goddess, they shouted. Look at my bird's nest! Check out my digamma!

She ignored them. He nestled, absolutely happy, knowing she was taking him to the place where he belonged. Where that place was he didn't know, never having been there, but it would be just right. He couldn't think of a fucking thing that was wrong or could go wrong. He couldn't think of a fucking thing. He couldn't.

"Take me, Goddess." He had said it, so she took him. There would be consequences.

Rosenblum Reborn

When liberated in midmorning, Sheldon and Derek were rapt in slumbers so deep that the rescue crews thought both were dead, making them fatalities ninety-two and ninety-three in the near total collapse of the Sir Walter Raleigh Inn. Placed on gurneys, each suddenly awoke, startling the first responders and catching the attention of the media. Neither said much, but though Derek couldn't think of a lot to say, he was polite to their questioners, while Sheldon rudely refused to utter anything besides an occasional curt yes or no.

As he was being interviewed, Derek noticed dark Priya and fair Tracy wandering past the long line of ambulances. They had survived the earthquake without injury and received none during the ensuing riot. Well, they were survivor types. It seemed to him that they were holding hands. They never looked his way. Both were headed for big things, while he didn't think he was; but they, all three, would gladly teach and go to meetings and do other stuff that professors do. Before getting stuck in the elevator, he'd thought becoming one was impossible for him, but now his prospects for employment seemed much less grim. Nothing specific. It was just a feeling he had. He watched the pretty ladies pull away. He wished them well, all the well there was.

"Uh, Mr. Glick?"

"Yes?" He didn't bother correcting them. It didn't matter what they called him.

He felt good, but not just because he was alive and unharmed while so many others had perished. Such satisfaction would have been only human, sure, but that wasn't it. He simply knew that things were going to be okay from now on. Yes, it was that simple.

"What did you think about in the elevator?"

"Think?" he replied. "Oh. I didn't do much of that. Mostly slept, I think. Was it really ten hours?"

Assured that it was, he shook his head. Had they asked him if he'd dreamed, rather than thought, he might have said that perhaps he had. At least he had this strange, hazy recollection of someone gaining access to their cage and assuring him that he need not worry, ever again, about anything. There may have been other people in the dream, he wasn't sure; but if so, he was the special one.

He was different upon waking, and so was Sheldon Glick, though not in the same way. Now Sheldon was grim and monosyllabic, quite the reverse of the quick-witted little guy Derek remembered. Maybe he was just upset, Derek thought, because the TV and newspaper people kept referring to them as Derek Glick and Sheldon Rosenblum. Whatever the reason, he wasn't fun anymore. It was a shame. Derek, however, had changed for the better, or so it seemed to him. Formerly desperate and anxious, sometimes quite irate about one thing or another, now he had a disposition that was sunny. No longer would it be his habit to imagine future successes that invariably turned out to be flops. No, in his post-Loma Prieta existence, he would just roll along, trusting that whatever happened would be good. Whatever is, is right. Now, who said that?

When told, after several weeks had passed, that there was as yet no trace of Lucia Luteplucker alive or dead, he said, "Oh. That's too bad."

At about the same time he learned that his friend, Sheldon, no longer wished to teach literature or teach anything and had asked the administration at Enola Gay State to let him serve out his pre-pension time on the campus gardening crew.

"Oh," said Derek. "That's too bad."

But not too bad for Derek. It turned out that the English Chair at EGSU was a great admirer of his work on Laurence Eusden, and thus he was offered the position that Sheldon Glick had chosen to vacate. The Chair's last name was Morton, so she just possibly might have been the M who accepted his seminal Eusden essay for *Poetics Now*, but he didn't bother to ask.

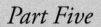

Part Five

Professor Rosenblum

Derek put in thirty-five tranquil years at Enola Gay. Early in his life there he published, in a little journal, his little paper on the *Scribleriad*. No one at the conventions he occasionally attended ever mentioned it, so he assumed it went completely unread. It was enough to gain him a full professorship, which was all that mattered. He had no further ambitions, so he never wrote anything else.

For some time he lived with a female assistant prof; when she left to become a wealth counselor in another state, he was unaffected. He didn't need anybody or anything, including money. When George and Mimi died, they left their professor son the store in Santa Monica as well as the condo in Malibu, both of which he sold. He was so well off that he didn't need to work, but he liked teaching. Well, it was hardly work, just sitting in class with his students. Giving them A's, as long as they kept their noses clean.

Derek never told anyone, but things had worked out so well for him that he was almost convinced he had some kind of guardian angel, a female one. The presence in the elevator who had assured him that all would be well just struck him as being female. Could that really be what she was, an angel? Once he asked Sheldon, who now wore a green uniform with "Shelley" inscribed over one of the pockets, if he remembered anyone visiting them; but his old friend turned and mounted his mower without a word.

I fit into this life, thought Derek. He thought this often. He was what he'd always wanted to be, a college English professor. There was absolutely nothing to worry about. Oh, his doctor tried to rile him, claiming that his blood pressure was too high. But how could that be? He never felt anxious or overly excited about anything.

Yes, his was a life of ease, and not just for him. It extended to the entire profession.

Nothing resembling the tooth and claw anarchy that overtook the professoriat in the Sir Walter Raleigh Inn ever happened again. What a hideous waste of energy, thought all the surviving participants, looking back. Such a senseless squandering! To make up for it, back on their home campuses the eighteenth-century scholars did everything they could to institute a permanent reign of calm. Everyone was surprised by how rapidly it spread to other areas within literary studies and soon reached beyond them. Oh, there was still some petty squabbling over parking privileges and office space, but everything always worked out okay.

Nor did the students cause any serious trouble, as long as they weren't overworked. What passed for acts of student rebellion in the nineties and after, often with a bow toward the activist sixties, were trivial events and went unnoticed by the media. Thus they served only to deepen the prevailing mood of quietus.

Something parallel occurred in the area of literary theory. Even before the time of the earthquake, an originally well-conceived resistance to the old New Criticism had spun out of control. Every reader could take on the writer's role, displacing the original pen or typewriter or computer. At first this had caused a flood tide of print to roll across the land. Soon, however, it became clear that if all were equally free in this way, no reading (which is to say, writing) could be either right or wrong, or even merely interesting except to the original critic. There seemed, then, to be no excuse for saying anything about anything, and the scholarly journals swiftly declined in both bulk and number.

English, more than any other subject, was easy and restful for students and professors alike. The Spitfire College of Higher Education had been ahead of the curve, but Enola Gay was just as nice, and everyone was nice to Derek.

He enjoyed his tranquil days and rarely thought of Lucia Luteplucker or Margaret Thatcher. He never thought about Dulness or assigned her poem in his eighteenth-century seminar, preferring Pope's lesser works such as "On a Lady who Pi—st at the Tragedy of *Cato*." That was always good for a few weeks. But somehow the *Dunciad* appeared on the reading list for what proved to be the last class he ever taught, and it surprised him, as if someone else had put it there. Nonetheless, he went bravely ahead with it. When they got to Book 4, that's when it got dark early and he ran out of his classroom.

Rosenblum Solus

He had been unable to rouse his students, who remained in the room, apparently asleep. Shelley the gardener had seemed neither to see nor hear him.

The prof looked up at the mid-afternoon sky. As he watched, it turned from dirty gray in color to black, with just a little gray in it. He'd never seen such a unidirectional transformation of the heavens, as if someone were turning a dial. Before his class, the sky had been blue.

Having walked in a circle around Bombardier Quad looking for someone, anyone, to tell him what was happening, now Rosenblum stood at its center beneath the flightless replica of the plane that dropped the bomb. He wished it would give him strength, but felt nothing of the kind. His legs were frighteningly weak, but the worst thing was having to be alone in the silence. Alone, except for such odd thoughts, bits of thoughts. My Empress. My Goddess. What the heck? Should at least be a campus cop in evidence somewhere. He'd been one once. He knew what they were supposed to do, help people who were lost and confused.

Yes, it was terrible to be alone here. Then, without a second of transition, he was trapped within a scrambling horde. They pushed at him and made ugly faces and held up their prizes. "A Nest, a Toad, a Fungus, or a Flow'r!" Far across the dismal plain he saw a monstrous chair, as yet unoccupied. He knew then. He knew.

The professor felt panic in every inch of his being. He had nothing! She was about to appear, any minute now, and he had nothing for her, not even an old scroll. Ah, no! Now he remembered—how odd that he'd ever forgotten—how during the hours in that elevator she had come for him and given him her lap. Him. Only him, Rosenblum. She was his angel.

As for the rest of you, he thought, mentally addressing the mob, all you hot shots: go fuck yourselves with your nests and toads and research grants. Stuff them up your asses, dunces. I am the One. And Rosenblum looked around him, and he saw that every dunce now lay upon the ground and did not even twitch.

He couldn't guess what the goddess would do for him this time, but he knew it would be great. He didn't need to give her anything. He was enough all by himself.

But she never came. The chair stayed empty. She had done what she wanted to do. All done.

And what became of Derek?

Who?

A feeble blast that no one hears, since no one is left. It echoes upon itself, most forlorn and promptly dies. Fame's final fart. The last kazoot. Goodbye! Goodbye!

Give the closer to the poet.

"And Universal Darkness buries All."[1]

[1.] *The Dunciad*, Book 4, line 656.

About the Author

A former professor of English, Jake Fuchs has written scholarly books, short fiction, two satiric mysteries, *Death of a Dad* and *Death of a Prof,* and the semi-autobiographical novel, *Conrad in Beverly Hills.* The son of Daniel Fuchs, the novelist and screenwriter, he lives in Berkeley, California with his wife, Freya.